Blood Games

Woody Tanger

BRANDEN PUBLISHING COMPANY
Boston

Library of Congress Cataloging in Publication Data

Tanger, Woody.
Blood games / Woody Tanger.
p. cm.
ISBN 0-8283-2022-5 (pbk. : alk. paper)
I. Title.
PS3570.A524B57 1994
813'.54--dc21
97-27587
CIP

The story, all names, characters and incidents depicted in this book are fictional. Any similarities to actual persons or events is purely coincidental and is not intended or should be inferred

BP

BRANDEN PUBLISHING COMPANY
17 Station Street
Box 843 Brookline Village
Boston, MA 02147

CONTENTS

4 -- Woody Tanger

Author's Note

Primum Non Nocere--first do no harm. These are the sacred words of the Hippocratic Oath sworn by those beginning practice as a physician.

I dedicate this book to the good physicians who live by these words.

Other physicians swear allegiance to Mephistopheles, the evil spirit to whom Faust sold his soul. These women and men cower under their medical degrees and oscillate between trickery, treason, tyranny of ego and trespass into the darkest crevices of humanity. Their minds are filled with memorabilia of past misery, some crocheted from a youth of intergenerational sex and drug orgies. Many of these are young physicians who are emboldened with their medical degrees and the blind idolatry offered them by society. They flock to the major teaching hospitals of the northeast. Some gravitate to clinical medicine. Others embrace psychiatry as a private killing field, whose undergrowth of lost souls offer them a chance to camouflage their own schizophrenia.

These physicians partnered up with the exotica of America today, legal powers who have embarked on an expeditionary search for justice as they define it. They use the might and majesty of the Government in their blitzkrieg. The corpses of civil liberties lie strewn across America's once-fruited plains.

Blood Games is written in a dangerous America. Your civil liberties are in menopause. Can you feel the cramps and see the menses? Free speech is government blood sport.

There are powerful forces in the U.S. who do not want the story of *Blood Games* told. 1984 has come and gone and returned in a mutated, more insidious form. When authors and journalists are not free to write and create without fear, how safe are you?

6 -- Woody Tanger

The knock at your door in the morning, is it Federal Express in blue with greetings from the Vermont Teddy Bear Company or the Federal Government with guns and gold badges? When you are stopped for a traffic offense, yanked from your car and spread-eagled like a serial killer, AAA can't help.

Are you fearful? Is someone watching as you browse in a bookstore? What books will the Government allow you to view? Is there some arcane law out there that will empower the 'Enforcers' to slam you to the floor, handcuff your hands, and carry you out of a bookstore like so much discarded trash. America the Beautiful which was, once upon a time, free of speech and blessed with fruited plains, is bleeding.

You comfort up and say, "No, not here in America."

Government is listening to your telephone calls and watching your computer screen, monitoring what you say, censoring what you can see and read.

What about sanctuary?

Traditionally, hospitals and their doctors were sought out, sub rosa, as a place. They offered a sympathetic setting for healing amongst doctors whose white coats conveyed a clerical-like calm.

Josef Mengel also wore a white coat when he dissected Jews alive.

The *menage à trois* of killing doctors, legal authorities in heat, and law enforcers with a grudge has produced a megawatt of evil in America.

1997 Woody Tanger

INTRODUCTION

This is a story about doctors and nurses who kill with a smile, a gentle touch, and a feel-good look. These are doctors stitched together with blackmail. You will meet 'kill' doctors and nurses whose habits of choice are drug use, twisted sex games, gambling, theft, and a lust for reaching out to children on the Internet. They hide under white coats, Latin-loaded degrees, and the revered title, M.D. If you live in a big city near an acclaimed teaching hospital, it's better than 'lottery odds' that you've already given them blood.

Welcome to Ridge Hospital. Check out the EMERGENCY EXIT; it could save your life.

The Ridge is a 530 bed hospital that towers over nearby cobblestone streets and the quaint rare book shops of Philadelphia's exclusive Chestnut Hill. The Ridge is 20 stories high and its brick facade, covered with thick streams of ivy, gives the main buildings a campus-like look of academic serenity. New research buildings reach out from the main campus in a star-shaped pattern.

Unlike other hospitals, compensation was never a problem at the Ridge and acquisition of the newest medical equipment was easy. As many hospitals sunk in decaying financial orbits, the Ridge was a bright star whose finances glistened like a diamond in the night sky.

The Ridge's Magnetic Resonance Imaging complex was one example of its financial muscle. Only the Ridge in Philadelphia had the funds to acquire GE's 'SIGNA' MRT (Magnetic Resonance Therapy) system enabling doctors to see patient images within 1/30th of a second. The total cost was $50 million dollars and was acquired without debt.

Ridge Hospital was a cash machine that made city bankers blush in envy.

8 -- Woody Tanger

A former thoracic surgeon, Dr. Walter Hagen, took command of the Ridge in 1985. Hagen created the élite 'Crystal Club' and limited membership to 100 of Philadelphia's wealthiest families. Members donated $250,000 upon acceptance, $100-,000 a year for life, and designated the Ridge as beneficiary of five million dollars upon their death. Crystal Club members and their immediate families received free lifetime medical care at the Ridge, their names carved into the granite facade of the medical complex, and endless accolades in the local papers.

The Ridge was a new breed, 'predator-hospital.' Hagen ambushed competing hospitals by acquiring their most prominent physicians using signing bonuses copied verbatim from major league baseball. When the 'victim-hospitals' were wounded, Hagen bought or killed them.

Battleship-hospitals like the Ridge were never naive. They understood the rules of health care reform were more akin to war than an academic debate in Congress. Doctors are soldiers, patients are ammunition and blood is money.

On October 15, 1995, Mrs. Ginny Choate and her three young children watched as Dr. Hagen dedicated a bronze plaque in memory of her late husband. Steven Choate died June 30th during a routine surgical procedure to repair his 'tennis elbow.'

Choate was 45 and in excellent health when he suffered cardiac arrest during surgery. A 'Code Blue' was called and within two minutes the operating suite was swarming with people running in controlled panic. The 'crash cart' was already in the operating suite where Choate had been intubated--his breathing done by machine. Tubes were connected to his arms and mouth.

"Fuck, it's Vfib. Paddles. 200. All Clear. Hit him. 360. All clear. 360 again. All clear."

"Give him 10 cc of epi." Epinephrine.

Behind Choate a pile of space-age look machines spit out data in greens and red. Blood pressure. Heart rate. Oxygen saturation. Respiratory rate.

Two weeks before his death, Choate's husband had told her about a Crystal Club member who died June 2nd after angioplasty.

After the dedication ceremony, Ginny Choate sent her children home with their nanny and chauffeur and remained at the Ridge.

One invited guest at the dedication ceremony, Philadelphia homicide detective, Lisa Marie Cooper, was neither family nor friend--Choate had begged her to come and watch.

PART ONE

Chapter One:
SO YOUNG

Mr. Hagen escorted Ginny Choate to his 20th floor office. Choate was silent as she walked inside.

Hagen's office was decorated with more TV monitors and computer screens than she had ever seen. It looked like something from the Star Trek movies her late husband loved to watch.

"Mrs. Choate, relax. Sometimes all these gadgets intimidate people."

"What are they?"

"The TV monitors provide me with a view of our operating rooms, the ER, ICU, labs and so forth. Anything you see can be recorded. I had today's dedication ceremony recorded for you."

"Why all this stuff?"

"Control, Mrs. Choate, control! Look up there. Those are my doctors and patients.

"The monitors keep everyone sharp. They know I'm watching."

"Were you watching?"

"Was I watching when Steven was in the operating room? Yes. He was a Crystal Club member. Of course, I was watching. Everything was going fine."

"Well, Dr. Hagen, it didn't. And he was so young."

"Steven had epicondylitis...tennis elbow. Almost always we can control it with drugs. If not, it's surgery or they can live with it."

Mrs. Choate glared at Hagen, "Or live with it, doctor?"

"Steven had a severe case. Surgery was the proper course. Did you ever hear the saying, 'a chance to cut is a chance to cure'? Steven wanted a cure."

"Who decided to operate?"

"Steven and his doctor. I assumed he had told you. Let's see who that was."

Hagen punched CHOATE, STEVEN into one of his computers. He printed the computer screen and handed it to Ginny Choate.

Ridge Patient Profile Date: 06-10-95
Patient Name: Choate, Steven Bates
38 Ruggles Farm
Plymouth Meeting, PA

Physician: Dr. Markus Harmon
Condition: Epicondylitis
Other: CRYSTAL CLUB
Consents: S. Choate
M. Cinners, RN

"Mrs. Choate, see for yourself. Dr. Harmon is a superb orthopedic surgeon and one of the best in the country. Markus has cut and cured so many baseball players they could fill a dug out. You can't go to a Phillies baseball game and not see one of his trophies on the field. Didn't you meet Dr. Harmon before the surgery?"

Now, angry and frustrated with Hagen's nonchalant attitude, Choate said, "No, Dr. Hagen, I never met him. I was in your waiting room reading *People* magazine when you and a minister came and got me. Don't you even remember that you met me at the pre-operative appointment."

"Mrs. Choate, I do remember, but it's been a tough day. You don't remember everything, either. We brought Dr. Tara Tuls with us. She's our Chief of Psychiatry. Long, red hair. Speaks with a distinct Boston accent. She gave you some medication. You seemed to connect with her."

Choate looked at Hagen with an angry stare.

"Maybe she gave me too much medication. And there's something else Dr. Hagen."

Hagen crossed his arms and waited for the question.

"My husband said he knew someone else in your Crystal Club who died this June. Two in one month?"

"I don't know what you mean. Mrs. Choate, this is a hospital. People die in hospitals. Even Crystal Club members. Most people die in hospitals. This isn't Club Med. That's life. This was supposed to be a time for us to have some tea and talk."

"Steven's just a name to you with $5 million tossed in. He's just a fuckin' ATM machine." Choate stormed out the door without looking back.

●●●

"Detective Cooper, this is Ginny Choate. I saw you at the dedication today and thanks for coming. I just finished talking with Dr. Hagen. Can we meet? It's really important."

"I've got your home address. Is that OK?"

"When?"

"One hour."

Cooper drove her unmarked Ford Taurus west from Philadelphia into fabled horse country. The drive from headquarters to 38 Ruggles Farm took Cooper through some of the most beautiful parts of America. She saw the sights of country inns, antique shops and farmhouses amidst gently rolling hills. Cooper drove past a red and black wooden gateway and down a one mile private road to the Choate residence.

"Mrs. Choate, I'm Detective Cooper, Philadelphia homicide."

Both women were in their early thirties. Each was about five feet five inches in height and trim. Beyond that fact, they lived in different worlds.

"Detective Cooper, I've never met a detective in my life; so, this is a little scary."

"A lot of people get that feeling. Call me Lisa and that'll help."

As they walked into an enormous country styled kitchen filled with the aroma of coffee and cookies, Cooper heard the sound of kids in the house.

"How many, Mrs. Choate?"

"It's Ginny. I have three kids: two boys and a girl. The youngest is only two and the oldest five and now they'll never know their father."

"Mrs. Choate, I'm really sorry about your husband, but I'm a homicide detective and your husband died in a hospital during surgery. Why am I here?"

"Well, my husband died in June at the Ridge. They operated on him for tennis elbow. He loved tennis. In high school he won varsity letters on his team; then, a couple of years ago, his elbow started to hurt when he played. The doctors gave him all kinds of medication but the pain got worse. Once, I remember he came home with tears in his eyes and Steven threw his tennis racket out the door. The doctors at the Ridge told him about an operation that might help. They said it was risk free and his best chance to play tennis without pain. That's what they told us. Steven was excited and said he wanted the operation. Well, he had it and Dr. Hagen comes out and tells me Steven is dead."

Cooper kept focused on Choate's eyes, "And..."

"And they said his heart stopped. Hagen saw it all."

"He was the surgeon?"

"No, no. His office has all these TV monitors. He watched Steven's surgery from his office."

"You mean he sits in his office and watches surgery all day?"

"Steven was a Crystal Club member; they get special treatment. I told you about the Crystal Club on the phone."

"Ginny, is that all?"

Choate reached out and gripped the detective's hands. "Someone else in that Crystal Club also died in June. Steven told me. That's pretty lucky for the Ridge." Choate spoke sarcastically, "Club members pledge five million from their estates. June was a good month for the Ridge. They picked up an extra ten million dollars."

"Who was the other person who died in June?"

I don't know. And Dr. Hagen didn't know. I asked him.

"Ginny, do you have any of your husband's hospital papers in the house?"

"Just copies of the consent forms."

"May I see them?"

The Ridge consent forms were titled:

CONSENT TO OPERATION or
OTHER SPECIAL PROCEDURE.

Line 6 read: **FOR THE PURPOSE OF ADVANCING MEDICAL EDUCATION, I CONSENT TO THE ADMITTANCE OF OBSERVERS TO THE OPERATING ROOM.**

Line 7 said: **I CONSENT TO THE DISPOSAL BY HOSPITAL AUTHORITIES OF ANY TISSUES OR PARTS THAT MAY BE REMOVED.**

"Ginny, I'll stop by the Ridge on the way back to headquarters; but, there's not much I can do." Choate acknowledged that fact but managed a slight smile of 'thanks.'

Chapter Two:
LOADING ZONE

Dr. Markus Harmon, please."

The hospital operator said he was on his pager and asked for a call back number.

"Tell him it's Detective Lisa Cooper. I'm on my way to the Ridge and I need a minute of his time. Here's my car phone number."

It was a beautiful fall day and the drive was a lot better than pushing papers at headquarters. Cooper's cellular phone rang.

"Detective Cooper, this is Dr. Harmon. What's the problem? I understand you're coming over."

"You said, 'there's a problem,' Dr. Harmon, not me. I need to clear something up."

"Detective, I'll save you the trip. I'm very busy. Let's do it by phone."

Cooper thought Harmon's voice had an uneasy edge to it. Maybe it was a bad day for him or just a normal reaction to hearing the word 'detective'. Whatever it was, Cooper did not suffer the answer 'NO' easily.

"Dr. Harmon, I'll be arriving in five minutes. Either meet me or I'll get the information from someone else."

•••

Cooper pulled out her police ID and parked in the LOADING ZONE. Standing in the front doorway was a man in his late 50's with arms crossed and a scowl imbedded on his face. His hair was a mess.

"Dr. Harmon, right?"

"Right."

Harmon looked like he had an attitude problem.

Cooper skipped any pleasantries as she so often did.

"Dr. Harmon, what happened to your patient, Steven Choate?"

"Not again, detective. Our hospital M & M investigated. They spent hours going over everything. Doesn't his wife have anything better to do? Why doesn't she play with her horses and rich friends and leave medicine to the doctors?"

"You said 'M & M'. What's that?"

"We have a hospital Morbidity and Mortality Oversight Committee. Any time we lose someone, that committee reviews the what, where, when and why--like hound dogs. Nothing gets past them. They check into things like Choate's death."

"Dr. Harmon, do you make house calls? How'd you know she has horses?"

"She lives in horse country. Good guess, right!"

"So, what happened to her husband? And what about the tissue removed during the surgery? And were there medical students in the operating room?"

"Detective, all this is in our protocol--just like you have at headquarters. Ask your Chief. Ellen Rome has rules and you follow them, right? Visit our legal department. It's all standard operating procedure."

"Dr. Harmon, no pun intended? Are you playing with me?"

Harmon turned and walked away.

Cooper shouted, "Dr. Harmon, did you lose another patient in June? Did you lose another Crystal Club member? Can you hear me, Harmon?"

"That's 'Dr. Harmon', lady, and this is a hospital, not a spa! Lots of people die here."

•••

Upstairs in his 20th floor office, Dr. Hagen asked his secretary, Emily Rosoff, "Did we tape that conversation with Harmon and the detective?"

18 -- Woody Tanger

"Just as you ordered."

Chapter Three: SHOE SIZE

She was a celebrity on the police force. Cooper was a Yale Law School graduate, who loved the law but hated the paperwork and endless hours in court. She had worked in the Manhattan District Attorney's office when she heard about a special police intern program in Philadelphia. The police were seeking diversity with a unique hiring program that had attracted former FBI agents, sports figures and a local TV newscaster. The pay was lousy but the challenge was great. Recruits went through a boot camp not far from the Gettysburg battleground. Cooper received her personal invitation from Philadelphia's maverick Chief of Police and former practicing attorney, Ellen Rome.

A graduate of George Washington University, Rome spent several years bouncing around as a political appointee in the Justice Department. She was impetuous and bored easily. Power never seemed to be the aphrodisiac for Rome that it was for so many others in Washington, DC. She was a native of Portland, Maine. Rome developed a lasting taste for the nice things in life like fashionable clothes, great restaurants, nice cars, and in college days, a healthy appetite for cocaine. The starving-young-lawyer-stories never intrigued her.

Her big chance came when a former FBI official and friend took command of a federal commission investigating the Philadelphia police. Rome was named general counsel for the investigation. When the inquiry ended after two years, it was called the Rome Commission. The report weeded out areas of corruption and influence peddling in the force, but also resulted in a strong endorsement of the core values and systems in that same force. She got involved with Sam Gentry's race for Mayor of Philadelphia and when he won, she was offered the chance to become the city's first female Chief of Police. With no children and a very messy divorce behind her, the job offer was a golden opportunity to immerse herself in a new life.

Cooper joined the program in 1990 as a clone of Chief Rome, a female lawyer turned cop. Six months, later she was a desk jockey detective paired with two veteran detectives.

Charlie Smith and Rudy Levin were an odd pair. Smith was a wannabe former center for the Philadelphia Eagles. He was six feet three inches and 250 pounds. At 58, he continued to work out, toning his huge biceps. His biceps were bigger than Cooper's waist. Smith's partner was small, flabby and shorter than Cooper. Rudy Levin was also 58, a conservative Jew. For the past twenty years Charlie Smith never missed a Passover Seder at Rudy's home.

Charlie and Rudy were inseparable because their love and respect had been forged in turmoil. Many years ago, a sergeant called Smith the 'house nigger.' Smith was stunned and kept his cool, but Rudy tossed his five foot body at the sergeant and landed one punch. That earned him a six month suspension without pay. Since that time, both detectives had been in and out of trouble. Now, Charlie and Rudy planned long winters in Boca Raton with their families, both having less than one year until retirement.

"Charlie, have you ever been to the Ridge?"

"Sure, Lisa, lots of times to visit folks."

"What about you, Rudy?"

"Same. Nice hospital. Great cafeteria."

Cooper briefed them on her day and asked for help. She needed the name of the other Crystal Club member who died in June.

"Guys, it won't be easy. I need that name. I can't get a court order. Maybe the three of us can do it together."

Cooper and her two partners rehearsed a plan as they drove to the Ridge.

•••

At four PM, Cooper returned to the Ridge with Smith and Levin. They walked down a long corridor, past the Hospital's 'kiss and cry' waiting room, to a circular patient information desk.

Flashing their gold detective badges, Cooper said, "We'd like some information on a patient who was here in June."

"Detectives, we don't release patient information to the police unless there's a crime, a court order or we have a patient's permission. You know the rules. I'll call legal and they'll send someone down."

Cooper knew that answer was coming. Smith edged Cooper to the side and tossed a football-mean look to the receptionist, who caught it right in the face. Smith looked at xher and straddled the indefinable threshold between silence and the quietest sound with some indiscernible muttering sounds. Then his voice thundered and the receptionist looked at Smith while thinking, "Where did this guy come from?"

"Give us the name or we'll get a court order."

"Come on, Charlie; ease up. It's not her fault. She's trying."

Cooper watched Rudy drift away to the side like he was a little kid ready to raid the cookie jar.

"Rudy, what are you doing? Come back."

Flashing a charming smile, Rudy answered, "Lisa, I'm talking with some of the nurses."

Cooper noticed that the TV monitor had followed Rudy as he walked to the side and it was not automatically sweeping side to side.

Charlie boomed his deep voice towards Rudy. "Let's get going. This is a waste of time. We'll get the court order and come back tonight."

Suddenly, Cooper felt someone standing behind her.

"Detectives, I'm Dr. Walter Hagen. I'm President of the Ridge. They paged me. What's wrong?"

"Dr. Hagen, I'm Detective Cooper and these are detectives Smith and Levin. We're all from the Philadelphia police."

Cooper intentionally left out the word homicide.

"Oh, yes, you've been with Mrs. Choate, right? She's so young. At least money isn't a problem. Her husband was a great benefactor of the Ridge. We miss him. You want to ask me about him?"

Cooper shook her head, No.

"Then, why are you here?"

"Mrs. Choate told me another Crystal Club member died in June. Who was it?"

"Detective, if that's so, I can't recall now. We've got thousands of patients."

Cooper was trained as a lawyer and imagined Hagen under cross examination.

"With all due respect, Dr. Hagen, you should remember because this was one of your Crystal Club members. There are only 100."

Hagen did not back off. "Detective Cooper, this is a giant teaching hospital. Think of us like a *Fortune 500* business. We've got hundreds of doctors, thousands of nurses, and tens of thousands of patients. Do you know everyone at police headquarters?"

"I know the 100 most important people!"

Smith took his giant right hand and slid it on Cooper's tiny waist, gently pushing her to the side. He peered down at Hagen, who was at least six inches shorter and 80 pounds lighter. Smith moved close enough for Hagen to feel the breeze coming from his mouth.

"Lisa, Dr. Hagen here doesn't remember. Let's get the court order. We'll come back tonight. Rudy says the food is great here."

●●●

"Detective Cooper, I remember! How could I forget. What a day."

Rudy winked and cut a broad smile aimed at his partners.

"Mrs. Choate is probably referring to Jonathan Roberts. We lost him at the end of June."

"What happened?"

"PCTA...percutaneous transluminal angioplasty. Roberts was overweight and a smoker. His arteries had narrowed. We inserted a catheter with an attached balloon and tried to open the artery and clean out the plaque. It's a delicate procedure with risk. Then, boom: arrest! He would have died within months anyway. We did our best."

Cooper's face was red with anger nourished from her experience as a trial lawyer.

"Dr. Hagen, first you tell me you don't remember a patient's name; now you tell me everything about Jonathan Roberts *except* his shoe size!"

Chapter Four:
JIMMY STREET

Cooper turned to Charlie, "Smooth Charlie. I didn't think he'd budge; but you guys really have the touch."

Rudy added, "Lisa, you're learning. Like the 'SureKill' (Schuykill River), you gotta take the twists and turns. This Hagen is cocky. He's smart. He's rich. He's a jerk. Hell, he's a doctor! He's even a surgeon. But that's all, no more. This is a dead end."

Cooper looked disappointed with that answer and thought Charlie might reinforce her doubts about Hagen.

"Charlie, talk to me."

"Maybe this guy's skimming the Hospital. Maybe he's got a thing with a nurse. But, Lisa, you've got zippo."

•••

Cooper called Ginny Choate and told her about her visit with Hagen. Cooper heard the laughing of kids in the background and wondered what their first Thanksgiving without a father would be like.

"I don't care how much money they have; this must be tough for her."

Cooper drifted through October and November while her partners counted down to retirement in July.

In January, 1995, Cooper joined two girlfriends and flew on Delta to St. John's Island. She carried the *Philadelphia Inquirer* on board and gazed outside. Somewhere over the south Atlantic, a bell awoke her and the FASTEN SEAT BELT sign came on. Seconds later the captain spoke:

"Ladies and Gentlemen, this is the captain. We're at 37,-000 feet about 300 miles east of Jacksonville. Planes ahead are reporting some scattered turbulence; so, we've flipped the seat belt sign on. Thanks."

Cooper hated to fly because the loss of control was her ultimate surrender. She started to breathe faster with anticipatory anxiety, remembering a fear of flying course she took and tried to concentrate on the newspaper. She looked at the words but could not read them. Suddenly, the wide body 767 started to jerk up and down.

"This is the captain, again. Sorry about this. It won't last long. We've asked ATC for an altitude change. Flight attendants, please take your seats."

Cooper fixed her eyes on the newspaper as friends grabbed her hands, trying to reassure her.

"Oh, my God!" Cooper screamed.

Her friends thought she had flipped out. Flying was not her thing. Not for a control freak. Cooper's scream terrified other passengers. A flight attendant asked if she was OK.

"My God, it's Dr. Hagen!" Cooper yelled, pointing to his picture.

"Who?"

"It's Dr. Hagen from the Ridge. Look! Here's his picture. He's signing a deal to buy the Philadelphia Health Institute."

> **(Philadelphia, PA 12/31/94): RIDGE BUYS PHILA HEALTH INST.** Pictured above is Dr. Walter Hagen, President of the Ridge Hospital, handing over a check to acquire the PHI. A second payment will be made before June 30th, the end of Ridge's fiscal year. Dr. Hagen predicted another hospital acquisition in the current fiscal year.

"He wrote out a check and bought it all. That son of a bitch! Bet I know where the money came from. And June 30th. June--Hagen's favorite month."

Cooper carried the picture with her until she returned home.

•••

It took Cooper only one hour to get an appointment with the Chief of Police.

"Chief, you gave me a chance on the police force because I brought something special to the table. We're lawyers, you and I, and you know we have different instincts. Those instincts tell me there's a bad deal going down at the Ridge."

Chief Rome felt a special kinship with Cooper. Both were around the same age and witnessed firsthand the subtle ways in which women were treated differently. Rome was a labeled a 'bitch' while rough speaking men on the force were characterized as 'tough' or 'determined." On the other hand, Rome was very much a woman's woman. She worked out regularly at the police gym and loved to lift weights with the young, ex-marine rookie cops. No one ever saw her wearing the same workout outfit twice, and she had a hard, voluptuous and very sexy look. She never dated inside the force, but was often seen on the arm of high-priced lawyers and socialites.

A couple of years earlier, Rome and friends chartered a sailboat out of St. Barts and spent a week cruising through the Caribbean islands. According to a retired detective who was vacationing in the same area, he saw Chief Rome lying topless on the beach, smoking marijuana. Since the detective was forced into early retirement as a result of the Rome Commission, his reporting skills were always put in the same basket as the *National Inquirer.*

Whoever or whatever Chief Rome was outside the Department, inside she ruled with vigor and innovation, winning the loyalty of most cops.

"Detective Cooper, I read your report on the Ridge and it's empty. There's no crime. Mrs. Choate may need a negligence lawyer, but she doesn't need a homicide detective."

"Chief, give me a chance and you won't be sorry. I've sat with Hagen and watched his video tapes of Crystal Club members dying on Ridge operating tables."

Rome saw the intensity in Cooper's eyes and made an instant decision. She was never afraid to take chances and go with her instincts.

"Cooper, I'll let you dig into it, with conditions. Budget your time. Take no time from active cases. You've got no money for this. Maybe you'll learn a lesson."

"Yahoo. Thanks, Chief."

Rome, however, wanted something from Cooper. "Mayor Gentry needs a favor. There's a detective from Boston named Jimmy Street. He handled that Charles River thing. Remember, it made the papers and morning news shows. Our Mayor is friendly with the Mayor of Boston. Seems this Street is a hero up there. Guess the Mayor in Boston thinks he may catch the political bug. So, he wants Street out of town for a while. We call it a police exchange program even though I call it a sham. So, Street is all ours for a while. Actually, he's all yours. So, let him work on the Ridge case."

"No problem, Chief. Where is this guy?"

"He's parked in homicide and he's not happy here."

Chapter Five: OPERATION END ZONE

Where's Street?"

Charlie and Rudy shrugged their shoulders and pointed towards the windows.

Cooper imagined that she would have to baby sit a 'coffee, booze, half-shaven, and foul-mouthed' detective.

"Cooper? he's gone."

"Gone?"

"He changed into his running gear and took off. He's nuts. It's 25 degrees outside. He asked directions to the Art Museum. Too many ROCKY movies."

•••

Street bundled against the freezing weather and headed west towards a mystical shrine for runners everywhere. He was dressed in New England Patriot blue and silver. The wind was howling and a mix of freezing rain and snow accumulated around his eyes and lips. Street ran down Franklin Parkway and through the falling snow and sleet he saw the Art Museum whose steps were immortalized in ROCKY.

Street had been running for 30 minutes when he heard a honking noise from the car trailing behind him.

"Damn, can't a guy run in peace."

Street shouted, "Hey, buddy, what's your problem?"

"Is that you, Street? Come on, I'll give you a ride. It's freezing. Even the dogs are inside."

Street looked to the right and saw Cooper at the wheel with her head half out the window, her windshield wipers tossing bits of ice and snow towards Street.

"Turn those wipers off; you're whacking me with ice balls."

Cooper thought Street looked like a candidate for a mountain rescue effort. Most of his face was layered in snow and ice, his nostrils ringing with ice. He was running without goggles, and his eyebrows formed ridges of snow.

"Get in, Street; you'll never make it."

"How do you know my name?"

"Street, I'm Detective Cooper, Philadelphia Homicide."

Street kept running towards the Art Museum.

"Meet you at headquarters in an hour."

Cooper's car skidded on the ice and rammed into the curb. The last words Street heard were, "you jerk..."

●●●

Cooper sat in her cubicle talking with her partners.

"Guys, how come you don't run like this guy from Boston?"

"Because we're not nuts. Lisa, he's your problem. We talked with him and he's angry. He says they wanted him out of Boston until things blew over with the big case he solved."

"The Chief says he's staying here; so, get used to him. More important, I've got an OK to check out the Ridge."

A pounding noise rocked the squad room as a big white shaped figure moved inside. From head to toe 'it' was a mixture of ice and snow: a little skin, bright red from the freezing winds, was visible. Then 'it' shook and a pool of snow fell to the floor five feet from Cooper.

Jimmy Street fashioned a big, innocent smile, like the dirty little kid in the laundry commercial, who comes inside covered with dirt.

"Outstanding. Freezing cold. Wind. I had the whole road to myself except for Cooper here. Say, Cooper, do you always drive like that? What a run. I ran those steps at the museum. Just like the movie. I wish they could have seen this in Boston. I'm gonna do that run again."

Cooper asked Street and her partners to join her in the interrogation room.

"Cooper, you weren't always a cop?" Street asked.

She noticed that, unlike most of the other detectives, Street was built rock hard with no visible flab. "Street, you really work at keeping in shape? How much do you weigh?"

He pondered the question for a moment and shot back sarcastically. "4,500 pounds less than a Mercedes S 420 'curb weight', that is. Now, answer my question: you weren't always a cop, right?"

"So what, Street? And how'd you know that?"

"No big deal; but it shows. You're sort of delicate. And you sure are smarter than your two partners here. Cooper, I know your type. You're on the fast track and so busy you actually know how to program your VCR. You go to bed at night with the next day's 'TO DO' list. And you know your friends by their last names. Sound familiar, Detective Cooper?"

"So, you've got me all figured out? Well, I was a lawyer; but I can shoot your eyes out from 200 yards. And don't be too tough on my partners. Charlie could toss you around like a football."

Everyone laughed as Charlie imitated a quarterback dropping back to pass.

"Cooper, I've been briefed on the Ridge. You've got nothing."

"Street, I've been briefed about you, too. I'll bet someone told you the same thing about the Charles River Hospital. Street, you were too damn stubborn to listen. You knew you had a case. It was a feeling inside. You had the guts to stay with it and you never backed off. I respect that. Street, I carried a newspaper picture of Hagen with me on vacation. I looked at his face every day. I hear the sounds of kids in Ginny Choate's house. Her husband died of tennis elbow and the Ridge picks up a cool five million dollars just before the end of their fiscal year. June was a great month for the Ridge. Two of their Crystal Club donors died. Two widows, ten million dollars, and a bunch of kids crying themselves to sleep. I'll bet there are more victims coming. So, Street?"

Cooper delivered a 'tour de force' performance, a Perry Mason winner-take-all speech, and she knew it.

"Cooper, two things. First, call me Jimmy. Second, maybe you ought to give your investigation a name. It's like wearing a uniform."

"Jimmy, in honor of your Patriot jogging outfit, I hereby announce the start of OPERATION END ZONE."

Cooper then whispered to Smith. "Charlie, how much does one of those Mercedes weigh?"

Chapter Six: THALIDOMIDE NIGHTS

At the Ridge, the dead of night is called 'Thalidomide' quiet. The drug known for causing birth defects and deformities is actually a sedative. A quiet night is 'T' time.

In the ICU (Intensive Care Unit) rhythmic hip-hop heart tracings dance in green across video monitors. Babies no bigger than softballs do a 'high wire' between life and death in the NICU (Neonatal Intensive Care Unit). Parents pace back and forth across linoleum floors while their babies hang between life and death. Across the landscape of the Ridge, nurses and doctors feel the danger of the night.

The room is bathed in white. The babies are connected with wires that dress them like puppets. They're fetuses that should still be in the womb, surrounded by nurturing fluids and fed quietly through the umbilical cord. The womb is black but safe. The NICU is white and dangerous.

They cannot see the micro-organisms that sweep across the Hospital visiting the sick. NOSOCOMIAL infections catch up to ten percent of all patients and kill about three percent. Nosocomial bacteria transfer from the sick to the sick.

How many sleeping in the Ridge are twisting the night away with iatrogenic nightmares? One of the deepest secrets in medicine is the doctor-caused or iatrogenic deaths. These are the demons of the night. No secret is more closely guarded than this.

The Ridge was 'T' quiet on that January night, as Cooper bundled against the cold in her Chestnut Street apartment not far from Philadelphia's waterfront. Her apartment was only a couple of miles from the million- dollar duplex condo in Rittenhouse Square owned by Dr. Walter Hagen. It was a glorious night to be home as chill winds moved through the patchwork of city streets. Cooper was asleep.

Dr. Walter Hagen was in his office at the Ridge.

The 20th floor was empty when Dr. Hagen had locked his door and reached into a video storage rack and pulled out two tapes.

Roberts, Jonathan 6/3/95 Dr Stoltz/Harmon
Choate, Steven 6/19/95 Dr James/Harmon

He checked both tapes.

"OK, Markus; they're fine."

Chapter Seven:
BE MY VALENTINE

Each year, the Ridge had a charity night dance on Valentine's Day called the 'Crystal Ball'.

Dr. Hagen and his staff planned the dinner dance with a surgeon's care. The wine list, the food, the orchestra and flower arrangements were first class. Each year, the party began with an elaborate video presentation by a local advertising agency. The video was ten minutes in length and chronicled achievements at the Ridge. So polished is the presentation that a pharmaceutical company pays all expenses and gets a 15-second infomercial at the end.

The dinner dance was always black tie and held at the Ritz. Invited guests include all members of the Crystal Club and their guests; plus, His Honor, the single non-paying member of the Club, the Mayor of Philadelphia, the honorary chairman of the Crystal Club.

During the evening, the Mayor welcomes new members and remembers any members who died. Dr. Hagen delivers his annual 'State of the Ridge' speech.

●●●

Valentine's Day was Monday, February 14th and OPERATION END ZONE was ready for the Crystal Ball.

Street, Smith and Levin wore their tuxedos. Cooper was dressed in a long, black, formal gown. The formal wear would enable them to mingle with the guests before dinner.

Chief Rome had briefed the Mayor on what her detectives had planned. He was not pleased that his friend, Dr. Hagen, and the Ridge were under investigation.

Cooper asked both police photographers to meet her in the Ritz Garage at 6 PM. As guests arrived, their cars were whisked to the underground garage. Below-ground photographers took pictures of license plates as the cars were parked.

The detectives moved around the hotel lobby as guests entered. Local TV stations had crews on the scene. Eric C. Goodman, President of KEYSTONE Broadcasting and Channel 31, was a Crystal Club member of long standing. The annual Crystal Ball always 'managed' great coverage on his Channel 31's early 10 PM news. Goodman and his wife, Carol, were Mayor Gentry's largest political contributors. The Goodmans and Gentrys were never far apart at functions like the Crystal Ball. Tonight, as usual, they sat at the head table with Dr. Hagen.

Goodman was the odd-face out at functions like the high society Crystal Ball and the blue blood of Philadelphia. He grew up in Brooklyn and worked his way into a series of weekend jobs as an announcer on small radio stations. He was the anonymous voice introducing paid half hours of religious programs on Sundays or tossing out weather forecasts at 4 AM when the only people who cared were already waist deep in water with their fishing poles. He graduated from Brooklyn College and won a scholarship to a communications school in Philadelphia. That's when he learned finance and there was never any chance he'd return to the broadcast business as an announcer.

Goodman met an undergraduate student in Philadelphia named Carol Wizer. She was manicured and well dressed in contrast to Goodman and his 'Brooklyn' look of hustle and struggle. When they married one year later, Goodman had managed to climb the first rung of Philadelphia's social ladder. It was his wife's family that introduced him to the 'good' things in Philadelphia society, including fitting into a tuxedo. By the time he graduated school, Goodman had put together a circle of contacts that he wove into a venture fund for the acquisition of broadcast properties. KEYSTONE struggled during his early years with small market radio stations. He had that same sense of frustration and annoyance that he was missing the big show. Then Goodman struck it rich as he tapped into a couple of *financial pools that were not satisfied ordinary returns. Goodman offered higher risk combined with a much higher return on investment and a small equity 'kicker' a piece of the action in KEYSTONE Broadcasting. Within one year he assembled a $15 million pool of equity which he leveraged into a total of $100 million with bank funds. Now there was no turning back.*

Goodman pushed KEYSTONE Broadcasting like an old-world farmer directing his donkey uphill. He never looked back; he never looked away, and never said 'quit'.

Unlike his friend Goodman, Gentry was 'down loaded' into Philadelphia society 100 years before he was born into the perfect family. Gentry's family, while not rich, enjoyed an elevated position in society through years of upwardly mobile marriages and endless charity balls. Everyone thought they were rich, even though they were not. Gentry had no taste for the acquisition of money but an insatiable passion for its pleasures. Winning the race for Mayor of Philadelphia was another move up in the society games he enjoyed so much.

Goodman and Gentry used each other's money and political position in open and lustful pleasure. They were naked and unashamed, and so were their wives.

Most of the guests had assembled in the Grand Ballroom by 7 PM.

The detectives went downstairs to the parking garage where the police photographers had just finished. The pictures would be ready by Tuesday and the license numbers matched with Crystal Club names.

The quartet of Cooper, Smith, Levin, and Street spent much of the night in the Ritz bathrooms. Of the 300 guests, almost a third used a bathroom before everyone assembled for the dinner portion of the evening. With a mix of alcohol and gossip, the detectives were learning much about the Ridge.

Then, the unexpected happened: Eric Goodman grabbed Hagen's arm. "Walter, these parties keep getting bigger. The Mayor tells me you've got police in formal wear hanging around."

Hagen's face blushed.

"Eric, hang on for just a moment; I'll be back."

Hagen asked the Mayor for a private moment.

"Sam, what's going on. Eric tells me you've got police in the hotel. Is that true?"

"Now, calm down, Walter. Relax. My police chief told me there would be some detectives here tonight. She said they were completing an investigation. She asked about you. I set her straight."

"Sam, where are these detectives?"

Goodman watched as the Mayor and Hagen's conversation grew more animated.

"Hey, guys, did I start this?"

Hagen held Goodman's hand. "Eric, you didn't start anything. You did the Ridge a big favor."

"Sam, I'm going to offer a brief welcome and then introduce you. Let's start."

●●●

Hagen took the microphone.

Ladies and Gentlemen, welcome to the 9th annual Crystal Ball, a night in which we honor the guardians of the Ridge. We honor the men and women whose generosity have made the Ridge a world class hospital. I'll introduce Mayor Sam Gentry in a moment. I know you're hungry and can't wait to hit the dance floor. First, a special welcome to some unexpected guests. We have four of Philadelphia's finest detectives here tonight. Instead of catching bad guys, they're trying to figure out why people die in hospitals.

Everyone burst into laughter. Hagen delivered the line with Jay Leno's timing. Everyone thought it was a scripted joke. Cooper and the others heard Hagen's remarks in the hall and stood in silence.

"Who told him? Must be that fat-lipped mayor. What an asshole!"

"Lisa, we got what we wanted here. We'll have the names of most Crystal Club members by tomorrow. Hagen may be smiling but I'll bet he wet his pants when he found out you were here. Enjoy the night. Happy Valentine's Day!"

Chapter Eight: NIGHT SWEATS

Street, how about Locust?"

"You eat those things?"

Cooper escorted Street down to Locust and 17th Street in Philadelphia's upscale 'meet market' where the fashionable gather for after-work drinks. Street unwound his life with ease. He talked about the Charles investigation in Boston; mostly, he talked about personal things like his ex-wife, and about his partner, who was gunned down when they stumbled onto a drug deal.

Street talked and Cooper listened. She was a great listener. Then, he asked questions.

"Lisa, you're pretty, young, and smart. Why aren't you dancing with lawyers in trendy Manhattan bars?"

"I did and didn't like it. This police work is fun. I can always pack my bags and get back into law. Right now, I'm in the right place."

"What about dating?"

"I do; but, no one special."

"And you, Jimmy?"

"Yeah, I was dating, emphasis on past tense. I dated this really sharp lady in Boston. She was beautiful. She was a captain in the military. I met her during the Charles River case."

"Are you still seeing her?"

"Only if I want to visit her in jail. Lisa, she killed those doctors."

"Whoops. Sorry."

"No problem. She tried to kill me, too. How's that for a reason to end a relationship?"

They both laughed.

"Jimmy, it's getting late. Let's call it a night."

"Lisa, want to make me some coffee at your place?"

"Jimmy, you've got to improve your lines. I'll take you back to your hotel."

"Lisa, I wonder how Hagen's 'big night' is going. You may catch some flack from your chief tomorrow. Your mayor seems tight with Hagen."

Cooper drove Street to his hotel and returned home to her condo.

●●●

"OK, Lisa, get the energy and light a fire. Then fill the bath-tub up with warm water and oils. Light some candles. And try not to fall asleep in the tub."

As she walked to the bathroom, Cooper hit REPLAY on her answering machine. There were three messages.

7:19 PM: LISA, IT'S YOUR PARENTS. REMEMBER US? HOW ARE YOU? CALL. HOW ABOUT DINNER THIS WEEK? TAKE CARE. LOVE YOU. MOM AND DAD. 10:45 PM:

HI LISA. IT'S RICK. REMEMBER ME? WE MET IN ST JOHN. WELL, I'M COMING TO PHILADELPHIA NEXT WEEK. HOW ABOUT DINNER. YOU'VE GOT MY NUMBER. HOPE TO HEAR FROM YOU. 12:10 AM:

DETECTIVE. THIS IS DR. HAGEN. THE MAYOR GOT ME YOUR HOME NUMBER. I NEED TO SEE YOU TONIGHT. I'LL BE AT THE RIDGE IN MY OFFICE. 20TH FLOOR. I'LL BE THERE AFTER 11 PM. SECURITY WILL BRING YOU UP. PLEASE COME ALONE. THANKS.

"Wow. That cancels the bath."

Should she call Street or her partners? Hagen said 'alone'. The Hospital's not some dark alley. She'd be safe there.

●●●

When Cooper arrived at the Ridge, it was 1:05 AM. She signed in at the security desk.

"Detective Cooper to see Dr. Hagen."

The guard was startled. "You mean the man is here, now? I didn't see him sign in. I'll ring upstairs."

"Sorry, no answer. Are you sure he said tonight and not today?"

At that instant, a black Jaguar drove to the front door. The front license plate said it all--RIDGE.

"Well, there he is, detective."

Hagen walked to Cooper in his tuxedo. The guard spoke. "Dr. Hagen, how was tonight's party?"

"Hey, it was great. Would you log me in?"

Cooper followed Hagen as he led her around a corner and down a long green corridor.

"We'll take the private elevator up."

The red EXIT lights gave the area a serene look. Cooper saw a huge fish tank in front. They walked past some offices and into a large reception area. Then Hagen guided her to a locked door. He slid a computer access card and punched in a code. The door opened and the lights came on automatically.

"Detective, the lights come on when the sensors detect body heat."

Hagen very gently touched her back and guided her towards a chair.

"Detective, please sit down. Thanks for coming. I've got something to give you. But first, we talk."

Cooper felt uncomfortable and wondered. "Was this where Ginny Choate sat?" She looked up and saw the row of TV monitors that Choate had described.

Hagen took his tie and jacket off and settled behind his desk.

"Tonight's little escapade, Cooper--that wasn't smart. It embarrassed me. It didn't help your career. And it was a waste of time."

Cooper stood. "Dr. Hagen, if this is a lecture, you can cut it short. Is that why you called?"

"No. Your silly game tonight convinced me that you don't understand. If I don't do something to straighten you out, you won't quit. I don't want you distracting us at the Ridge from our mission. Cooper, you're a classic case of a little knowledge and a lot of harm."

Hagen was never diplomatic in tone or substance with anyone, including his staff at the Ridge.

"Again, Dr. Hagen, you're lecturing. It's late. If that's all, you can show me back to the elevator."

Cooper saw that Hagen was simmering inside. He was fighting to control his anger. Beads of sweat poured down his face.

"Detective Cooper, you assume that because two Crystal Club members died in June there's evil here. You listened to Mrs. Choate and all her phobias. Did you consider that she was angry because her husband gave us so much money? Maybe that meant fewer horses for her."

Hagen was focused. His brown eyes glared at her. He reached under his desk and removed the two tapes labeled ROBERTS and CHOATE.

"Detective, see these?" he said, holding them high over his head in defiance. "These, detective, are the videos taken during surgery on Roberts and Choate. I'm going to show them to you. Maybe I'll even give them to you. You can show Mrs. Choate the way her husband died and what we did to try to save him. Maybe that will shut her up."

Hagen took the Roberts tape, lowered the lights in his office, and played it. Cooper's eyes focused on a big TV monitor behind Hagen.

"Cooper, have you ever watched what happens in an operating room?"

"No."

"Fine. This tape was made June 3, 1993. See over there in the lower left hand corner? That's what we call the 'IBOX'--the tape's ID."

Roberts, Jonathan
6/3/95 09:30:00
Cath Lab Four
ID #: 93063954
Dr. Harmon/Dr. Stoltz
Macky, Jones, Joy

Cooper watched as she saw a man wheeled into a gray colored room with a large clock visible in the background. The doctors and nurses looked like astronauts. They were covered from head to toe in white space suits with a purple and yellow logo, The RIDGE.

"I can't see his face. How do you know that's Roberts?"

"Roberts has an ID bracelet on his arm. It's bar coded like cereal in your supermarket. When they wheeled him into Cath Lab #4, the bar code was scanned by an electronic device in the door. It flashed his name, ID, and blood type on a monitor in the Cath Lab. It also appeared on the video monitor we're watching. The surgeon must record that the patient's identity has been positively confirmed. Cooper, this is foolproof. We paid a million dollars to install it throughout the hospital."

The tape continued to roll. The IBOX read 09:54:23.

Someone took a large syringe with a 3 inch needle and buried it into Roberts' right groin. The cardiologist took a scalpel and cut. Cooper looked away as drips of blood spilled onto the surgical drapes.

"Cooper, now they're inserting a catheter through that incision near his groin and snaking it up to the heart and into the narrowed coronary artery. See, the doctors are guided by the picture on that X-ray screen."

Cooper nodded.

"Whoops. Careful. See that monitor. Looks like a spasm. Watch those ST segments on the monitor."

"Dr. Hagen, what's 'ST'? How come there's no noise? It's so silent."

"ST looks like that heart's not getting enough blood. Yank that catheter. That's it; looks better. See those numbers. ST's coming back. Great."

Cooper thought. "Damn, he's doing play by play. He's into it."

"I don't usually record audio in the Cath Lab. We actually have two way communication. We only use audio if there's some extraordinary procedure."

Cath Lab is the Cardiac Catheterization Suite. It's two rooms split with leaded glass. On one side, the patient and the doctors; on the other side, the monitoring technicians record the data, evaluate blood samples. On one side, the astronauts; the other side, Mission Control.

Cooper looked a bit queasy.

"Are you OK, detective?"

Cooper nodded.

"See his heart? It's a shadowy outline on the X-ray. The arteries are those white lines. They sent a contrast agent through his arteries. That's a dye that shows up on our fluoro and xray. The narrowing indicates plaque. Some of those lines narrow to nothingness. That part of the artery is partially blocked by atheroma, a fatty substance. Roberts had poor left ventricular function. He probably had a 'silent' heart attack. Too many nachos. That added risk. Not a winning ticket for surgery."

Cooper watched the X-ray screen and saw Roberts' heart rhythmically contracting. The IBOX read 10:13:27.

"Roberts crashed."

Hagen narrated the next few minutes of video terror. Cooper felt chills climbing her spine.

"The muscles in the two atria, the upper chambers of his heart, started to electrically fire at about 400 pulsations a minute. Cooper, anything over 180 is deep shit. See the alarm lights on those monitors? This is too fast. Those impulses won't all make it through the atrioventricular node to the ventricles, but too many of them do. Overload. The wiring in his heart won't

let it happen but it sure is trying. His heart's beating like a drugged-out drummer in a rock band. Faster! Faster! Faster! Look at that sucker move. Detective, he's in trouble."

The Cath Lab was in turmoil. She couldn't read lips but the panic was naked.

Hagen pulled the tape.

"Detective. Had enough? You don't look so great."

"That's terrible. You get off on this kind of stuff, right Hagen?"

"Look detective, Roberts knew the risks. This wasn't a trip to the dentist."

Cooper settled back in her seat. It was almost 2 AM. Her face was drenched with sweat.

"Dr. Hagen, you have Choate's tape. I'd like to see that."

"Cooper, haven't you had enough? You want more, brave little girl!"

"Show me, Dr. Hagen."

"OK."

Choate, Steven
6/19/95
10:15:00
OR East Two
ID #: 06194155
Dr. Harmon/Dr. James
Macky, Jones, Joy

Hagen played the second tape.

"Detective, Choate had damaged his tendon on the outside of the elbow. The tendon connects muscle to bone. He developed tendinitis. Choate tried a nonsteroidal anti inflammatory drug but that didn't help. After consulting with a sports surgeon, Dr. Billy James, he decided on surgery. Choate knew Dr. Harmon and asked him to 'scrub in' as a favor. Typical Harmon, wherever he goes in this hospital, he takes over. Throws his weight around. Harmon is our mench here at Ridge. He knows everyone. He would have made a damn good politician."

"Yeah, well, he didn't get my vote."

Hagen stopped the tape.

"Detective, Dr. Harmon knew Roberts. He knows all the Crystal Club members. Many of our Crystal Club members feel better having him around. He speaks their language, you know: money, stocks, real estate investment trusts."

"Go ahead, Dr. Hagen, start the tape again."

Choate's surgery began at 10:17 AM.

Within two minutes, she saw panic again.

"What happened?"

"Choate crashed at the beginning."

"Dr. Hagen, I don't want to see more."

"Yes, you do; you're a veteran."

Hagen fast forwarded the tape. The time read 11:33:03.

"Detective, they worked on Choate for more than an hour. They fought to save him. They tried everything. It was heroic."

"I've seen enough."

Cooper slumped in her seat. It was 2:30 AM.

"Detective, you've seen it. We took you inside the OR. Are you satisfied?"

Cooper was soaked in sweat with her blonde hair a mess. Her makeup was off. She still wore her long black evening dress.

"Detective, I'm sure you'll hear from Chief Rome tomorrow and maybe even the Mayor. You were out-of-bounds last night. Enough is enough. So, are you satisfied? Maybe even an apology?"

Cooper went into a rage as Hagen lectured her like a little girl in school.

"Dr. Hagen, I want a copy of those tapes."

"No way. Not possible."

"What's the problem? I'll make copies and get them back."

"So, Detective, you enjoyed them? You want our confidential hospital tapes to take home and play on your VCR? Maybe a side show at police headquarters?"

Hagen stuffed his hands in his coat and fiddled with his black tie and started to put it on.

"Dr. Hagen, getting dressed for another party? Are you nervous?"

Cooper was not ready to go quietly into the night and, in fact, she never went quietly into the night. She went through law school with a scholarship and a night job as a waitress. Cooper grew up in a very affluent part of Long Island and then watched helplessly as her family's chain of drug stores was wiped out by large discount stores. In high school she had everything including Florida vacations and ski trips, new clothes and a nice car. At that time in her life, she never thought of law school. Then her family finances and lifestyle came crashing down, and by the time she settled into law school, her parents were divorced and her childhood home was gone. 'Coopers Drug Stores: Where FAMILY comes FIRST' was gone from city streets across Long Island. She cried whenever she drove by one of the boarded up drug stores where so many of her childhood memories were incubated. Law school was a mission of redemption for Cooper and a chance to take back part of the good life that she missed very much. But, when she could have moved from the DA's office in New York into a fancy Park Avenue law firm she changed course from a high paying job and U-turned to join the Philadelphia police. It made no sense to her friends and family but she didn't give a damn what anyone thought.

"Why didn't the state medical examiner check these people out? It's the law you die within 24 hours of admittance to a hospital and the coroner gets a call. I want the medical examiner to look at these tapes. You should have had him check this out. Why not?"

"Well, they're confidential, detective. We don't release video tapes helter skelter. And these are Crystal Club members, not just anyone off the street."

"'Helter skelter', are you a Charles Manson fan? Who made you God?"

"That's a dirty little thing to say, my sweet Detective Cooper."

"You just showed me some ugly tapes. Either give me the tapes or I'll get a judge's order. Does Mrs. Choate know these tapes exist? Maybe her lawyer should know."

Hagen handed the tapes to Cooper. "You know, I'm good friends of Mayor Gentry and I've even met your boss, Chief of Detectives, Ellen Rome. I assume they're aware of what you're doing?"

Cooper flashed her gold detective's badge. "See this? It means I don't have baby sitters any more. Would you like me to call the Mayor and Police Chief and wake them up at 3 AM and get their OK? I can call some friends at the papers. I'll put you on the phone, Dr. Hagen. Now, please show me downstairs."

●●●

Cooper raced back to her condo with the tapes. The city streets were deserted and snow plows were clearing gutters. It was a strange and uncomfortable night for Cooper. There was nothing nocturnal about watching videos of people dying on operating tables.

Driving home, she passed a drug store near city hall and spotted a few people inside. She remembered all those nights when her dad would get a call in the middle of the night from the police asking him to open up his drug store and fill an emergency prescription. Never did he say 'no.' When the calls came, especially if it wasn't a school night, she'd go with her dad and watch as he opened the drug store. She saw the faces of people in the night in trouble and her dad was the hero. He always looked tallest in the middle of the night when he filled a prescription. Sometimes parents would bring their little children with them to the drug store. Most vivid in her mind were the police who waited for her dad at the drug store. They wore uniforms and had guns and their police cars had lights flashing. Maybe that's why she ditched a Park Avenue law firm for the grimy scenes a detective looks at each day. Cooper was daydreaming in the middle of the night.

Cooper was having night sweats in the middle of winter.

Chapter Nine: BOWELS OF THE RIDGE

Where's Lisa?"

"Relax Charlie; it's just 9 AM." Rudy called her at home.

There was no answer. Street entered the squad room.

"Hey guys, hell of a night."

Charlie wasted no time. "Street, you went with Lisa after the Ritz, right?"

"Sure did. We had a few drinks; talked. Then she took me to my hotel, around midnight. Say, she's a great listener. A classy lady."

"Well, we can't find her."

Street reminded them it was 9 AM and they all had had a late night. Worry was Charlie's specialty.

"Rudy, do me a favor. Call communications; see if they can reach her."

Rudy put the operator on speaker phone.

"Detective, she doesn't answer in her car. Hold on, let's check the log. I've got it. She called in at 12:30 AM and said she was going to the Ridge."

The three detectives drove to Cooper's place.

Smith dialed the Ridge from a cellular phone.

"This is Detective Smith, Philadelphia Homicide. Get me Dr. Hagen."

A secretary answered. "Dr. Hagen's office. He's in a meeting right now. Do you have a call back number?"

"You get Hagen, now. No, call back. Get him."

Smith's voice thundered through the line.

"Dr. Hagen here."

"This is Detective Smith. Where's Cooper?"

"What?"

"She logged out to the Ridge after midnight. Did you see her?"

"Yes. She left around 3 AM."

"Doctor, she better turn up fast and with a big smile. Get the drift?"

They arrived at Cooper's condo as Smith hung up. The detectives raced inside, buzzing her unit. There was no answer. Then Levin pushed every button and someone buzzed them into the building.

Smith pushed her doorbell while Levin banged on the door. Street watched from behind. They waited and there was no response. Levin took out his portable phone and called homicide's hot line.

"Has Cooper arrived?"

"No."

"Has she called?"

"No."

Smith turned to Levin and Street. "Back up guys, I'm gonna take this door down."

Street grabbed Smith. "Wait. Let me try."

Street got on a knee and pulled some slim silver metal sticks from his pocket. He picked her lock. The dead bolt was not in place. Cooper's door swung open. Smith and Levin pulled their guns and walked inside.

"Cooper, are you there?"

Street moved to the right and towards a closed door. As it slowly opened, Street heard a noise.

"Guys, over here."

Street lifted his right foot and rammed the door open, shattering a mirror. Street pushed so hard the door handle dug into the wall.

Cooper shot up from under the covers.

"What the..."

Street smiled. "Good morning, Lisa. Cooper, we thought Hagen did you in last night. You had us worried."

Cooper looked at the three rough and tumble detectives standing at her bedroom door, guns at their side. They looked so humble that she started to laugh and put her arms up.

"I give up! You guys are the greatest. You were worried. I overslept. Sorry. I feel so special. And you, Jimmy, you can get me a new mirror and fix the door."

"OK, sleeping beauty, get dressed."

"Guys, get comfortable in the kitchen. Make some coffee. Wait till you see what Hagen gave me."

While Smith and Levin went into the kitchen, Street paused and looked at her bedroom, littered with pictures.

"Well, Street, that was an invitation to leave so I can get dressed."

"Who's that little girl in this picture?"

"That's me and my dad in front of a drug store he owned on Long Island."

"What's it called?"

"It was called Cooper's, but it's gone now."

"How about your dad? And is that your mom in this picture?"

"My parents are fine. They're divorced but they still live on Long Island. Detective, you sure ask a lot of questions."

"I love pictures of families and people and dogs and cats and kids. And you've got a sampling of everything here."

"No one ever peered at my pictures like this. You're easily amused. No, forget I said that. Take it as a compliment. I'll bet there's a side to you that most people never get to see. You can learn a lot about people by the way they look at things. I'm surprised."

Smith yelled from the kitchen. "What's going on in there?"

"Relax, Charlie. Jimmy's looking at some of my pictures."

"What pictures?"

"Jimmy, see what I mean? Typical male!"

●●●

In fifteen minutes, Cooper emerged from her bedroom wearing a tight green and yellow skirt at least 3 inches above her knees. Street noticed that when she sat at the coffee table another three inches of leg showed.

"Street, stop staring at my legs."

Cooper told the story of her night at the Ridge with Dr. Hagen.

"Look at this, guys. Two video tapes from Hagen. He showed them to me last night. Hagen's a video nut and he tapes everything, including surgery. I've got tapes of Roberts and Choate when they died on the operating table."

Cooper described the call from Hagen and the hours she spent at the Ridge watching the tapes.

"So, Lisa, you didn't call me. You dumped me off, came home, and went over by yourself. Thanks for the confidence."

"Come on, Jimmy. He asked to see me alone. It's a hospital. If you're not safe in a hospital, then where?"

"Lisa, people die in hospitals."

"Jimmy, that's not the question. The question is: Do they get killed in hospitals?"

Chapter Ten: JOKER'S WILD

On the way to headquarters, Cooper radioed the medical examiner's office. She wanted a doctor to see the tapes. Cooper received a code SIX-FOUR call, shorthand for the 'devil' and it meant that she was in trouble.

"Detective Cooper, Chief Rome wants you in her office when you arrive. Copy that?"

"Roger"

●●●

"So, Cooper, you had your own Valentine's Massacre last night?"

"I'm making progress. We just caught a bad break. The Mayor must have told Hagen about our license plate sting."

"Cooper, it wasn't the Mayor; it was Goodman. He owns KEYSTONE Broadcasting and he probably owns Mayor Gentry too! Forget I just said that."

"Chief, I'll bet the Mayor called you."

The Chief signaled, "Yes".

"And you promised to hammer me."

Again she indicated, "Yes".

"I've got news for you. Downstairs we've got two video tapes. They're tapes from the operating rooms at the Ridge. They show Roberts and Choate when they died and I've got the ME coming to watch them."

"And how did you get those tapes? You didn't take them without authority, did you?"

"Chief, you'll like the answer. Hagen gave them to me."

"Cooper, I want to see those tapes. Then we can put this Ridge fascination of yours away and you can get back to work."

Chief Rome and Cooper went downstairs and joined Smith, Levin, and Street in a small room with a TV and VCR. In the corner was Dracula, Drake Cula, one of ten medical examiners on the Philadelphia police force.

Cula was in his early 70's. There is no forced retirement for ME's. He was popular with cops and always had a smile unlike other ME's. He was a snappy dresser with a quick walk.

Street was introduced to Cula.

"Say, Cula, you don't happen to know *Dead Face* McCann up in Boston. He's one of our ME's. I've never seen him smile."

Cula shook his head.

Smith went over and high-fived Cula.

"Dracula, man, where did you get that tie?" He was wearing a bright yellow tie and white shirt.

Rome spoke. "OK, enough. Play these tapes. Cula tell me what you see. Or, what you don't see."

Cooper played the Roberts and Choate tapes.

"So, Cula, what have we got?"

"Well, Chief, we've got two tapes with good video and no sound. No Academy Awards here."

"Cula, I'm not asking for your movie review."

Smith hoisted the movie section of the newspaper, held it high and said. "Dracula gives 3 stars to *Showdown at the Ridge* starring Lisa Marie Cooper.

"This isn't funny, Cula; did you see anything strange?"

"Chief, other than the results, the tapes look fine."

"Cula, educate me; tell me what we saw."

"It's an OR. I see a 3 channel monitor, a cart of medications, anesthesia gear, intubation equipment, suction apparatus, overhead lights, scrub station, sheets, tape, gauze, foley catheters, needles, IV, syringes. It's the real thing."

Cooper looked disappointed with Dracula's explanation.

"Come on Dracula, think. Isn't anything unusual in those tapes?"

Cula sat and put his hands over his eyes while everyone watched in silence.

"One thing, Cooper. These procedure rooms have very bright overhead lights. I mean bright like the sun over the Equator. I didn't see anyone sweating in the videos. That makes no sense."

Chief Rome had an answer. "Cula, maybe they weren't in there long enough."

"Maybe."

"Cula, thanks for your help. I want to talk privately with my detectives."

Cula left the room and Rome spoke with the detectives.

"Enough, Detective Cooper. In the real world I have a boss, and Mayor Gentry is mad. That episode last night was a horror show. That broadcast guy, Goodman, is a huge contributor to the Mayor and he's friends with Hagen. There's a lot of political muscle out there and unless you have something solid, this Ridge case is over."

Rome walked out of the room with some last words for Cooper. "Lisa, you tried. No harm done."

Cooper looked at Smith. "Charlie, I guess **OPERATION END ZONE** is over."

●●●

Street and Cooper were alone in the room.

"Lisa, I've been where you are now. Give me the videos."

"Why?"

"Don't ask."

"I need them back."

Cooper walked out of the room and Street knew how she felt. He made a phone call and then entered a series of numbers from the touch tone phone into a beeper. In ten minutes Street got the return phone call.

One of the secretaries said, "Street, there's a phone call for you from Boston. Maybe it's April Fool's Day. The guy says his name is JOKER. Is this one of your card-shark friends up in Boston?"

Chapter Eleven:
NEVER SAY DIE

Street, so they exiled you to Philly. You're too hot to handle here in Boston. Now that you're a jazzed-up hero, the Mayor thinks you want to mug his job. Street, you're nutso if you try and score in politics. Leave that to the schmucks."

"Joker, I'm not going into politics. The Mayor is paranoid. So what if my picture was in the papers and I made the talk shows? So the jerk asks the Chief to FEDX me to Philly till things cool off. I don't mind. This isn't so bad."

Street continued. "You know, I owe you big time. Your big blue pens with the radio transmitters saved my tail. Your gadgets are golden and I want you to know..."

"Now, don't get mushy on me, Street. What's cooking down there? What trouble have you met in Philly? How's the junk food?"

"Between classes at MIT and your job at headquarters, can you cut me some time? It's important. I need your help."

"Street, are you in trouble already? Don't you like those seventh inning stretches. How about half-times or commercial breaks. What about plain old time-out? How do you find trouble so fast?"

"Can you get down here this week?"

"Who's paying?"

"I am."

"I'll be there; but Street, don't blindside me."

"Joker. I need some stuff."

"Street, I've got that Alka Seltzer feeling."

Street wrote out his list. "Joker where are you now?"

"My palatial estate on the MIT campus overlooking the beautiful Charles River."

"Give me your fax number on campus." Street asked Joker to stand by while he faxed his shopping list.

> *Hey, Joker, here's the list: Computer program to search OBIT pages of Phila Inquirer last ten years: match up with words--CRYSTAL CLUB. Electronic equipment to analyze two video tapes. Uniform from Fire Department (ask McCauley to get you one). Bunch of those finger print transmitter pens with Philly Police logo. Call me back. I'll wait. Street.*

"Street, you forgot a few things like, should I pack up Old Ironsides, the Boston Garden and Fenway Park? You're nuts?"

"Joker, I know it's a tall order. Keep this to yourself."

"Street, when do you want me?"

"I'll get my partner McCoy to cut you a plane ticket on his credit card. How about tomorrow?"

"Get me some of those Philly Hoagies. I'm hungry already.

●●●

"Lisa, we need to talk. Have you heard on the license plate numbers?"

"We'll have them later this afternoon. What difference does it make? This case was over before it started."

"Lisa, you're not a quitter. You know I'm not. Sure we ruffle feathers. We're not finished. Never say die. Bad choice of words..."

Cooper's eye brightened, "...unless it's June at the Ridge."

Street told her about Joker in Boston. "Lisa, this is a whiz kid. His computers and electronic gizmos are bionic appendages. He's probably got an atomic bomb hidden under his bed at MIT. He made big blue and white Boston Police pens and implanted little transmitters in them. I asked people to write their names and addresses using the pens. Then I took them back...with fingerprints. The signal covered about ten miles. The transmitter was inactive unless a little bubble inside was damaged or, in my case, crushed. That pen saved my life."

Cooper couldn't understand why Street offered his little speech.

"I called Joker. He's coming down tomorrow."

For the first time since his exile to Philadelphia, Street felt like he was a detective again.

"Lisa, I asked Joker to create a computer program."

"You lost me."

"He'll write a computer program. He'll customize it to search for the words CRYSTAL CLUB from the *Inquirer*'s obituary pages. That'll give us a list of people in the Club who died in the last ten years. We can check when they died and see if there's a pattern. Like, Club members who died in June."

Street described how Joker would review the video tapes. With a fire department uniform on loan, Joker might find his way into the Ridge for a first hand look. Joker would also bring some of his fabled transmitter pens.

"Street, he can do all this in 24 hours?"

"He doesn't sleep. Or he does so with his eyes open. My partner up in Boston will help him."

"Charlie and Rudy, come on over here."

Cooper called her partners over, and, as Street listened, she explained what was in the works.

Smith reached for Street's hand. "Hey, Street, you're a stand up guy. I take back what I said about the Celtics."

"Charlie, I didn't hear you say anything."

"I know."

Chapter Twelve:
THE SIXTH MONTH

Street and Cooper met Joker at the airport. Cooper watched as he lumbered through the gangway lugging three oversized bags and bumping into every other person.

"Joker, I'm Detective Cooper and you can call me Lisa. How'd you get all that stuff on the plane?"

Street interrupted. "Lisa, one thing you'll learn about Joker is not to ask too many questions because it's better not to know."

Cooper watched as Street and Joker embraced like two long-lost brothers.

Pointing to Street, Joker said, "Lisa, you realize that Philadelphia has hi-jacked the man, like he's the whole party. This is not just another pretty face; he's the high water mark up in Boston...a legend. We call him the hunter because he catches animals with two legs."

Cooper looked inquisitively at Street.

Joker had not finished. "He could probably run for mayor and win." Street did not think anything to do with politics was funny. "A little meshugana, but a..."

Street put his hand over Joker's mouth. "Enough!"

Joker's eyes blazed in adoration for Street as they peered from behind thick rimmed glasses. His tattered brown sports jacket, wrinkled blue shirt and gray-yellow tie looked like the perfect college uniform. Jack, the Joker, was Edward J. Wilson III, the son of two world- famous University of San Francisco astronomers. Brilliance was a family habit. The nickname, Joker, was earned with his brilliantly orchestrated practical jokes like placing a car atop MIT's main building or laser light shows that disrupted the Cambridge night but disappeared before police arrived.

"Tell me, what does the 'hunter' really mean?"

Joker gladly accommodated her question.

"Lisa, Street is a tracer of shadows in the night. He's a nightmare for the bad guys. Five years ago, the Isabella Stewart Gardner Museum in Boston was robbed. The papers called it the greatest art heist in history. Street was working robbery homicide on St. Patrick's Day when they hit the museum and he was assigned the case. It's the only case he hasn't solved, yet! Street, our hunter is rapped so tight inside that if he didn't jog, he'd explode."

"OK, Joker, stop exaggerating."

"Jimmy, pull out your wallet. I dare you; go ahead."

"Lisa, he's exaggerating. Joker's nuts. The only trouble is, he's also a computer with a social security number and so we tolerate him. Hell, we even pay him."

Street pulled out his wallet and Joker went for something inside.

"Hey, get out of there. What are you doing?"

"Showing the detective, here, why you're called the hunter in Boston."

Inside Street's wallet Joker found a yellowed and tattered piece of old newspaper. He unfolded it and began to read from it:

> STOLEN FROM THE GARDNER MUSEUM WERE THE PAINTINGS *A LADY AND A GENTLEMAN IN BLACK, STORM ON THE SEA OF GALILEE* AND *A SELF PORTRAIT* by Rembrandt. 3/19/90

"Five years after the robbery he still carries a news clipping. He's the hunter, and then some!"

"OK, you've had your fun; now, give me my wallet, cyberface."

Cooper listened with amusement and watched as Street grimaced like a kid caught in the cookie jar. This tall, lean, 40 something hard-edged Boston detective had Dennis the Menace written all over his face.

"Street, let's go visit that newspaper, *The Inquirer*."

"Joker, why not your hotel?"

"Street, relent, repent, release. Joker is here. I talked with the computer folks at the paper. They got approval from management. Or they claimed that they did. I've got my cyber sleuth stuff ready to go. They'll let me take whatever I want."

"Joker, how'd you pull that off?"

"I created a customized piece of software for the newspaper. It's a little gift. I'm giving them a cryptographic security protocol. Not like the Mickey Mouse software they have now. They can deploy it and protect their computer programs from hackers. It'll change their passwords from letter only to alphanumeric. Letter only passwords are prehistoric. You know, like you, Jimmy."

By 10:30 AM, Joker was settled next to one of the newspaper's computers. A crowd watched as he inserted the CRYSTAL CLUB search program he crafted at MIT. Joker dazzled the newspaper's computer junkies with a hat trick of double click razzle dazzle. Cooper and Street watched in silence as Joker took control of the computer room. While he worked, Joker talked in computer speak. The scene was reminiscent of a World Series baseball star talking about batting styles. Words like *dueling security schemes*, *migration paths* and *networks* were tossed like baseballs around the room.

At 11:00 AM, Joker handed a 20-page report to Street.

"That's it, Street. Names. Dates. Addresses. The works. Every mention of the CRYSTAL CLUB in the obituary pages since 1985. And, it's alphabetized on one list and in chronological order on the other."

Cooper looked in amazement at the list.

"Lisa, that's our Joker."

Joker rose to a chorus of ringing applause from the newspaper's computer team. He signed a few autographs and then entered his computer e-mail address in the newspaper's computer.

The next stop was police headquarters for a chance to review the CRYSTAL CLUB list.

June is the sixth month.

36 names listed in *The Inquirer's* obituary page from 1985 through 1994 included the words CRYSTAL CLUB:

CRYSTAL CLUB/Cross Reference Phila Inquirer
01/01/8512/31/95 Obituary Page/Joker

NAME	DATE OF BIRTH
Anderson, James	**August 12, 1987**
Apple, Robert	**January 3, 1988**
Artben, Allen	**April 5, 1986**
Azinger, Michae	**March 3, 1990**
Ballinger, Paula	**June 10, 1992**
Bittman, Ben	**September 24, 1989**
Bullocks, Bradley	**June 3, 1991**
Choate, Steven	**June 12, 1995**
Collins, Martha	**December 20, 1985**
Crisler, Jensen	**June 1, 1993**
Dempsey, Ernest	**July 6, 1990**
Dwight, David	**June 8, 1989**
Eisenhower, Margaret	**October 13, 1986**
Erickson, Philip	**February 9, 1994**
Fell, Jason	**May 30, 1990**
Franklin, James	**June 23, 1991**
Franklin, Richard	**June 7, 1989**
Fuchs, Jackson	**August 7, 1991**
Grissom, Thomas	**June 12, 1989**
Gutten, Ernst	**January 3, 1994**
Hatten, Judy	**June 5, 1988**
Hershey, James	**March 14, 1990**
Holliston, Ralph	**October 3, 1987**
Iverson, William	**June 22, 1988**
Jackson, Stephen	**June 5, 1991**
Klemp, Lyndon	**June 26, 1987**
Lafleur, George	**August 3, 1995**
Macy, George	**December 12, 1990**

Northern, Jennifer	**June 2, 1986**
Oppenheimer, Michael	**April 19, 1990**
Pincus, Phillip	**March 9, 1986**
Richardson, Richard	**June 13, 1989**
Roberts, Jonathan	**June 3, 1995**
Stack, James	**July 4, 1992**
Welles, Jack	**February 3, 1990**
Zell, Peter	**July 23, 1989**

36 Crystal Club members died between January 1, 1985 and December 31, 1994; 36 members died in ten years. 16 or 40 percent died in the month of June.

Cooper looked at Joker's list.

"Joker, give me one of your MIT formulas. Could this be a coincidence?"

"There are 365 days in the year. Death rates vary slightly according to such factors as weather. On a monthly average, slightly more people in the northern hemisphere die in January and February. The same is true in July and August. Severe weather is the common denominator in those four months." Joker saw all eyes were focused on him. "According to statistical probabilities, we have a problem. Unless you tell me that June is Russian Roulette month in this city, then something weird is happening at this hospital."

Street added, "We know when these folks died, not where."

"Charlie, check records at City Hall. Fax them a copy of your list. We'll wait for the info before we take this whole thing to the Chief."

The answer took less than 30 minutes.

Smith handed the list to Levin. "You tell them Rudy."

"Well, it says here that 29 died at the Ridge. The ages varied from mid 40's to late 80's. Seven others died out of the city. One in London, LA, St. Thomas, two in New York City and two in Miami."

Smith looked at Rudy with a smirk. "Rudy, come on? You're holding back. I saw the list. Quit the dramatics."

Cooper spoke before Rudy uttered another word.

"...and all 16 who died in June died at the Ridge. Right?"

Rudy nodded, "yes."

"What else is going on? Same doctors? Same operations? Joker, we need answers."

Street pondered the question he had tossed at Joker. All these deaths. OK, people die in hospitals. But these are very rich people and every one carried a Crystal Club card that expired in June.

"Joker, maybe all these Crystal Club folks ate some bad Chinese food."

"Cute."

"Street, we're going up to see the Chief. Joker, you're great."

"Joker, we've got more things to do. Let's go."

Chapter Thirteen: TERPSICHOREAN PLEASURES

"Good morning, CHARLES RIVER MEDICAL CENTER."

"Dr. Ernie Green, please. Tell him it's Detective Jimmy Street in Philadelphia."

"He's on pager."

"Beep him and give him this return number."

"Are you a patient?"

"Better than that. Beep him."

"Detective Street, what are you doing in Philadelphia?"

"Ernie, that's a story you don't need to hear. I need your help. It's a medical question. You better sit down for this one."

"What! Street; you're crazy."

Street had popped the question. How would a doctor kill a patient in an operating room and not get caught? How could they do it while the president of the hospital, a doctor, was watching. How could they do it with nurses and another doctor in the room.

"Street, you're kidding, right?"

"Ernie, does it sound like that?"

"Street, you gotta give me a minute. No one ever asked me that."

"Ernie, take all the time you want. But make it the right answer."

Ernie Green was named temporary Chief of the 7th Floor at the Charles River Medical Center after the death of Dr. Timothy Marks. Green had survived the dead cure rampage at the famed Boston hospital that killed his two best friends and his mentor, Dr. Marks. Green knew that he owed his life to Street.

"Street, I'm a doctor. Your question is sick. Doctors don't kill. Not on purpose."

"Ernie, we know each other. We came through a lot at the Charles. Trust me on this. I need that answer."

Green asked a couple of questions. "What kind of surgery?"

"Angioplasty and arthroscopy for tennis elbow."

"What hospital?"

"The Ridge in Philadelphia. A big teaching hospital."

"Street, that's a great hospital. It's the biggest one in Philadelphia. They've got a fabulous reputation."

"Ernie, answer the question." Street looked at Joker while the phone was silent. "Ernie, Joker says hi. He's down here, too."

"Street, what's going on? You called the cavalry in on this?"

"Some other time Ernie."

Green then gave Street the draconian answer. "Street, I'd bolus them with a drug or air."

"Ernie, explain. I don't wear one of your white coats, remember."

"This is way out, Street. I'd put a big bolus of air into an IV. The air could hit the heart and disperse. There'd be no trace. They'd die. The air bubble could jam up the works. Wack out the lungs or worse, the brain; you'd stoke them out--kill them. Kind of like an air lock in a submarine. Ever see *Hunt for Red October*?"

"Street, forget that. No good. Might be hard to put in enough air without anyone seeing. Shit, I can't believe I'm even thinking this way."

"You still there, Ernie?"

"I could also give them a bolus of pancuronium. That's a paralytic agent. Like one big, bad snake bite. Like those blow darts in the movies. Small syringe, same result. I might be able to do it without anyone seeing me. That would be the tough part. It could be done."

Silence on the phone.

"You still hanging in there, Ernie?"

"Thinking, Street. Another idea. Potassium. Lot's of it. 100 mg right into an IV. We use it all the time in cardiac surgery to stop the heart. Street, you eat a lot of bananas?"

"I don't get it."

"Street, bananas, a great way to get potassium. Don't sweat it. You couldn't eat that many in a day."

"Thanks a bunch, Ernie; talk with you later."

"Street, not so fast. What you're describing doesn't work if someone is going solo. You'd need a bunch of people working together. Your patients wouldn't die in such neat and orderly ways. It's too complicated. Someone would notice that there was trouble. Someone would intervene."

"Ernie, what you describe is a conspiracy."

"Street, doctors aren't going to dance to money. At least, I don't think so. You couldn't pay them to kill. I take that back. Let me think about it. We've got some strange people in white coats walking around here. Money still doesn't sound right, though."

"Maybe it wasn't money. Maybe it was sex or drugs. Maybe they were under the gun."

"Street, I don't believe it."

"That's because you think all doctors are God. It's a new world. Times have changed. I wouldn't call the Charles tranquility base."

"You're still crazy, Street."

"That's me. Crazy Jimmy Street. Never say no; never give up. Talk with you soon."

Street reached Cooper upstairs as she waited to talk with the Chief.

"Lisa, I've got more information. Get your dancing shoes ready. Isn't this Chubby Checker's hometown? We're going to twist and shout. How about your place at seven?"

"Street, maybe you'll fix the mirror, too."

Chapter Fourteen: MUSCARINE

The chemists label it C9H20NO2. It's a highly toxic alkaloid derived from the mushroom Amanita muscaria and it is found in decaying animal tissue.

A decaying hospital can be a toxic source. Jimmy Street had seen a Boston hospital decay.

While Street planned a night with Cooper, he also planned a middle of the night visit to the Ridge with Joker.

•••

When Street arrived at Cooper's condo, she was dressed and ready for dinner.

"How'd it go with Chief Rome? What'd she think of Joker's computer printout?"

Cooper said she was both thrilled and in turmoil. Chief Rome okayed a formal investigation. OPERATION END ZONE was back. She told Street there were so many thoughts speeding through her head, she had a headache. She was scared. She was excited. Cooper had her tonsils removed at the Ridge. Her nephew, Andrew, had been born at the Ridge. A retired detective she knew had a bullet removed from his leg at the Ridge. The Vice President of the United States had visited the Ridge last year and honored Dr. Hagen and his pioneering ways. The Ridge was part of the fabric of the city she loved.

"Lisa, you did it. Congratulations."

"For what? Jimmy, this isn't a game. I don't want to uncover any demons at the Ridge. Do you understand?"

Street was intimate with the dilemma Cooper confronted. She landed herself in a quadrangle and had to get out. Getting out of a case was always harder than getting into one. Street flashed back to his first moments with Dirk Eldridge and Ernie Green in Boston. A beautiful and brilliant 27 year old doctor was dead at the world famous Charles Hospital. The medical examiner said it was accidental. Street knew there was more to the story. He believed Cooper knew the same thing.

"Hey, where are those dancing shoes? Dinner and dancing tonight."

Cooper burst into tears and Street guided her into a chair

"Lisa, I'm here to listen. Talk to me. Let it go."

Street saw some bottles of wine stacked in the kitchen. He uncorked a white California and grabbed two glasses. Cooper watched as he juggled the wine and glasses. Then one glass fell to the floor. After a second of silence, Cooper started to laugh.

"Jimmy, after you clean that up, you can do the same in the bedroom. You are a lot of things. Smooth is not one of them."

Street reached for another glass without cleaning up the broken glass. He sat next to Cooper.

"Jimmy, the kitchen."

Street would not let her eyes wander from his.

"Lisa, broken glass is good luck."

With those words, Street slid his hands behind Cooper and turned her back towards him. He started to roll his long fingers across her shoulders. His fingers played across her neck and shoulders. Cooper's hair was knotted with a yellow and green band. Street tossed it to the floor. His fingers moved from her neck and into her hair. Cooper felt the strength of his fingers as her head rolled from side to side.

With her back to him, Street guided his fingers through her hair and onto her face. His right fingers touched her forehead and eyes with a rhythmic push and release. His left fingers cuddled her chin and mouth. Cooper opened her mouth.

Her tongue was dripping with fluids as she rolled it around his middle finger. Street's finger coasted inside her mouth. Cooper's tongue cradled his finger and she drew it deeper inside. She sucked his finger and drew it in and out.

Street's eyes closed. He turned Cooper towards him. Street opened his eyes. Now facing each other, Street watched as Coo-

per placed another finger in her mouth. Street looked down and watched as she lowered her head.

He eased his finger from her mouth and straddled her head with his hands. Their lips were only an inch apart. The wet tips of their tongues touched.

With a powerful surge, Street moved his lips onto hers. Her tongue moved inside his mouth and then his into hers. She wrapped her arms around his head, tightening the embrace. Street rolled his fingers around and behind her ears. Their eyes were open. Their lips were locked. The juices in her mouth spilled into his and he swallowed. He sucked her tongue deep inside his mouth.

Cooper groaned in ecstasy. Street slipped his hands inside her white silk blouse and moved across the buttons. Cooper lifted her hands inside her blouse and ripped it apart. Street pushed the blouse over her shoulders and down. Street's eyes looked down and he saw her nipples bulging in outline against her white lace bra.

Their lips did not separate.

Little streams of juices flowed from the edges of their lips.

Cooper slowly moved her lips from Street and took off his tie and shirt. He was bare chested. His upper body was hard and well shaped. She bent forward and moved her tongue across his hairy chest. Her lips settled on one nipple and then the other. Cooper straightened her back and moved Street's hand to the clip on her bra. It fell to the floor.

Street looked at her breasts. They were rounded and perfectly shaped. The nipples were small and hard. Street wet his right middle finger and then oozed it around Cooper's right nipple. Cooper looked down as her nipple hardened and pointed upward. Street took the same finger, placed it in his mouth, and then moved it in a circling pattern around Cooper's left nipple. She took her hands and cuddled her own breasts. Street looked on in frozen ecstasy.

Street reached his hand out and guided Cooper towards the bedroom. They walked towards the bed, naked from the waist up. Cooper held the wine and glasses.

Her bedroom had a king-sized bed with wooden posts and two large white chairs on either side.

Cooper released Street's hand and slumped into one of the white chairs. Street stood in front of her. He extended his hands and she pulled him closer to the chair.

"Lisa..."

She put her fingers to his mouth and touched his lips.

"Jimmy, watch."

Street was still.

Cooper lifted her legs and placed one over each leg of the chair. She wore sugar colored nylons. Her blue and white high heeled shoes pointed at the ceiling. Her blue skirt was up at her waist. Cooper moved her hands under her knees and pushed them up and wider. Street crumbled to his knees. His legs were rubber.

"Jimmy, take my shoes off."

Cooper's shoes fell to the floor. Street held each foot and massaged them. Cooper moved her toes and wiggled in the chair.

"Jimmy, that tickles."

Street's hands moved up Cooper's legs and settled behind her knees. He saw her white panties silhouetted under her nylons. Cooper guided her nylons and panties down her legs and tossed them away. Her blue and white skirt was draped across her waist. Street was naked.

Cooper had a surprise for Street. "Jimmy, reach over and hit that button."

"What is it?"

"Just do it."

Street recognized the device. He had seen it on pianos. It was a metronome. When he hit the button it started to click at a fixed interval.

"Lisa, what's that for?"

"It helps me with rhythm for sit-ups. It's good for other things, too."

CLICK. Three seconds. CLICK. Three seconds. CLICK.

Street climbed fully onto the chair and brushed against Cooper's body. He moved to the beat of CLICK, CLICK, CLICK. Cooper did the same.

For the next two hours, Street and Cooper were wrapped around each other, their bodies covered in sweat and juices, the room reverberating with groans and laughs. They made love first on the chair, then on the floor and finally in bed.

Street spilled some of the wine on Cooper as she lay on the bed and fell asleep in each other's arms.

Street awoke. It was almost 12 midnight.

"Lisa, I have to go."

"Street, hit and run?"

"Not so. This is great."

"Why leave?"

"You don't want to know."

"Jimmy, we've shared everything tonight. Don't stop now."

Street explained that he and Joker planned to go inside the Ridge. Joker had a fire department uniform and would masquerade as a fire inspector. Joker had set up two-way radio communication. Street would be his safety man positioned in the hospital waiting room while Joker looked at the ORs used in Roberts and Choate's surgery.

"OK, now Joker has extra protection. We're both coming. And, by the way, Jimmy, I noticed your eyes are different colors. You've got dog eyes. That's really wild. Do you have other secrets?"

Cooper put on a pair of jeans and a polo shirt. Street got dressed, minus his jacket and tie. At 12:33 AM, they arrived at the Ridge. Joker was in his rented car.

"Street and Cooper, Philly's new dynamic duo."

Joker was dressed in blue shirt and pants. Somehow he had acquired a Philadelphia Fire Department logo patch and hat. He carried official looking papers and a small bag. Joker looked like a fire department inspector.

"Street, this fire department pin has a microphone. There's no ON/OFF switch. Put this in your ear. It's like a hearing aid."

"Go get 'em, Joker. Be careful inside. I'm here for you. Just say the word."

"What word?"

"I'll know."

Joker walked through the labyrinthine glass doors and headed to the security desk. Two security guards were at the desk.

"So what's up? You're with the Fire Department?"

Joker never answered.

"I'm here to do a spot check of the Ridge. You know the new rules. We have surprise inspections. This is a Category III; so, it's no big deal."

The guards looked puzzled. "What's a Category III?"

"That's an after-hours walk through of hospitals with more than 300 beds. It's not a complete inspection. We just check fire extinguishers, alarm systems, and the heating and cooling."

Street heard everything Joker said. "Lisa, Joker's really piling it on. This guy's always prepared. Maybe he was a Boy Scout."

The security guards asked for ID and Joker pulled out a picture ID with the Philadelphia Fire Department logo, signed with his legal name, Edward Wilson III.

One of the guards motioned for Joker to sit down while they verified his ID.

"Tell you what, folks. If you're going to make this a big deal and make a night of it, then, screw it; I'm going to make this a Category I inspection--let me use that phone."

"What's a Category I?"

"That's a big deal. We'll bring some fire trucks over here. You'll call whoever is in charge...get 'em out of bed. We'll bring in the whole inspection crew. And we'll be here when the sun rises. So, let's get to it. You call whatever and I'll call headquarters."

"Wait a minute. Let's go back to that Category III. How long would it take?"

"Half an hour and I'm out of here. You can come along, if you wish."

The guards signaled OK and paged an off-duty nurse as escort.

Street looked at Cooper. "He's in!"

Joker noticed an odor when he entered elevator 2 C. He thought the smell was musklike. The smell was hidden under the disinfectant that was the primary scent. Words came to his mind as he traveled in the elevator to one of the operating rooms. He thought of words like decay, gloomy, dark, and hellish. For Joker and his super-human sensory tools, this was a stygian ride equal to his worst nightmare. Joker spoke softly so that Street could hear his commentary.

The nurse who accompanied Joker thought he mumbled his words.

"Inspector, did you say anything?"

"Nurse, not a word. Just thinking."

The nurse pointed him towards several operating rooms. Her coffee break had ended.

"Can you find your way back down?"

"Easy. Thanks."

"Street, I know you can hear me. That elevator was a box. It smelled like decay, covered up with deodorizer. I'm going into the OR where Roberts died."

After ten minutes inside, Joker spoke into his transmitter pin.

"Street, I swept the room for electronic gadgets. Nothing. I saw the TV monitor sweep back and forth. I looked at all those medical toys."

"Wow, they've even got a mass spec on the anesthesia gizmo."

"They're real neat. I read the labels. Seems like good stuff. Some of them are made outside Boston. They calibrate these machines in the hospital. Someone signed M. JOY/Ridge.

"And who are you?"

"Lady, we're doing a fire inspection. Category III. Is that a problem?"

"Just curious. It goes with the job. I'm Dr. Tara Tuls."

"Nice to meet you. What keeps you here so late. My goof. This is a hospital. Silly me. We do so many inspections they just become a blur."

"Actually, I am here late. I'm the Chief of Psychiatry. Can you believe it? I just finished for the day. Night. Whatever it is."

"You're a shrink?"

"And you've got a name?"

"Eddie Wilson, Philadelphia Fire Department. Say, your red hair almost matches our fire trucks." Joker watched as she walked away.

Tuls was tall, about 5 feet 10 inches, very pretty, with cute legs and a dangerous half smile. She was all that Joker saw and a lot more.

She was an expert in a field of drugs called psychic energizers. This was a protocol of drugs used to treat depression. Tuls had a lot of experience from her days in junior high school outside of Boston. Her father was a giant in the Boston field of psychiatry and he was also her first lover. She was 13. The trauma of those early years propelled Tuls into a patron of older men. She was gifted with nice clothes, fine restaurants, and vacations to elegant resorts. By the time she was 21 and entering medical school in Boston, Tuls had several hundred sexual partners. Her partners were male, female and combinations of both. Her drug of choice was sex.

Marriage changed her life, if only for a couple of years. She married a Boston criminal lawyer. She soaked up the culture jewels of Boston like the Symphony and Museum of Fine Arts. She had her first affair one month after returning from a honeymoon in Rio. Her lover was a construction worker who gave her powerful, muscled sex and a lasting item to remember him. Herpes.

From that moment on, her hatred of men was insatiable. She was an accomplished sexual predator and her targets of choice were married men. Dr. Walter Hagen, Dr. Markus Harmon and seven other staff members at the Ridge had all enjoyed her gifts of flesh.

Street and Cooper were in the waiting room. They were holding hands and talking. Joker walked past them and into the parking lot. After a couple of minutes, Street and Cooper walked outside.

"Hey, guys, that hand holding was a nice little touch. Very smart. What a babe I met upstairs. Red hair unlike any you've ever seen."

Street and Cooper did not dare look at each other.

"Joker, let's talk this out tomorrow. I don't think getting friendly with doctors at the Ridge is too smart."

"I won't forget that smell."

"You smelled her?"

"Street, the elevators! Get your mind out of the gutter."

Chapter Fifteen: VORTEX

OPERATION END ZONE assembled the next day. Joker had his bags packed for his flight to Boston.

"Street, it's back to school. The Technodrome awaits."

Cooper smiled. "Joker, I heard a lot about you from Jimmy. You're all he said and...then some."

Joker pulled a piece of paper from his pocket.

"Street, one more thing. I called one of the medical companies listed on the OR equipment. It's called DATAX and they're in Lexington, outside Boston. They said there's a field representative for this region trained in calibration of their BP Monitors and they have a 24 hour hot line for repair. Their representative is Darlene Evers. The name I saw on that equipment was 'M. JOY'. DATAX has no M. JOY."

"Joker, no joy, right?"

"Street, don't take my lines."

•••

Cooper's beeper rang and she saw a familiar call back number. "Choate residence."

"This is Detective Cooper."

"Mrs. Choate, it's that detective on the line."

"Detective Cooper, this is Ginny Choate. Thanks for calling back."

"What can I do for you?"

"I hired a lawyer and he notified the Ridge we're filing a $20 million suit for negligence in my husband's death. I wanted you to know."

"Which firm?"

"Carmen, White & Choate. My husband's brother is a senior partner."

"Mrs. Choate, we'll talk later. I appreciate the call."

Cooper had Mrs. Choate on speaker phone. If there were evil spirits loose in the Ridge, a lawsuit might make it tougher to get the facts. Subjects of a possible police investigation would be extra careful if they were facing a civil lawsuit.

•••

"Detective Street, there's a call for you on line two."

"Street."

"Chief, how's the weather up in Boston? Yeah, I'm doing fine down here. Working on a good case. Maybe this exchange program wasn't such a bad idea."

Street was silent.

"No fuckin' way! You can tell the Mayor he can kiss my ass. He's not gonna lead me around like some traveling pet show. I know he wanted me out of town. I know why. Now all of sudden he wants me back. Bullshit. I know what's coming down. His buddy Mayor Gentry down here must have called him. They want me out. Well, no way."

Street slammed the phone down and growled.

Cooper's face went blank and Smith and Levin grimaced.

•••

Smith and Levin saw Cooper's blank look. Street put his arm around her.

"Babe, I'm not going anywhere."

"Homicide...this is Detective Smith. Can I help you?"

"Yeah. When? Right away."

"Guys, I told you about my friend inside the Ridge. The one who works in administration. Guess what? They just admitted a Mr. Eric C. Goodman for observation. CRYSTAL CLUB flashed on her computer screen. Guess they have an alert system when club members are admitted."

Street looked outside the window at falling snow. "Well, it sure isn't June. Lucky Goodman."

Chapter Sixteen: MISTY, THE PROZAC DOG

Big city detectives are like windshield wipers moving across a dirty window in winter.

Street thought he had seen everything that was dirty. He had knelt on wet pavement while a junkie held the cold steel of a revolver against his head. He remembered a young Jimmy Street in the doorway of his New York home when they came because his dad had been gunned down on a police stake out. Street saw the face of his wife saying goodbye. He saw madness at the Charles Hospital in Boston as a great doctor self destructed. It was a rare day when Street was surprised.

"Street, you won't believe this. Cooper, listen up...this is new."

Smith read from his note pad.

"You know Goodman checked into the Ridge. Well, he didn't check in alone."

That made no sense.

"Seems Goodman was admitted to a private room reserved for Crystal Club members. He came with his dog, Misty."

"Go ahead, ask me how I knew he brought his dog?"

"Your source at the hospital?"

"Yeah, but what made this story wild?"

There was a moment of silence; then Smith continued. "Goodman's dog takes Prozac. She's an eleven year old beagle mutt. Goodman's office told the Hospital his dog takes Prozac. They set up a little dog house in Goodman's room and they feed his dog and give her Prozac. Goodman's wife gave them special meal instructions for the dog."

Street threw his hands in the air.

"Thank you, Mr. Goodman. Just when the world's coming apart, you get touched by a hero. A guy who reminds you that no matter how crazy things get, it can always get worse. Good-

man turns the Ridge into a Prozac-pushing dog kennel. I'd like to shake this guy's hand."

Cooper leaned over. "Jimmy, first we better find out why he's in the Ridge."

Smith had the answer: "Admitting papers say 'Ulcer?'"

"Lisa, given a choice of going back to Boston or visiting Mr. Goodman and his Prozac dog Misty, I'm staying. This cinches it."

Street made reservations to fly home on Friday. He had an appointment in Boston with the Chief of Police. On his way to the Ridge, Street imagined a Prozac-hooked beagle getting Crystal Club VIP treatment while other patients waited to see their doctor. Street could not erase his smile.

"Mr. Goodman, I'm Detective Street and this is Detective Cooper."

Goodman was sitting in a chair with Misty in his lap, his wife in another chair and a fax machine churning out memos from his Philadelphia TV station. The scene was preposterous and, if it was not the Ridge, amusing.

"Mr. Goodman, we understand you've got an ulcer. So, how do you feel?"

"How would you feel? Lousy! I've had it before. I'll be out fast."

Cooper wondered if that last remark was just a coincidence. Street thought to himself. "Damn straight, buddy; I'd get out fast, too."

Cooper clapped her hands and Misty looked over.

"Here, Misty; come here."

Misty stayed in Goodman's lap.

"I agreed to see you, detectives, because the police are always helpful to our people in news at Channel 31. We've got a great relationship with the police. You've got questions on our Crystal Club?"

"We do."

Goodman started talking about Dr. Hagen. "He's a genius. He's made the Ridge into one of the great hospitals in our country. And I'm here getting all this special care, free of charge."

Street interrupted. "Well, not really free."

"Listen, young man. I'm getting up there in age. I've got to do something with my money. I've been lucky. KEYSTONE Broadcasting started with one small radio station outside Philadelphia. Now, we've got 15 radio stations and 9 TV stations coast to coast. We're listed on the stock exchange. It's an honor to be in this Crystal Club."

As Goodman spoke, a dietitian, dressed in white with a CC emblem, walked into his room. CC personnel specialized in care for Crystal Club members.

"Detectives, look at this menu. They give me some lousy tasting liquid. Here Carol, pick something out for yourself and Misty."

Street and Cooper looked at the menu in amazement.

Crystal Club Menu

Grilled Shanks Braised/Apricots and Spices
Cannelloni
Braised Melange of Vegetables
Grilled Bread and Goat Cheese
Scallops with Shaved Truffles

Goodman's wife ordered as if she were dinning at the Ritz. Misty settled for the leftovers.

As the dietitian left, a doctor entered Goodman's room. Her name tag read, Dr. Rundy.

"Mr. Goodman, it's always an honor to meet someone from the Crystal Club. Dr. Hagen will be visiting with you in a little while. I want to do a few tests and make sure you're comfortable. We'll take care of this problem. Mrs. Goodman, you and these guests must leave. I know your husband has permission for the dog to stay. We'll bathe her to make sure there are no bugs or ticks."

"Detectives, thanks for the visit. Now, how can you beat this?"

Goodman sported a wide grin and pointed to the door.

Street and Cooper looked at each other and wondered if they'd get another chance to question Goodman.

●●●

Street was in his hotel room when the phone rang at 9:30 PM.

"It's Charlie; how are you Street? Good luck back in Boston."

"So, what's up, Charlie."

"Thought you'd like to know. Goodman was discharged from the Ridge tonight. Goodman and his wife and that Prozac pooch are all home safe and sound."

Chapter Seventeen: CRI DU COEUR

In his flight to Boston, Street asked for a dictionary. Bibles, Sports Illustrated and Forbes were never a problem on planes. Street found his dictionary and looked up words like 'mad' and 'angry'. He saw the synonym Cri du Coeur and loaded the French words into his vocabulary. He also wrote it down.

"Let's see how the Chief likes this." Street pulled a piece of paper from his pocket. "Chief, this is a cri du coeur! And I'm not kidding."

The Chief laughed.

"Jimmy, maybe you caught some bug down in that bunker at the Charles Hospital."

Street and the Chief liked each other. The Chief was a political animal and Street was not. Both knew the ground rules of the meeting.

"Street, this is off the record. You wanted the meeting. Agreed?"

"Yes sir!"

The Chief defined the political landscape in Boston and Philadelphia. "Street, our Mayor has eyes on the State House. That ego-maniac, Gentry, in Philadelphia has eyes everywhere. These hacks are friends. They scratch each other's back so often they ought to leave their initials. Mayor Gentry is friends with this Dr. Hagen and some broadcast mogul, Goodface or something..."

"...It's Goodman, sir."

"Hagen claims there's a detective down there named Cooper. He says she's a hot boiled bitch and he thinks you're pushing her. Hagen called Goodman and he got the Mayor.

The Mayor calls our Mayor. Can you guess the next call? You can finish the story yourself."

"What'd you tell him?"

"I said we'd talk. I told him you wanted to get back to Boston. I told him I didn't think calling you back was a problem."

Street pulled out his badge and gun and placed them on the Chief's desk.

"Street, no theatrics, please."

"Sir, may I speak openly?"

"This is all off the record. Let it hang out."

"Our kissass Mayor is nothing but a suit and tie whore. He's a political sleaze ball. He's a wimp. First he wanted me out of Boston. Guess he figured with all the publicity from the Charles I might have a political urge. No way. Then he got a call from the Mayor in Philadelphia and he wet his pants. Get Street out of there. Well, with all due respect, sir, no fucking way."

"Street, you don't have a choice."

"Yes, I do. You can keep that badge and gun and I'll take my retirement. I like the idea of newspaper reporting. My first story will be about the Charles Hospital and the Mayor's coverup. How many people in Boston know there's a decaying corpse and killer viruses and bacterium in the bunker?" Street never bluffed. "One more thing, Chief, tell the Mayor that in the course of human events, he's nothing but lost luggage."

"Street, I'll skip your speech. Take your badge and gun. I'll handle things. Just get back to Boston soon."

"Chief, I'm coming back to run the Marathon in April."

"That's not what I meant."

"And Chief, what did Hagen call detective Cooper?"

"Street, don't get involved with Cooper. We want you back at work in Boston."

•••

"Lisa, it's Jimmy. I just finished with the Chief. We're on the same page. I'm still part of OPERATION END ZONE."

"Jimmy, I'm smiling."

"I'll meet you at the airport. The drive from Logan to Hyannis is about 90 minutes. We'll be on Nantucket by midnight."

Chapter Eighteen:
NANTUCKET CROSSING

Street and Cooper boarded the last ferry of the night. The crossing from Hyannis to Nantucket took two hours in ten foot seas. Cooper was bundled in a yellow wind breaker and slept while Street nursed a cup of coffee.

It was midnight when a cab dropped them off at Street's cottage. Nantucket Island was deserted; Street's refrigerator empty. He grabbed every blanket and both cuddled for warmth. It was a typical Nantucket winter night with a strong, wet howling wind, the taste of a salty mist everywhere. When they awoke around eight AM, the sky was gray.

Street had some bicycles in the laundry room and they went in town for breakfast at the Donut. Nantucket in the winter was a special sanctuary for Street. Cooper loved everything she saw and understood why Street could not stop talking about the Island's magic.

After breakfast, they returned to Street's cottage. Street planned a long walk along a beach and then an afternoon of tranquillity. He was changing clothes when the phone rang.

"Lisa, you get it."

"Charlie, what's wrong?

She knew Charlie would never call unless there was trouble.

"When? I'll talk with Jimmy and call you back."

"Jimmy, Charlie says Goodman was re admitted to the Ridge. He's on a respirator. That's all I know."

"Lisa, I don't care if Goodman's dog Misty overdosed on Prozac. We're taking that walk on the beach. We'll catch the last ferry back. We can be in Philly tomorrow afternoon."

Cooper felt a huge wave of contentment sweep over her. Street had instantly put her topsyturvy world in perspective.

She felt a blanket of Nantucket *mellow* and it was so comfortable.

"Lisa, this is our time on Nantucket. No one is gonna take it. Let's walk."

●●●

"We're becoming *last ferry* travelers."

After the ferry landed in Hyannis, they drove to Boston and arrived at Street's Beacon Hill condo as a cold mist settled across the city. Street had reservations on the first Sunday flight to Philadelphia. According to Smith, Goodman was fighting for his life at the Ridge.

"Lisa, it's not June. Bet Goodman makes it."

Chapter Nineteen: NIGHT CRAWLER

For the evildoer, a chance to vandalize the night is vindication. While some sanctify the night with sleep, others congregate in the dark and contemplate unholy acts.

At 2:34 AM, five computer screens in Philadelphia networked in a bootstrap security protocol.

SYS is on. TERMINAL standing by. RAZOR here. CHASE is awake. SATAN on line. ACID feels your pain.

COBOL welcomes the team. Kill the humor.

RAZOR identify your firewall. RAZOR confirms with code word cull and challenges TERMINAL. This is TERMINAL and our platform is ^ ^ ^.

COBOL requests unlock sequence from team.

SYS is 3. RAZOR is 7. CHASE is 9. TERMINAL is 9. SATAN is 3. ACID is 3.

This is COBOL. We confirm 379933. That is an unlock. We are go for chatter.

We have 60 seconds folks. What about that detective?

He's out of it. Lollipop is pushing for his transfer back to Boston. Detective Street won't be a problem.

And Cooper?

She's got nothing.

Do we have a leak at the Ridge? Is someone feeding info to the cops?

We'll check. How many votes to terminate if we confirm leak?

This is COBOL. Two votes required for termination.

Question for COBOL... Date set for next Crystal Club DISCONNECT?

Pending. Will advise.

Team members receive $50,000 quarterly payment on 15th. Other payments in kind processed. Questions?

CHASE is green. RAZOR OK. SYS OK. TERMINAL is happy. SATAN. ACID

COBOL orders sign off in 10987654321.

Chapter Twenty: GOODMAN REDUX

OPERATION END ZONE was full throttle Monday morning with the return of Street and Cooper. Smith and Levin greeted them at the airport.

"So, how was your weekend?"

"This Jimmy of mine, he took me on a ferry in ten foot seas and showed me his no-heat cottage on Nantucket. We had breakfast, took a walk on the beach and caught another ferry back to Hyannis. He sure knows how to show someone a good time."

"Charlie, tell me about your source at the Ridge."

"Jimmy, I've got a friend there. Her name is Celia. She worked at headquarters but a job placement outfit put her in the Ridge and got her more money. We stay in touch. Sometimes I fix a ticket. I told her we were looking around the Hospital and not to talk about it. She called and told me about Goodman."

"What about him."

"Hey, Jimmy, I didn't want to call her at the Ridge. I don't want to get her involved. I called patient information. Now, he can have visitors. Isn't that a fast recovery?"

"Damn straight, it is. Let's try and visit him. Can you and Charlie get us a list of those Crystal Club license plate numbers at the Ritz?"

●●●

The detectives flashed their ID and headed to the 5th floor. When they walked in Goodman's room, they were amazed to find him walking around and barking commands into a speaker phone. He had an unlit cigar in his mouth.

"That's right. My computer says the overnights put us three points behind. This is a sweeps period. Jazz our news up. More crime. More pictures. More sex. More perverts. Get a good fire."

Goodman was in a room with elegance that would embarrass the Ritz. His room overlooked trolley cars moving through Chestnut Hill. The furnishings were rich mahogany. He had several TV's, a computer and fax machine.

"Detectives, you're back."

"Yes, and, Mr. Goodman, you're back."

Goodman's wife Carol and Misty sat on an elegant white chair.

"It was nothing. They say respirator and everyone panics. Guess I got some sedatives mixed up. What, me worry? This is the Ridge."

As Goodman spoke, one of his doctors entered.

"I see we have a full house here. Mr. Goodman, I'll come back."

"No, doc, these two are detectives. Maybe I could put them on my TV station. You know, hot news story at the Ridge. That might kick those numbers up. Only trouble is, there's no story here. Doc, tell these folks what happened."

He said Goodman complained of confusion, anxiety, and was delirious. When he arrived at the Ridge, there were symptoms of hypercapnia. The doctors who examined Goodman were suspicious that he was in acute respiratory failure. So, they helped him breathe. After a little while it was apparent that his drug regimen was the cause. Along with too much vodka.

"Whatever drugs they gave me for the ulcer must have goofed things up inside. I slept great last night. I'll be out of here tomorrow. You folks seem really interested in the Ridge. Haven't you got better things to do?"

Dr. Hagen walked in Goodman's room, but did not seem surprised to see Street and Cooper.

"Eric, you look great. The doctors kept me informed. I see our favorite detectives are still around. Are they bothering you?"

"Walter, they're no problem. We work with cops all the time at the TV station. I don't mind."

"Well, Eric, I do mind. This is a hospital. Detectives, should I call the Mayor or are you leaving?"

"Dr. Hagen, it's always so special to see you. I've got the video tapes you gave me. We'll mail them back. Registered."

Goodman looked at Hagen and asked, "What video tapes?"

Cooper hoped Goodman would ask that question.

"They're video tapes of Jonathan Roberts and Steven Choate, two Crystal Club members who died last June. Did you know them, Mr. Goodman?"

Goodman nodded with a look of dismay.

"Sure, I knew them. What happened to them was awful."

Hagen knew what game Cooper was playing for Goodman.

"Cooper, you and your partner can leave. Say, Street, I thought you were sent back to Boston?"

"Doc, that's what you'd like. Talk it out with the Mayor. I'm here for the duration. You and I are going to become best of friends."

Cooper turned to Carol Goodman. "Mrs. Goodman, take care of Misty. And take care of your husband. You're lucky it's not June."

Goodman turned to Hagen. "What does that mean? Who cares if it's June?"

Chapter Twenty One: PROSTHESIS

There was a telephone message waiting for Street at headquarters.

Joker left a one word message, PROSTHESIS.

"Joker, I got your message. I don't understand it. But I've got it. Translate it for me."

"Street, dictionaries! I heard you read them on planes. Prosthesis is the replacement of a body part. OK, I took some liberty with that definition. The key word, Jimmy, is replacement. Maybe things at the Ridge have been replaced. Maybe things are not what they appear." Joker had a copy of the Ridge Cath Lab and OR tapes. He knew the BP monitors were calibrated by the Hospital and not the manufacturer. "Street, I've got a simple theory. Can't prove anything. Want to hear it?"

"Your simple theories tend to get complex. I'm listening."

Joker asked Street to remember Star Trek and Mr. Spock. He wanted Street to recall Spock's refrain: *Not logical.*

"Street, logic is the study of reasoning. It's also the non-arithmetic sorting of computers. It's the fundamental choice between yes/no, black/white, up/down. Do you follow me so far?"

"Joker, get to the point."

"Street, we saw medical instruments on the OR video tapes. We assumed they were accurate. You were told there is a specific patient in the OR despite the fact you can't see a face. You assume it's who the Hospital said it was. You may be assuming a lot. Get my drift? What happens before the OR? They don't just walk in off the street and zip into the OR. Don't assume anything. Question everything. Trust no one. How's that for logic?"

Joker went on with a list of what ifs.

"Street, we need to get back inside the Ridge. Can we get court OK to place some electronic equipment inside the Hospital? Get me back in there and I'll put some traps in their computers."

"What are traps?"

"Street, they're like electronic mouse traps except the mouse doesn't know it's caught."

"Joker, I doubt we can get court OK for anything. I'll ask Cooper to try. Can you come back this week?"

"Give me a couple of days. I'll get some whizbangs from one of our laboratories. Street, the grapevine says they tried to yank you back to Boston. True?"

"Yup. It didn't work."

•••

"Guess who called?"

"No idea."

"Our lady in red. The shrink with the red hair. Dr. Tara Tuls called and left a message for me at Philly Fire Department headquarters. She asked for Eddie Wilson."

"And?"

"And, our cover worked. They confirmed my story."

"Joker, I'm not real comfortable with her calling."

"Relax, Street. I called back. She invited me to join her for a drink. You're not the only stud from Boston working in Philly."

"Joker, a word of advice. Don't go. We don't know who all the players are at that hospital."

"I'm thinking about it."

"Joker, you're out of your league. Stay away from her. This is not a game."

"OK, chill out Street. I'll back off. Her loss."

"Maybe your gain."

Cooper called the 'END ZONE' team together.

"Well, here it is. Jimmy has Joker coming back. Can we get a court order that let's us set up some bugs in the Hospital?"

Smith answered, "Cooper, you're a lawyer. You know the rules of evidence. No way!"

"Well, let's try anyway and maybe we'll get lucky with a judge."

One hour later Cooper and Street met an assistant DA in the chambers of Judge Malcolm Soto. Such meetings in chamber are usually informal. The assistant DA was Jack Adams, a former classmate of Cooper in law school. What Street did not know was that Adams had also been a former fiancee of Lisa Cooper.

"This must be my lucky day, Jack; how are you? Long time no see."

"You look great, Lisa. And here we are together using all those thousands of dollars in education to save a little piece of humanity. Well, what part of humanity do you want to bite off today?"

"Cute, Jack; you're still the most sarcastic person I ever met."

Judge Soto had been organizing papers on his desk and caught some of the give and take between Cooper and her ex classmate, Adams.

"OK, is it a class reunion? If so, you're in the wrong room."

"Judge, we want a limited order that permits us to place listening devices in three specific areas. One is Dr. Walter Hagen's office; he's the President of the Hospital. We also want devices in two operating rooms."

Soto jumped to his feet.

"Whose garbage is this? Have you read the Constitution lately? You want to listen in while people are in an operating room. What about their rights? What about the doctors and nurses. And you want a device in this Dr. Hagen's office? Why? Because the Ridge is so successful. I've been a patient at the Ridge. It's a great hospital."

"Say, judge, do you belong to the Crystal Club?"

"Heard about it. No. So what?"

Cooper smiled, "Lucky you."

She saw the aggravation on his face.

"Lucky you, sir, your honor."

"Judge, we can prove that almost half of the Crystal Club members who died in the last nine years have died in June."

"So what? Don't try and sterilize something that's clean. Your request is DENIED. Hell, I should order you back to law school. Now get out of my chambers."

Outside Judge Soto's chambers, the 'END ZONE' team formed a small circle.

"Hey, Lisa, I'm not surprised."

Cooper found a wooden bench and sat with her hands on her knees. Street moved next to her. He leaned over and whispered.

"Lisa, get real. This is where the fun begins."

"Street, we're at a dead end. Let's face it. This is it. We've got nothing. The judge was right."

"Lisa, we've got Joker coming back to Philly. We've got our wits. And we've got more."

"What's that, Jimmy?"

"We've got two, not one, two detectives who believe there's something rotten at the Ridge."

"Jimmy, you believe."

"Lisa, I believe. I know. I feel it. Like I told Hagen, he and I are going to become best of friends."

Chapter Twenty Two: ON THE EDGE

Street knew that everyone lives on the edge of death. A big city cop has no choice except to descend into the cesspool. Cesspools are not taught at the police academy. Cooper was refined, intelligent and gutsy. She had never experienced Street's world. Smith and Levin knew about Street's cesspools. They could twist good cops into bad cops.

The cesspools that Street encountered were metaphysical. There were only subtle differences. He endured the death of his partner by a drug dealer. He entered the privileged world of high tech medicine in Boston and found demons in the corridors.

Street owned a set of principles that kept his head above the slime. His principles were basic. They were the glue that kept him centered. He accepted that evil existed in an infinite variety of forms. He never stereotyped the Lucifers. His fundamental principle was to capture evil, having the instincts of an African hunter.

As lawyer-turned-detective, Cooper never lived on the edge. She had Street's hunter instincts, but not his creativity. She did not know, or share, his willingness to work at the edge of the law.

The time had arrived for Cooper to meet a new Jimmy Street, a Street that worked the edges--the edge of the envelope, and then some. He felt no remorse for she had exposed him to the Ridge and carried the Ridge baggage until others started to believe. It was too late to detour, too late to forget. It was too late to escape. Jimmy Street and Lisa Cooper were now part of the Ridge and Street never let go.

•••

Everyone assembled in Street's hotel room. It was 7:30 PM. Sandwiches and coffee were spread across the bed, tables, and chairs. Then, Joker knocked on the door.

"Hey, folks, round two."

Joker held five foot square sheets of paper that he attached to the walls. Street's room started to look like a wartime command center.

"Lisa, Charlie, and Rudy, I want you to listen hard. Maybe it's time for some of you to take a walk away from the Ridge. Joker and I are just visitors. Charlie, you and Rudy are almost out. You've got retirement coming. You don't need this. And Lisa, you're a cop and also a lawyer. Think about that. Before we start, you need to think."

He offered everyone a chance to get out. In fact, he offered them a chance to kick him out of town.

"Before we go any further, Joker and I are going downstairs for a walk. You talk it out. If you're in, you're taking a big chance. If you're out, that's no problem."

Street and Joker took the elevator downstairs and walked around the hotel lobby.

"Street, I've got everything you asked for and more."

"Joker, this is their city and their situation. Hey, we can ride off into the sunset and back to Boston. The worst is I'll get a slap. You'll be fine. Those folks upstairs have a lot at stake. Smith and Levin can smell their retirement. And Cooper may not have the stomach for this."

Fifteen minutes later they returned to Street's room. The three Philadelphia detectives were sitting together.

"Well?"

Smith lifted his huge frame and stood. He left a crater in his chair.

"OK, here's the deal. Rudy and I are leaving the room. We didn't see anything. We're older. We've got families and responsibilities. Do you understand, Street?"

"You bet. What about you, Lisa?"

"Street, I'm in. I'll take my chances."

With those words, Smith and Levin got up and gave Lisa a kiss. They high-fived Street and Joker, and left.

"Street, I'm scared."

"Lisa, that makes three of us."

•••

COBOL opens the gate. Logon request for RAZOR, TERMINAL, CHASE, SYS, SATAN, ACID. Enter onboard authenticate upon arrival. Meeting tonight at midnight. Urgent. COBOL is clear.

•••

Cooper and Street listened as Joker explained.

"Jimmy, this is ultrahot. Remember, we talked about *logic*. Lisa, think where you've taken us. Consider the logic. Almost half of the Crystal Club deaths in the past nine years occurred in June. I ran a computer program on those probabilities. It's the same chance of winning every state lottery in the United States on the same day. Not one state. Every one! You got some video tapes from Hagen. They have no audio. Can we read lips? No. These doctors and nurses wear masks. And their patients sure aren't talking in the OR. How convenient! Why no audio? I've got a world class nose. That elevator at the Ridge smelled like some guy who smoked a cigar and then took a bathe in cologne to hide it from his wife. The cigar smell is there even if he showers in cologne. We need to get inside the Ridge. I want to look at the equipment in the OR again. And I'd like about 30 minutes in their computer control center."

"Lisa, can Charlie call his friend who works there?"

"He wants to keep her clean. I can ask. Isn't there another way in?"

"Maybe."

Cooper picked up the phone and reached Charlie at home. His wife answered and said her husband and Rudy were out for a drink. Cooper dialed his cellular phone.

"Charlie, I know you and Rudy are out of the Ridge thing. One favor: can you call your friend at home and ask her to do something?"

"Guess so. Why don't I call her at work tomorrow?"

"Charlie, calling her at home is a lot safer for her. I don't trust anything inside that hospital."

"Tell me what you want from her."

Joker got on the line.

"Charlie, it's simple. We need to know who works on their computers. I need the company name."

"I'll call back."

Smith called back in 15 minutes. "Celia made a phone call. She stuck her neck out for me. The name of the company is VALLEY FORGE SYSTEMS."

"Street, let's start with the Ridge computers. I've got some software that is like a vacuum cleaner. It is a timed sequence search. It'll lie around unseen until the middle of the night when it'll sweep all the main computers for words like *Crystal* or *Hagen* or whatever else you want. Then it'll dial out on a hospital modem and dump the data into my portable. They'll never discover my little computer virus."

"When do we go, Joker?"

"Hey, Jimmy, why wait. Let's go hunting, *amigo*."

Joker left and Cooper stayed.

"Jimmy, this is taking a big chance. I'm in. I told you so."

"Lisa, there are no guarantees. Hey, if it all goes bad, maybe we can retreat to Nantucket."

"Jimmy, I wish I wasn't so tired tonight. This Ridge thing is really taking it out of me."

"Lisa, invite me back to your place and we'll fall asleep together. I'll get some oils and grease your back. How's that sound?"

"Jimmy, all ten fingers?"

●●●

COBOL with time check. 00:33:15. Confirm online. Punch your access code at 00:35:00. COBOL standing by.

00:35:00: 455435 logged. Everyone is on chatter. Update on leak inside Ridge

This is CHASE. . Employment records confirm new hire at Ridge was Philadelphia police secretary. Computer log shows calls to police department.

Computer identifies incoming calls from homicide at police headquarters.

COBOL seeks risk assessment. Enter risk level number using your password. COBOL has number. Team assessment of risk is 9. Vote to terminate. Tally at 00:39:00. COBOL awaits results.

00:39:00: COBOL back on line. Vote is 51 for termination. RAZOR confirm mission is accepted.

●●●

Street and Joker prepared to leave for the Ridge. Joker planned to enter the Ridge late in the afternoon. Thanks to Smith's friend Celia, Joker was logged through the Hospital's administration department for a routine computer repair call from VALLEY FORGE SYSTEMS. Celia found VALLEY FORGE SYSTEMS listed in the Ridge directory of vendors.

Cooper ran a quick background check on VALLEY FORGE SYSTEMS. Police files showed SYSTEMS on a list authorized to repair police and other city computer systems. Their pricing was competitive and the Company's founder, Rick Cone, was an acquaintance of Mayor Gentry. She visited SYSTEMS offices in Valley Forge and told Cone there was an ongoing police investigation at the Ridge Hospital. After some questions about liability, Cone agreed that Joker could enter the Ridge with a SYSTEMS ID. Several times Cone asked for assurances that SYSTEMS was not involved in any police sting that could make the 11 PM news. Cooper down-played everything and explained that the police were doing a survey of computer fraud. She reminded him that SYSTEMS did a lot of business with the city and that the Mayor would appreciate his help. Cooper knew that if the Mayor found out about SYSTEMS so called help, he'd probably ban them from city contracts.

Cone looked uneasy when Cooper left his office. Cone was nondescript in appearance and was very nervous and hyper. She thought his demeanor seemed logical under the circumstances. Cone's offices were in an idyllic location, not far from the Valley Forge National Historic Park. The area was crowded with monuments, historical markers and beautiful paved trails for jogging or bicycling. Cooper imagined Street would like to see Valley Forge some day.

"Detective, we're scheduled for a routine repair visit next week to the Ridge. Should that be changed?"

"No." Cooper was satisfied that Cone would remain silent about her visit after she advised him of the consequences if he interfered in a police investigation. She never told him that he had no obligation to cooperate.

"Street, Joker's all set. VALLEY FORGE SYSTEMS will confirm Joker is their employee. Have him use his real name, Edward Wilson. I'll meet you at the Ridge. I've got a VALLEY FORGE SYSTEMS ID for Joker."

Forty five minutes later, Cooper handed Joker his ID in the Ridge parking lot.

"Dispatch to mobile 89. CODE ALPHA OMEGA. Detective Smith standing by."

The AO code meant answer immediately.

"Charlie, this is Cooper. Why the AO?"

"Lisa, don't let Joker inside the Ridge."

Charlie's very powerful and rock solid voice was trembling and uneven.

"He's already through the doors?"

"My contact at the Ridge, Celia, didn't show up for work today. Her sister just found her at home. She's dead. Cooper, this is turning sour."

Street heard Charlie's message and instinctively put his hand on his revolver and clicked the safety off.

"Lisa, I'm gonna get Joker out of there."

"Street, Joker's got a microphone on. He's in a hospital. He'll be OK."

Cooper grabbed Street's hand and squeezed.

"Jimmy, I promise. Joker is safe."

Street's cellular phone buzzed.

"Jimmy, this is Charlie. Rudy and I will be at the Ridge in ten minutes."

"Guys, stay out. We already decided who's in and who's out."

"Street, my friend Celia from the Ridge is dead. Someone involved with that hospital tracked her down. Rudy and I are back in this case."

●●●

"Street, this is Joker. I'm inside. Going to security to check in. Stay tuned, *hunter*!"

Joker stopped at the security desk and signed his name:

Edward Wilson VALLEY FORGE SYSTEMS 5:30pm

The first thing Joker noticed was that the guards were different from the night he went in as a Philadelphia Fire inspector. If they were the same guards, Joker was prepared to turn and exit. They asked for ID and Joker gave it to them. "You're going to the computer room, right?"

"You got it."

"You know the way, don't you?"

"Sure."

Joker started in the direction of the elevators.

"Wrong way buddy. Are you sure you know?"

"Yeah, I'm just looking for a coffee machine."

"Keep going around the corner. It's on the right."

"Thanks."

At the coffee machine, Joker looked around and found a directory.

"Street, if you can hear me, I'm going inside the computer room. This should be fun."

The Ridge computer room had no windows. Two women were inside working with the computers.

"Hi, ladies. I'm from VALLEY FORGE SYSTEMS. Can you give me a couple of minutes on the computer? I'm going to run a couple of diagnostics."

Joker logged in and immediately surveyed the computer sub menu, scanning passwords, hosts, bootparams, protocols, security logons and commands. He tried to work in an easy going, nonchalant way so he would not attract attention.

"Well, folks, the computer looks fine. I'll just add some upgraded software and be on my way."

The women in the computer room were in a corner sipping coffee and talking. Joker opened his black briefcase and pulled out his personal density floppy disks--nondescript black, but actually fireballs with enough power to customize the Ridge computers so exquisitely that the Hospital would probably never know that command and control had been passed to Joker.

Joker had nine floppy disks to load in the computer. Each was a power plant that would churn out and interpret data with exhilarating speed. After twenty minutes, he inserted the command to automatically connect to the internal modems and dial to a direct telephone line installed in Street's hotel room. Joker engineered an incredibly intricate backup system for communication. If the Ridge computers failed to call at the appointed time, Joker's program instructed the computer to call an 800 number at MIT without a trace of long distance calls.

In 30 minutes, Joker was done and he left.

"All done, Street."

"Joker, we've sweated plenty. Charlie's contact in the Hospital was found murdered. We almost came in and pulled you out."

"Well, I'm sure glad you didn't. Jimmy we did it. Now, all we have to do is wait and watch. The first performance is tonight."

●●●

Street's hotel room was cluttered with twin computers installed by Joker. The time was almost 3:30 AM. Street, Cooper, and Joker were awake sipping coffee and waiting for the Ridge computer to check in. A green light started to flicker and Joker jumped up from his seat.

"OK, folks, here we go. That light means we're getting a phone call from the Ridge computers. Jimmy, this is great."

The first words to scroll across Street's computer screen were eerie.

COBOL to team. Check in. TERMINAL online. RAZOR is good. SYS is fine. CHASE is clean. RAZOR confirms leak is plugged. SATAN . ACID . Sleep well.
COBOL congratulates RAZOR

Suddenly, the message stopped.

"Joker, what happened?"

"Don't know. Looks like a line interrupt. The computer should redial."

For 15 minutes, everyone stared at an empty computer screen. Then, the green light started again.

"See, I told you. We've got more data coming on line."

COBOL to Philadelphia detectives: Welcome to Dunkirk. We caught you. No more peekaboo. Say goodbye. Your software is dead. Joker is an amateur. COBOL out.

Joker read each word. "No, Street, this isn't possible. This can't be. The software was foolproof. No, it's not possible."

Street reminded Joker about his earlier words about logic.

"Say anything you want, Joker, but, there it is--lLogical. Now, let's untangle it."

For the first time, Cooper observed the arrogance of Street and Joker combined. Separately, neither person was that way. Together, they acted like two mountain climbers. She saw they were stunned and, indeed, embarrassed.

As Street and Joker second guessed the computer message, Cooper offered a simple suggestion: "Don't you boys get tired. It's time for some sleep."

"Lisa, we're not finished. I'll see you in the morning."

Chapter Twenty Three: Ruggles Farm

Street looked exactly like a man who had stayed up all night. His face had a washed out look. His eyes were red and if he shaved, he did a lousy job. Street and Joker never did get to sleep. Joker was back at the hotel in Street's room trying to figure out what happened. He called his computer groupies at MIT and asked if anyone had put a prank message in his software. After talking with MIT, Joker was convinced the message they read in the early morning hours was terribly real.

Rudy Levin, the sometimes left out part of the Smith-Levin detective duo, had plenty to offer in the morning. Rudy's wife, Marjorie, was a big fan of the Philadelphia social elite. If there was no chance she could ever join it, and there was no chance, then at least she could devour its gossip. She read society pages each week and read the gossip columns in local newspapers. Her husband told her about the Ridge Hospital. One name registered with his wife and that was Virginia Ruggles Choate. Levin got an earful from his wife on the widow of Steven Choate.

As Rudy started, Cooper thought she would hear a tranquilizing story. Cooper changed her mind very quickly.

"Lisa, you went to this Ruggles Farm right after the dedication ceremony for his late husband, right?"

"Yup."

"And that was because his wife was all broken up about his death and wanted to talk. She insinuated that Dr. Hagen, or the Ridge, was somehow responsible for the death of her husband, right again?"

"Rudy, right again."

Rudy then told what he knew, prefacing it all by saying the words came from his wife, not a court of law.

"Well, Cooper, Marjorie told me last night that the Choate's marriage was a big headliner. She had left him a couple of times. She had accused him of being physically abusive although she never went to the police. They even had a separation and her husband lived alone in their Rittenhouse condo. This Virginia Choate was no wallflower either. She was born Virginia Ruggles, one of Hudson Ruggles five children. Does the name Ruggles ring any bells? It would if you knew something about Society Hill. Her father's family originally owned most of the land and buildings in Society Hill. Her family was worth hundreds of millions. Virginia Ruggles went to the best private schools here and in Europe. There's a catch: her father's family lost everything in the Depression and she goes through school living off a dwindling trust fund. Bingo! She marries Steven Choate, the Choates who built some of the railroads. From money to money."

"Rudy, you got all that from Marjorie?"

"And then some. This Virginia Ruggles Choate never lost the taste for horses, country estates, and society balls. Her husband left $5 million to the Ridge, $20 million in a trust fund for each of his children, and the remainder to his wife. And that remainder is another $100 million, give or take a few horses here and there. Not bad for an abused wife."

Cooper pondered Rudy's tale about the *Ginny* Choate she had met. It was the Ginny Choate who begged her to attend the dedication ceremony for her late husband. And this was the same woman who said she went to Hagen's office and stormed out in anger. If Choate's grief was an act then maybe she was using Dr. Walter Hagen as a waste basket for conspiratorial games. If that was true, then the grief torn Mrs. Choate had played Cooper like a first violin in the orchestra.

Cooper stormed out of the squad room en route to Ruggles Farm.

•••

"Ginny Choate please! Tell her it's Detective Cooper."

The maid partly closed the door and Cooper heard her talking with Choate.

"Mrs. Choate is busy right now. She wants to know if you can return at some other time."

"No, I can't. Tell her I'll wait."

After a few minutes, Ginny Choate emerged and greeted Cooper. She asked her inside for coffee.

Cooper looked at Choate's eyes and saw a woman of privilege, who appeared recovered from the mental trauma she exhibited when her husband was memorialized at the Ridge. She was composed and serene as Cooper sat across a country style wood kitchen table.

"Mrs. Choate, I'm not comfortable calling you Ginny. I never was. I've got some followup questions."

"Sure, detective, ask what you want."

"Someone provided me background on your married life, especially troubles you and your late husband had. I guess they were in the form of rumors. You know, things like abuse. Talk about that please."

"It had nothing to do with my husband's death."

"That's the point, Mrs. Choate; maybe it does. You called me. You asked for my help. So, Mrs. Choate, your life became my business."

"Detective, this conversation is off base. I don't know what rumors you've heard. It's a long way from troubles in a marriage to losing a 45 year old husband to tennis elbow in the OR at the Ridge."

"Mrs. Choate, I'll be blunt. You're about $100 million dollars richer. If your husband was abusive, he sure isn't now."

"I resent the implications. Detective, I didn't invite you here. I'd like you to leave. I want you to leave now."

"Sure, Mrs. Choate. Call me when you need me. Use me to create a firestorm at the Ridge. And, when it suits your desires, poof, see you later detective. Mrs. Choate, it doesn't work that way."

112 -- Woody Tanger

As Cooper drove back to headquarters, she tried to reconcile the strange happenings at the Ridge with a woman who benefited greatly from her husband's surgery for tennis elbow. Did the Ridge do her a favor?

Chapter Twenty Four: IMPATIENTS

If plants can be impatient, then, it is sacrosanct that humans should enjoy the same rights. Impatiens burst open when their ripe pods are touched. Humans open when raw nerves are touched. The comparison between impatiens and police is logical.

Cooper rushed to judgment when confronted by a grieving widow whose young husband died on an operating table. Joker concocted what he arrogantly predicted was a foolproof way to take possession of the Ridge computers. Jimmy Street, flush with praise for his handling of the Charles River murders, knew he was the best detective in America. Now all three were left with empty ideas and theories that went nowhere.

Street called Boston and said he was ready to return home. Joker had already retreated to the MIT campus and was modeling computer programs that matched the Ridge computer fiasco. Detectives Smith and Levin were left with the murder of a former police employee who worked at the Ridge. Cooper doubted the wisdom of her assumptions of guilt about Dr. Walter Hagen and the Ridge Hospital. OPERATION END ZONE had fizzled as the detectives and Joker went their separate ways.

Each one confronted one another in different ways.

Street looked forward to jogging along the Charles in preparation for the Boston Marathon. Street and Cooper agreed it was time to give themselves space and let events dictate what happened next. Smith and Levin had about five months until their retirement.

Detective Jimmy Street returned to Boston on March 5th.

PART TWO

Chapter Twenty Five: BOSTON HOMECOMING

Jimmy Street was home in Boston and he could already imagine the sounds of crowds jammed around Copley Square for the finish of the marathon. His partner, Mike *Mickey* McCoy, picked him up at the airport and they headed through the tunnel, the Boston Garden.

"Mickey, I'e got a giant favor the ask."

"Say it, Jimmy."

"Would you mind taking a cab back to headquarters and let me drive around...alone. Tell them I'l be in tomorrow. Tell headquarters I'e got the flu. Anything will do."

"You OK, Jimmy?"

"Fine. I just need some down time."

McCoy hopped out and Street drove past Beacon Hill and straight to a grimy side street in Boston' South End. This place was a quasi religious shrine for Street; it was the spot where he and his partner faced a druggedup Satan in which only Street survived the encounter. But the terror of that night continued to draw him to the site. Street got out of the squad car and looked at nothing in particular. He was lost in his memories of that night. As he drove away, he knew he'd return again and again and probably for the rest of his life.

Some detectives get tough with all the murders by putting bars between their innermost feelings and the dirty world in which they work. When that happens, the cops themselves are imprisoned. They are sentenced to life in prison within their own psyche with no chance ever of parole. Only the *female* side of a detective, male or female, kept them in touch with the goodness that defines most days. Street was determined to hold onto that *goodness* and not become cynical and closed.

The next stop for Street was no stop at all. He drove past the Charles Hospital in Boston's medical center; he saw the Hospital's ugly orange painted garage and thought of the violent storms that pounded everyone connected with the Charles Hospital. He was tempted to stop and say hello to Dr. Ernie Green and the President of the Charles, Dr. Irizone Shiri. Street did not feel like talking and kept driving. He turned on the radio and heard familiar voices. The radio voices were a welcome home sound that confirmed he was really back.

Jimmy Street drove west on Storrow Drive tracing the path of his favorite jogging trail. On the other side of the Charles River he saw the MIT campus and assumed that Joker was provoking more mischief. Street turned north and crossed the Charles and then drove past Joker's workshop. He wanted to say hello, but for now, the proximity to Joker and his world of wizardry would suffice. Street drove back into Boston and doubled parked outside DeLuca's at the base of Beacon Hill.

As he went inside to pick up some carry-me-to-tomorrow groceries, he saw a meter maid walking towards his unmarked car. He didn't give a damn whether she ticketed his car or not. In fact, as he was in the check out line, he saw her writing out a ticket. In mock horror, Street turned to a young and pretty woman behind him. "See outside, I'm getting a ticket." The woman thought that was a dumb way to meet someone. She turned away and Street continued. "I'm not trying to pick you up. No, I'm getting a Boston parking ticket. I'm really back in Boston." On seeing the woman become worried, he pulled out his gold detective badge and showed it to her. She looked only slightly reassured as he went to his car and tucked the ticket into his coat.

It was only mid afternoon; yet, it felt oddly like night. He was home in Boston but he kept thinking of excuses not to go home. When he finally went home, he understood why he felt so strange.

"Damn, Lisa, I'm home in Boston for a couple of hours and I miss you so much." He could not remember the last time in his life that he dared feel so vulnerable.

•••

Back in Philadelphia, Street's Boston homecoming punctuated Lisa Cooper's thoughts. Street was a bright light in the middle of her winter of selfdoubt and risk. Cooper remembered the 24 hours in Nantucket and especially the rocky ferry ride to the Island. She felt so warm and protected in his arms.

Cooper went home early and changed into some cut off jeans and a Philadelphia Phillies T shirt. Street had told her about the murdered Boston doctor who was found in a Detroit Tigers T shirt and how her death had turned his life into a whirlpool. Cooper laughed inside when she visualized Street running down Ben Franklin Parkway towards the Art Museum. She laughed when she pictured him bursting through her bedroom door, gun drawn, and smashing her mirror. Cooper laughed again when her memory flashed a picture of Street dropping a wine glass in her kitchen.

And with all those wonderful memories of Jimmy Street, Lisa Cooper sat on her hardwood floor and cried.

•••

Street's answering machine was loaded with messages when he returned home. Most of them were retrieved while he was in Philadelphia, but these were new messages within the last couple of days.

Message #1: Jack Gergen from the
***Boston Gazette*. We'd like to do a feature story for our Sunday magazine. Call back please.**

Message #2: Rick Salerno from Wine Importers. Just got a case of 1986 Chateau Talbot. Great price. Call if interested. We can put it on your credit card and ship FED X.

Message #3: Street, it's the Chief. Welcome back. See me when you're in the station.

Message #4: (voice synthesized) THIS IS COBOL. WE HAVE YOUR ADDRESS. WE KNOW WHERE YOUR SISTER LIVES. YOU HAVE NICE NEPHEWS. STAY IN BOSTON. YOU ARE FINISHED HERE. RETURN AND YOU'LL HAVE ANOTHER DEAD PARTNER. DETECTIVE COOPER WILL BE TERMINATED AND YOU WILL BE TO BLAME. YOUR FRIEND JOKER IS ALSO AT RISK. COBOL OUT.

"BOSTON POLICE HEADQUARTERS."

"This is Detective Street, Badge BP818, page Joker. Ask him to call me back at home." Then he called Cooper.

"Oh, Jimmy, I was just thinking about you."

"Lisa, do you have a cold? You're all stuffed up."

"No, you jerk, I was crying."

"About what?"

"Street, you probably wouldn't understand."

Then Street thought about the phone call. "If they have my number, they have Lisa's. Bet they're listening. "...Lisa, call me from a pay phone."

"Jimmy, it's snowing outside. Are you crazy?"

Street heard the click of call waiting and flipped the phone.

"Street, it's Joker. Welcome home. Have I got something..."

"Can't talk. Got a problem. Your place in one hour."

When Street flipped back, the phone line with Cooper was dead. Street did not want to call Cooper again and so he waited for her to call.

Detective Cooper. You just talked with Street in Boston. We heard every word. Stay away from him or he's dead. Move on.

"Who is this?"

Cooper, this call is over. Remember we can get to Street.

Cooper decided not to call Street and drove to police headquarters, right into the squad room. Charlie and Rudy were at their desks looking at boating magazines.

"Guys, I just got two phone calls. One from Jimmy in Boston; he wanted me to call him at home, but he asked that I do it from a pay phone. Then I get a call using a voice synthesizer to disguise the person. He or she warns me to stay away from Jimmy. The worst part is they knew Jimmy and I talked. My condo is wired."

Smith and Levin drove Cooper back home with a police debug team following. They found that Cooper's phone was tapped, but not in her apartment. The bug was installed in the basement by someone who was able to traverse the phone lines in the condo building.

"Cooper, you've got to call Street back."

Cooper dialed his home phone and there was no answer.

"Great. Now, he doesn't answer. Get the name of his partner up in Boston, and let's call police up there and have them check his place out."

•••

Street drove across the Charles River and maneuvered through the one way streets that are a trademark of Cambridge. He could not find a parking space, so he pulled out his police ID and parked in a loading zone a couple of blocks from Joker's office on the MIT campus.

Joker's large office looked like it had suffered an air strike by F14 jets that had lobbed their smart weapons through the windows. The floor was tile, covered with an eclectic combination of beat up Orientals, dirty quilts, and bathroom floor mats with names such as PLAZA HOTEL, BOSTON, SHE-

RATON, and MARRIOTT. *Scientific American* and dozens of computer magazines were piled against the walls. The furniture looked like it was stillborn. Boston Red Sox, Rolling Stones, and Mickey Mouse posters decorated the fading white walls. Another poster showed HYDRA.

"Joker, what the hell is that?"

"Street, you should study your Greek mythology. HYDRA is the many headed serpent that Hercules killed. It means a persistent and multi dimensional problem...just our cup of tea here at our resort spa, otherwise known as MIT."

One huge poster dominated the room and was pasted directly above the bank of computers. It was a five foot square black poster that showed a spread winged phoenix on it's funeral pyre. Under the graphic were the words:

"From the desert and into the fire,
rise Phoenix from your ashes
and renew yourself

A dozen computers were lined up next to each other on a long glass table. Computer cords snaked down from the ceiling, connecting the computers, monitors, printers and modems.

The smell of wood incense mixed with an unusual odor of birds together with a slight background smell of marijuana. Two parakeets chirped from inside a cage hanging near a window.

A couple of futons and some sleeping bags were stored in one corner of the room next to a small portable refrigerator.

"Joker, your office looks the same, except the smell of cannabis seems a little strong. Remind me never to take the Chief over here."

"Jimmy, I burned some extra incense to hide it. Maybe you should light up one of your cigars. I want to introduce you to some friends."

Joker scanned the room and motioned for his two friends to come over.

"Mark Toshi and Bill Deyoe, this is the hunter, the famous Detective, Jimmy Street. This is the man."

Toshi was short and oriental, although it was not easy to see his eyes through glasses that looked bulletproof thick. DeYoe was about the same size. Both wore blue jeans and shirts that had a lot of miles on them. Joker said they were undergraduates at MIT. Toshi was from San Francisco and DeYoe was from Detroit.

"Jimmy, these are my alteregos. Did you ever hear of PROJECT RHODOPSIN?"

"Joker, I haven't got time for this now. We need to talk about other things. We've got a wild card loose in Philadelphia."

Street pulled out his answering machine cassette and handed it to Joker.

"Nice little message, Jimmy. Do you know what COBOL means? It's computerspeak for business programming: COMMON BUSINESS ORIENTED LANGUAGE. Jimmy, whoever sent this was smart enough to synthesize his voice. This is no BOZO. That's the person who sent us the computer message in your hotel room. They had to get a tip or they never would have found the programs I loaded at the Ridge."

●●●

Street took one of Joker's phones and called Cooper. He let the phone ring and ring and there was no answer. "Maybe, she's there and not answering. Maybe, she's out. Maybe, she's in trouble."

"Charlie, am I glad to hear your voice. Where's Lisa? I've been trying to reach her."

"Hang on, Jimmy. She's cool. She's here."

"Jimmy, someone bugged my house and called after we talked. They threatened me and you. I left a message for you at headquarters."

"Lisa, some crawling little worm is not going to threaten us. I miss you, babe. Will you come up to Boston this weekend?"

"Jimmy, I miss you too. I'll take the flight that gets in at 6 PM."

"Be careful. No phone calls to me in Boston. Can you put Charlie back on the phone?"

"Charlie, Lisa doesn't know but some low life left a message that she's dead if she stays on the Ridge case. Whoever it was signed off with the name COBOL. Keep an eye on her?"

"Jimmy, take that to the bank!"

•••

Street walked in circles around Joker's office as Toshi and DeYoe sat at the bank of computers tapping the keyboards with the touch of some great virtuoso. Joker could see his friend was on fire inside. Street had not bothered with his blue or brown contact lens so he had his dog eyes of blue and brown.

"Jimmy my man this is focus time. This room is the big leagues, not little league. We'll figure things out. That PROJECT RHODOPSIN that I talked about, do you remember?"

"Yeah, but unless it has to do with Lisa and the Ridge; let's save it for another time."

"Well, hunter, maybe it does. Now sit down and give me five minutes or I'll blow some DELTA9TETRAHYDROCANNABINOL your way."

"Joker, you're off the wall. What's..."

"Don't bother trying Street, it's THC. Cannabis sativa. Weed. Grass. Happy Smoke. You need some. Chill."

"Toshi, DeYoe and I are reconstructing the work of a Soviet scientist named Yuri Ovchinnikov..."

"Joker don't you have any simple words in your vocabulary?"

"Street this scientist worked at the Shemyakin Institute of Bioorganic Chemistry in Moscow. He was working on protein for computers."

"You mean feeding computers food?"

"Street, it's a quasi military secret that bacteria can change due to light and can be what we call 'logic gates'...switches...in protein based optical computers. We're talking about computers that can calculate, relate, manipulate, clone and, ready for this Street, think and feel. And this isn't science fiction. This is way beyond all the gadgets of the Internet."

"Joker, so what?"

"The 'so what' is that some hybrids of this experimental technology, like writing and reading data, helped us create some software protocols like the kind I put in the Ridge's computers."

"That's great Joker, because they obviously didn't work. COBOL or whoever this nut is, found them."

"Street, stay in touch. This is the Joker. This kid is not lost. Get your good neighbor awards at headquarters and we'll handle this end. Unwind, Street. You're too tight my friend."

"Joker, you're on target there. I'm outta here. You can reach me Monday at headquarters. Lisa is coming to town this weekend."

"Stop by and visit, OK, Street?"

"Joker, she's coming tomorrow to relax. Talk to you Monday."

•••

The aftermidnight landscape is a time that can inspire poets and artists or be a sedative for people working at the edge. Nocturnal stillness can be inhaled like the bouquet of a 1976 Lafite Rothschild or savored as a ripened and open rose. Mysteries of night sensations can paint mind pictures of pastoral settings or rolling forest springs. If there is a sacred time, it is the night when so many escape the punishing reality of day. Street in Boston and Cooper in Philadelphia were asleep.

At exactly 12:30 AM, seven computer screens in Philadelphia networked, again.

•••

COBOL signon at 00:30:00. Team confirm status and logon. with security code. RAZOR is here. TERMINAL good. . SYS OK . CHASE ready. SATAN smiles . ACID just fine .

COBOL to team: all code numbers accepted. .

COBOL to RAZOR: well done . Hospital plumbing finished and leak repaired. . SYS excommunication of Joker was inspiring. COBOL informed Street and Cooper that we are unforgiving . Crystal disconnect scheduled. Candidate selection process. COBOL standing by for sign off codes.

COBOL has 27993 and confirms. COBOL to team: well done and goodnight.

•••

Jimmy Street was finally asleep in his own bed with his clock radio set for eight AM. The windows in his condo were sound proofed and there was a tiny hum from the automatic fans. Street managed to watch the first few minutes of the Tonight Show and after the Jay Leno monologue clicked the TV off. The next sound he heard was not his clock radio.

RING. RING. RING. RING. RING. RING. RING.

"Who the hell is that? It's 1 AM." Street did not answer the phone and it stopped. Then a minute later it started again.

RING. RING. RING. RING. RING.

"OK, whoever you are, this better be important. Speak."

"Street. Street. It's Joker. My place. Urgent. Street..."

The phone line was dead.

"Shit, they're killing the guy." Street jumped out of bed and got dressed while calling headquarters.

"Detective Street. ZEBRA emergency. Patch me through."

In less than thirty seconds Street was on the line with Boston's swat team.

"This is Street. ZEBRA team to MIT campus, Land Building, second floor. Contact is 'Joker'. I'll meet ZEBRA on scene."

Three navy colored sedans raced through Boston's empty streets and crossed the Charles. Two Cambridge police cars were waiting for them on the Cambridge side of the Mass. Avenue bridge. A small blue and white communications van was dispatched and trailed minutes behind the twelve Boston cops whose combat fatigues were labeled in yellow letters, **BOSTON POLICE ZEBRA**. As required by Boston police protocol, the Chief of Police was called and notified that a **ZEBRA** alert was activated by Street. Only a handful of detectives enjoyed this privilege to call a **ZEBRA** without authorization of a superior officer.

Street cut through Beacon Hill, down Cambridge Street past the Mass General Hospital and onto Storrow Drive. On the other side of the Charles he saw the gathering storm of flashing police lights.

"Go. Go. Go. Don't wait for me. I'll meet you at Joker's place."

Some of the ZEBRA team members had met Joker during his part time job at headquarters. Everyone likes the 'whizkid' from MIT who volunteered to fix broken VCR's, TV's and helped with computers. It seemed as if every Boston cop had Joker's home phone number and most used it. In less than five minutes from dispatch, the ZEBRA team arrived at Land Building on the MIT campus and charged upstairs to Joker's office with weapons deployed. Street was two minutes behind and monitored radio traffic from the ZEBRA team.

ZEBRA ONE: WE ARE IN THE BUILDING

ZEBRA COMMAND: WEAPONS UNLOCK

ZEBRA ONE: NEGATIVE CONTACT. APPROACHING DOOR. SEEK OK TO ENTER

ZEBRA COMMAND: STREET JUST ARRIVED. HE'S IN BUILDING. COMING TO YOUR LOCATION

ZEBRA ONE: STREET IS HERE. OK TO ENTER?

ZEBRA COMMAND: YOU HAVE AUTHORIZATION. ENTER.

SECURE. REPORT.

ZEBRA ONE: GOING IN.

Street watched as the **ZEBRA** team coordinated with a team member downstairs who cut the building's power. At that instant, they smashed through the door wearing night vision goggles.

"Get Street in here fast!"

Street rushed in and saw Joker, Toshi and DeYoe sitting at the bank of computers with a cloud of incense hanging near floor. The room was empty.

"Street, you don't travel lightly. Hey, Raymond, is that you behind the goggles? Where's Lisa?"

Raymond White, ZEBRA team captain flipped his goggles off, "Joker, Street thought you were zapped. What's going on here?"

"Hey, guys, I didn't call. I'm low key, high tech. Talk to Street."

"Guys, he sounded like someone was killing him. My fault. Write it up. I'll take the heat on this. Sorry."

It took the ZEBRA team only a couple of minutes to load their gear and head back into Boston.

Street looked at the trio and exploded in anger.

"Joker, damn you and your computers and your middle of the night phone calls and all your MIT crap. I thought you were dying. You said 'URGENT'. So here I am in the middle of the night. Now I'll be doing paperwork for the next month."

Toshi and DeYoe pointed to one of the computer screens. Joker stood with his hands crossed and a big smile on his face.

"Street, welcome to Philadelphia."

"What?"

"JOKER to Street. COBOL is checkmate. My backup software hidden in the Ridge computer transferred COBOL's message using the alternate 800 number. Whoever COBOL is doesn't know we're connected. Jimmy, get comfortable. It's time for bedtime magic."

●●●

"Toshi, show Jimmy the print out of COBOL's 12:30 AM message."

It looked like a wild west death warrant with Street and Cooper at the top of the list. Also on that list was a person without a name whose only mistake was their membership in the Crystal Club. Street had a list of COBOL's conspirators whose devilish names were engraved in Street's mind. ACID, SYS, UNIX, RAZOR, TERMINAL,CHASE and SATAN. Perhaps a sweaty nightmare would put faces on these synthetic names that curled across Joker's MIT computer.

"Joker, we'll search these names and try to unwind the codes. These names weren't picked out of a hat. I think we've got some ego at work here and let's use that to our benefit."

"Street, there's more news. Since our 800 backup program worked tonight, the chances are good it will sweep the Ridge computers again. When it calls us, we'll answer with our architecture here. COBOL is going to meet four new friends. We borrowed some names from the folks at MIT astronomy.

Joker lead Street to a table where Toshi and DeYoe had four folders with labels on them: ***WIMP, MACHO, BLACK, AND NEUT.*** DeYoe set up a response protocol so that COBOL would think some of his computer pen pals were horsing around.

"Look on the wall Street and you'll see a little biography on our four friends.

WIMP: Weakly Interacting Massive Particles...short for cold, dark matter.

MACHO: Massive Compact Halo Objects...dwarf stars.

BLACK: As in holes with gravity so intense light can't escape.

Neut: not Newt but neutrinos that interact only weakly with ordinary matter.

"Street we still don't understand how COBOL found the software so fast and disabled it. And we don't know how long this 800 backup program will function before they find it. Throwing our four astronomical friends at COBOL may distract him. This guy is into computer games. It's his amusement park."

•••

Now. Street could challenge anyone to deny that the Ridge was just another ordinary hospital.

"Jimmy, I'm sleeping. Call back tomorrow."

"Lisa, don't hang up. Don't go back to sleep. We've intercepted a message from the Ridge computer. Joker's back up 800 number worked. And what a message."

"OK, I'm up Jimmy. What's the message?"

"Try this one Lisa. This COBOL is going to kill another Crystal Club member and maybe you and me and Joker, too. And he congratulated someone code named SYS for catching what Joker did to the Ridge computer. Lisa, how could anyone know? Did you tell the Chief about Joker? Did you use a secure radio channel? We've got to find out."

"Hey, Jimmy, did you give Charlie a guilt complex? He's sleeping on the couch in the living room. He said he was worried about me and wanted to keep on eye on me until things settled down. Jimmy, you had a part in that, didn't you?"

"Sleep well, Lisa."

"Jimmy, you're so sweet. I can't wait to see you this weekend. Hey, you've had a wild Boston homecoming."

"Lisa, let's make sure we're both on the same planet this weekend. Talk to you in the morning. And think about SYS."

Chapter Twenty Six: HYDRA OF THE TIMES

When Street finally made it back home and climbed into bed, he closed his eyes but could not fall asleep. Instead, he kept seeing Joker's office with all its posters and then a ZEBRA team charging through the door to rescue three computer sleuths who were hacking away and having a good time. Street clearly saw the poster of HYDRA, the many-headed serpent. Then he drifted off and started to dream.

SERPENT LOOSE IN MY ROOM. IT HAS MANY HEADS. I LIE FROZEN IN FEAR. WILL HYDRA SEE ME? I SEE ANGEL CAKES. I SEE VANILLA ICE CREAM. I SEE COOKIES. I TAKE A BITE OF DESSERT AND IT TURNS INTO A SERPENT HEAD AS I SWALLOW. GOD SAVE ME--IT'S KILLING ME.

Street shot out of bed, soaked in sweat. He had drifted off for only a few moments of sleep and was punished with a dream that put him inside the Joker's poster of the serpent HYDRA. Street did not want to close his eyes and leave himself vulnerable to other dreams. The time was 4:45 AM and he started a long run down Beacon Hill and along the Charles River. He ran for more than one hour. When he got home, he plunked down on his bed and fell asleep.

"Jimmy, it's Lisa. Still in bed, lazy bones?"

"Lisa, you don't know half of my night!"

"When will you be at headquarters?"

"Thirty minutes."

"I've got a lead. I'll call you there. Joker already faxed me the computer printout he intercepted from the Ridge computer."

"Lisa, what time is it?"

"Well, if you make it to work in 30 minutes, you'll have one hour till lunch."

Street looked at his watch: it was 10:30 AM.

•••

Kill a Boston cop.

For extra measure, COBOL throws in a Philadelphia cop and Joker. Street was practicing for his meeting with the Chief. He held the computer print out that proves there is a COBOL who plans to terminate a Crystal Club member at the Ridge.

Lisa Cooper was practicing the same lines as she prepared to meet with Chief Rome.

"Cooper, what if all this is a prank? What if we have a computer hacker wishing everyone a happy April Fool's Day? We can't toss Philadelphia police resources around without evidence. And speaking of that, how did we get that computer print out from the Ridge?"

Cooper hoped that last question would get lost in the maze of what ifs that Chief Rome was navigating. Cooper, drawing on her legal experience, constructed a perfectly honest answer that simply left out the name Joker.

"Chief, I went to VALLEY FORGE SYSTEMS and asked their help. I met with Rick Cone, who owns the company, and he was very helpful. They do computer consulting and design work for both the Ridge and the City of Philadelphia, including the police. I understand this guy Cone is a political contributor to Mayor Gentry so he's wired into the system."

"Detective, what do you mean--wired into the system?"

"You know, Chief, the system of political I-do-for-you and you-do-for-me. That's the system."

Chief Rome was not amused with Cooper's insights into the political ins and outs of Philadelphia and of her mentor, Mayor Sam Gentry. She took a big piece of paper and wrote, SYSTEM, then crossed the word out with a magic marker. "Detective, there is no SYSTEM. That doesn't change the fact that you have some new data and it's worth checking out. Even if it turns out to be a hoax, I want you to catch the person who thinks offing police officers is a computer game. So, get to it, Lisa."

Chief Rome took a telephone call and motioned for Cooper to leave. As she was, Rome handed her the piece of paper with the word SYSTEM crossed out. "And don't forget, there is no SYSTEM. That's a playground in your mind."

Cooper hustled out of the office and into the arms of Smith and Levin, who were waiting.

"Lisa, you and Street make quite a combo. You sure were a lot more mellow before he came to town."

The three detectives took an elevator down to homicide. When Cooper sat down, she tossed out Rome's paper with the crossed out word SYSTEM. Cooper spent the rest of the morning on the telephone asking the staff psychologist about the code words COBOL, TERMINAL, CHASE, SYS, UNIX, RAZOR, and ACID.

Cooper kept staring at the Chief's crumpled note while she talked. Then, a thunderbolt exploded and she jumped out of her seat, yelling, "Oh shit, that's it! Damn, I know one of the code names. It's right in front of me. My God!" Cooper bolted past Smith and Charlie and tossed them the piece of paper with the word SYSTEM on it. "Get Jimmy in Boston. FAX him this paper. Then, read it to him over and over; he'll figure it out."

Chapter Twenty Seven: FRIEND OR FOE

Cooper raced through the police garage and sped west in her car, realizing that going alone was against police rules. She called headquarters on a scrambled frequency. "Communications, this is Cooper. Patch me through to homicide."

"Homicide."

"I need Charlie and Rudy."

"Wait."

"Lisa, we faxed the paper to Street. He figured it out in about ten seconds. And he's bull that you're going alone."

"That's why I'm calling. I need backup."

"We're on our way. We have the address. Don't go in without us. And call Street; he's all worried."

"OK, and tell Chief Rome, thanks. She won't understand but tell her anyway."

Lisa Cooper was on her way back to Valley Forge to visit with Rick Cone at VALLEY FORGE SYSTEMS. Cooper thought the code word SYS was short for SYSTEMS. And Cone knew exactly what and when Joker planned to do at the Ridge. Was Rick Cone SYS, one of the seven names in these computer *Blood Games*?

Three Philadelphia detectives entered VALLEY FORGE SYSTEMS while an unmarked cruiser waited at the rear. Local police were on hand to assist. The detectives approached the receptionist and asked for Rick Cone.

"He'd be very happy to see you, but he can't be reached now. He left a few days ago for a Caribbean cruise. He's expected back in one week."

Cooper could do nothing except retreat and contemplate a return visit to a judge's chambers in hopes of getting a search warrant. Based on her hunch that SYSTEM and the code word SYS were the same, she expected the answer would be a NO. As a lawyer, Cooper was practiced in the art of questions. She needed to confront and get Cone off guard and now maybe that chance was gone.

"Jimmy, we bottomed out at VALLEY FORGE SYSTEMS. The man I met, Cone, is on a cruise. Maybe I can get a search warrant."

"Lisa, we'll work it on this end. Let's see if Joker can help."

Chapter Twenty Eight: 20th FLOOR CIRCLE

As Cooper returned from Valley Forge, a collection of impressive cars was parked in front of the Ridge. Three PM was the scheduled start of the Ridge's quarterly board meeting, on the 20th floor adjacent to Dr. Hagen's office. The room was customized into a round shape with a twenty foot diameter circular mahogany table in the center. A crystal chandelier hung directly over the table and spread a soft off white glow throughout the room.

Not all twelve board members planned to attend the March meeting. In attendance were: Dr. Hagen, Chairman of the Board. The others represented a diverse and, for the most part, moneyed segment of Philadelphia society. Not all board members were in the Crystal Club.

Sitting next to Dr. Hagen was Eric C. Goodman, Chairman of KEYSTONE Broadcasting. Mayor Sam Gentry sat next to Goodman, his good friend and political benefactor. Drew Lewis, founder of Lewis & Stone Enterprises of New York City was serving his last year of a five year term. Julie Connelly, formerly a U.S. representative at the United Nations and onetime Congresswoman, was also present. Dr. Ernesto Seya, former U.S. Surgeon General, was the other physician on the board. Representing the Ridge's primary bank was Edmund Peters III, who sat next to his squash partner, James Kerr, Chief Counsel and partner in Kerr, Heinz and Smith.

Hagen read a quarterly report on the operations of the Ridge and asked for a financial summary from the Hospital's accounting firm. Kerr reported on the status of litigation, including the recently filed suit by Virginia Choate. Then, Hagen spoke for a few moments.

"For those of your present, and we have several not able to attend, I first ask that the quarterly report is adopted as reported without amendments. All in favor signify by raising your hands."

The vote for acceptance of the report was unanimous.

"I'm pleased to report that we estimate the Ridge will show an operating profit for the fiscal year ended June 30th of approximately $23 million dollars. In addition, the Ridge's endowment has increased substantially and now totals almost $100 million dollars. As reported earlier, most of those funds are invested in liquid government securities. The physical plant of the Ridge is in superb shape and all other continuing elements of our health empire are doing well."

Hagen then moved back to a chart that was covered with a blanket. He flipped the blanket off with the panache of a night club magician.

"I'm sure all of you recognize the photo of the Good Samaritan Hospital in Philadelphia. This medical institution was founded almost 150 years ago and still occupies it's original site, plus about 200 extra acres. The value of Good Sam's prime downtown land far exceeds its value as a medical enterprise. We commissioned an appraisal of this land and it exceeded one billion dollars. We believe our community would be better served if Good Sam became the next acquisition of the Ridge. We could expand our campus here in Chestnut Hill onto land we already own while demolishing the Good Sam buildings. They are too old to rehabilitate. Their time has come. We are already in the process of hiring the top doctors from the Good Sam. They know we intend to merge it into the Ridge, but they are resistant. As they witness the departure of their department heads and key fund raising personnel, we expect them to see more clearly the benefits of a merger. We expect to make a formal offer to purchase sometime around the end of our fiscal year. Dr. John Andersen at Good Sam has threatened to fight us all the way, but we believe that is more of an emotional response. Andersen is 82 years old and has been President of Good Sam since

World War II. He just can't let go. We expect to schedule a special board meeting in June to authorize the funding of our offer. This will be an expensive acquisition. But, when completed, it will make the Ridge the largest medical institution in the United States. That, my fellow board members, will complete my mission as your president and I will seek early retirement upon the successful takeover of Good Sam. I intend to spend the rest of my active days in medicine as a visiting professor and researcher."I've given you a lot to think about. On your way out, the staff will provide you with back up reading materials. If there are any questions, I'm ready."

Only one hand went up in the board room and it was Julie Connelly. "Walter, what happens if John Andersen at Good Sam decides to fight a takeover?"

"He will succumb. Excuse me, bad choice of words. He'll fail."

Chapter Twenty Nine: INK

And that's the story so far."

"Sure we'll protect your identity, but why give us the story and stay on the Board of Directors? That's a conflict of interest."

"He's going crazy over there. I can do this city more good by staying on the Board and trying to keep tabs on him. I'll leave at the appropriate time. My conscience is clear."

•••

RIDGE IN HOSTILE TAKEOVER BID FOR GOOD SAM HOSPITAL

EXCLUSIVE: Ridge Hospital is preparing another major hospital acquisition. A reliable source has confirmed that the Ridge will make a bid to buy Philadelphia's Good Samaritan Hospital and its enormous tract of downtown land. Under the proposed plan, the Good Sam will be swallowed by the Ridge this year. Dr. John Andersen, 82 year old longtime President of the Good Sam, is fighting the takeover bid.

It was not possible to reach either Dr. Andersen or Dr. Walter Hagen, President of the Ridge for comment. Andersen has regularly rejected all previous takeover bids, claiming they were an effort to acquire the hospital's priceless land and would leave thousands of patients without quality neighborhood care.

Shortly after 6 AM, the newspaper story was faxed to Hagen's home.

"Sam, you're the Mayor of this city. That story is treason. We've got a fuckin' blabbermouth on the Board. Someone spilled his guts. Can't you get the police to tap the telephones of our Board?"

"Calm down, Walter. You can't go around doing that; it's illegal. Relax, the story's no big deal."

"Sure, Sam, let's see how relaxed you are around election time when you need more money. Goodman has been your own private bank. Think about it, Sam."

Hagen called James Kerr, chief counsel for the Hospital. "Jimmy, did you see today's paper?"

"Sure did, Walter. I knew you'd be calling and the answer is NO. Like I've said before, you can't run around and sue the newspaper every time they print a story or get something wrong. And in this case, they got it right. You've got a leaky mouth on the Board."

"Yeah, and I'll bet it's one of those goodie-two-shoes we put on the Board so it looks pretty in our annual reports. Whoever leaked this is gonna get his mouth zipped up real tight. No one is going to stop me from buying Good Sam."

"Walter, you better take a nice long walk and cool down. And don't go making threats. When you can prove who it is, get him off the Board. And maybe it's not someone on the Board. It could be a secretary or someone in photo copying. In the meantime, Andersen can't do anything with the story. The guy is 82 years old. He's hanging on to the Sam because he still thinks he's some east coast, Nobel Prize winning Albert Schweitzer. Forget it! Andersen is history. You'll get his hospital."

"Jimmy, I'll stay cool. Watch!"

Hagen pushed some buttons to conference in his personal secretary and administrative assistant.

"I want you to do something."

"Yes, sir."

"Did you see the story in the *Inquirer* about our plans to buy the Good Sam?"

"Yes, it was..."

"How many secretaries do we have up here on the 20th floor?"

"Four."

"And downstairs in the photo copy room, how many people?

"Three."

"And how many people in document delivery services?"

"Two."

"By my count that's nine people who had access to the notes and documents prepared for my Board meeting. Is that right?"

"Dr. Hagen, ten people if you include me."

"Draft a document that informs the other nine people they are terminated effective immediately. Checks will be cut today and they are to be out by tonight. Collect their parking garage passes and their keys and inform security that all nine are to be supervised today while they clean out their personal effects."

"Dr. Hagen, these are good people and some have been here for years. What did they do? When they ask why they are fired, what do I say?"

"Tell them it's my decision and the reason is failure to keep hospital business confidential."

"Dr. Hagen, all of them? That makes no sense. They'll sue."

"Do what I instructed, or, shall I do it myself and, in that case, have ten terminations?"

"Sir, I'll do it."

•••

Julie Connelly read the morning edition of the *Inquirer*. "Yup, that's pretty much what I told them."

Dr. Andersen was tall, trim, and looked 60, not 82.

"Hagen is possessed. He's lost all sense of decency and perspective. He took the same oath I did: *First, do not harm*. That's the bullshit part of the Hippocratic Oath. How many do that now? Harm people? Hey, we kill them every day to clean out their beds and keep the money flowing. Got some pain? Here, take this and don't wake up. Now he's become a madman. I don't care how much the Sam is worth. We're a hospital not a real estate developer. We heal and comfort the sick and we do not sit down with speculators to guess how much our land is worth. Unlike the Ridge, we don't think like a FORTUNE 500 company . Hagen may be surprised what's left inside this 82 year old body. You did the right thing Julie."

"Be careful, Dr. Andersen. Hagen is crazy. He's mad and he'll do anything to feed his ego."

"Julie, Hagen's out of control. This Crystal Club of his is a monster. It's bigger and more powerful than the Hospital, and, it's dangerous. All that money and power in the hands of a doctor who is crazy. The damn club belongs on Wall Street, not in a hospital."

Chapter Thirty:
THE MATRIX

02:15:00: COBOL team alert. SYS is on trek. Cooper visited SYS location. SYS will be warned. Cooper termination. Will vote on issue. Off.

•••

Cooper waited a few minutes. Dr. John Andersen came out and greeted her. She knew he was in his 80's and yet his appearance stunned her. "Did he find the Fountain of Youth?"

Dr. Andersen walked with a brisk pace and head up high. He had a quick smile and glowing eyes. This was the man Cooper read about in the morning newspaper.

"Dr. Andersen, why is Dr. Hagen so intent on buying Good Sam? The Ridge just acquired another hospital and yours is not for sale, right?"

"Detective, Hagen is a machine and never forget that fact. He is obsessed with control, and, buying Good Sam would crown him king of medicine in the US. Some folks think he wants the Good Sam so he can sell off our real estate and profit from the acquisition. Those people don't know Hagen. Hagen would welcome the profit; but, it's the chance to enlarge his kingdom that appeals to him. He's an evildoer dressed in whites and crowned with a stethoscope who sees his patients as property and his doctors as tools. The man knows no boundary. Well, I am his boundary and he will not get **my** hospital".

"Dr. Andersen, do you know much about his Crystal Club and how that works?"

"It's simply an ego drenching money machine for rich social climbers who need to see their names bronzed and hear people say how wonderful they are. The Ridge has made a fortune from the club. And it's amazing, when a Crystal Club member dies, Hagen has no trouble getting a replacement. I heard he has a waiting list!"

"One last question, Dr. Andersen: How can you stop Hagen?"

"First, young lady, we have a board of directors and I believe they are loyal to me and the original charter of the Good Sam. We have a law firm that would block the Ridge. Most importantly, we have justice on our side, not to mention other resources. What it comes down to is fortitude and integrity. Not everyone in our world is cursed with the ego and ambition of Hagen. Some of us stand on our principles and believe that good will triumph, even if that sounds corny. Hagen and the Ridge are used to getting their way; that, my dear, will change. No one has written the final chapter on the Good Sam. Hagen may imagine this 82 year old crotchety doctor is going to fade away at his demand. We'll see. We'll see. Guess what, detective? I'm even good with computers--as good as my great grandson is with the Internet."

Cooper relished her few minutes with Dr. Andersen, especially since the contrast with Hagen was so vivid. Andersen was impressive, stately, witty, and confident. Cooper liked this father figure but doubted that Andersen understood the challenges.

●●●

Hagen plotted a new acquisition strategy in view of the premature publicity. Hagen's mind was infinitely more powerful than his peers, and his thought process was focused. By three PM, Hagen had prepared a confidential memo for distribution to a handful of people. He typed it out on his office computer while Emily Rosoff loaded the 20th floor with temporary help from a secretarial service. Several hospital security guards were stationed on the floor.

Confidential/Your Eyes Only

TO: James Kerr, Esq. General Counsel
Edmund Peters III
Eric C. Goodman
FR: Walter Hagen
RE: Acquisition of the Good Sam

Overview
Our plan to acquire the Good Sam was leaked to the media and we must move quickly before we face political opposition. As an FYI, all support staff that handled Good Sam documents for the board meeting have been terminated.

Positioning
Catalogue through our PR firm all negative publicity about the Good Sam and issue news release detailing such. Andersen. Is he senile? We'll ask the question...no one will remember the answer. Charts and financial overview of the Ridge. Quotes from political leaders about the Ridge. We'll get the Mayor to issue special proclamation.

Churn and Burn
We will allocate a $1 million dollar fund for signing bonuses of doctors at the Good Sam. Objective is to strip the Good Sam naked. We'll target every department head...good or bad.

Rumors
Circulate stories about the Good Sam and it's blood supplies, with focus on AIDS. These stories will originate from a source we use for such matters. Also stories about a high mortality rate at the Good Sam. Get names of prominent people who have died there.

Media
We need fast and strong publicity on radio/TV/newspapers. We'll contact our advertising agency and inform those media who get our ad dollars that we have important news releases. Any media that refuses to assist will lose all ad dollars.

Financial
Edmund, this is very important area. Can you talk with Good Sam bankers and get a feel about their finances. Where can we squeeze. We can move some of our $100 million cash to the Good Sam bank if they cooperate.

Political
Eric will contact Mayor Gentry. He'll call in some IOU's and get the Mayor to counter any political action opposite our objective.

Andersen's Board Members
We'll reach everyone of his board members through 3rd parties. Let's take apart the list of his board and find mutual friends. Objective is to force Andersen out. When he's gone, we'll try and lead their board to a successor who will cut a quick deal. We can offer the new Good Sam president a golden parachute when we acquire.

Andersen Personal
We have private investigators that will check out his family. Items like a child or grandchildren with drug abuse or police problems. They will check Andersen's life history. Check our sources at the police and Department of Justice. They leak like urinal. Flush them. When he goes down, the Good Sam goes down.

IMPORTANT: Read and destroy this memo.

By five PM, Jimmy Kerr, Edmund Peters and Eric Goodman had read their memos. At 5:05 PM, all three joined Hagen on a conference call.

"Gentlemen, have you each read the memo?"

"We have, Walter. It's a little dramatic, don't you think?"

Hagen exploded with a rage that had been building all day. "How dare you ask. Edmund, your bank holds about 50 million dollars of Ridge money. If I pull it out tomorrow, would that be dramatic? You'd be over here on your hands and knees. And, Jimmy Kerr, famous Philadelphia lawyer, you think I'm too dramatic? Have you checked your legal fees from the Ridge, lately? Eric C. Goodman, founder of KEYSTONE broadcasting--let's talk dramatics. We spent almost $500,000 with your TV station last year. And you've borrowed from our Crystal Venture Fund. Shall I continue? Now gentlemen, whoever thinks I'm being too dramatic, please speak up. I'm waiting. I'm waiting. I'm waiting." There was dead silence on the line as Hagen kept repeating, "I'm waiting... I'm waiting.

"Now, a reminder: Destroy your memos."

•••

Cooper's Sky Page beeper started to buzz and she pressed a couple of buttons to retrieve her message.

COBOL MESSAGE INTERCEPTED. THEY KNOW YOU VISITED SYSTEM LOCATION. BE CAREFUL. CALL ME. STREET.

Now there was proof that Rick Cone, or someone at VALLEY FORGE SYSTEMS, was one of names unearthed by Joker's intercept of COBOL. Cooper called the assistant DA office and prepared to go back into Judge Soto's chambers. This time, she thought they'd walk out with a signed order to search the premises of VALLEY FORGE SYSTEMS. Within a few hours, Cooper was in Judge Soto's chambers with Jack Adams at her side pleading again for a search warrant of VALLEY FORGE SYSTEMS.

"So, Adams, you think the police should get a search warrant? Tell me how you know all these computer messages are not some hacker playing ouja board with our Detective Cooper?"

"Your honor, you denied us before because you thought we had littleg. Now, we have a document that was produced by an MIT consultant to the Boston Police, someone they call Joker. We have an affidavit faxed from Boston that attests to the validity of this so called COBOL intercept."

"If I grant your request, it's going to be a very limited search warrant. It'll be a one-time visit and *no carte blanche.* Have you considered waiting until you develop more evidence before executing a search? If there is a conspiracy afoot, your search will send the rest of this group scurrying into the bushes for cover."

Adams looked at Cooper to see what she wanted. She clenched her fist in a go for it signal.

"Your honor, we do want that warrant executed now."

Judge Soto asked Adams and Cooper to leave his chambers while he considered the request. He told them to return in 30 minutes.

"OK, Cooper, your request for a search warrant at VALLEY FORGE SYSTEMS is granted with these conditions.

"First: you get one search and that is limited to Mr. Rick Cone's office. You may not search any other offices within that business.

"Second: the search warrant is good for 72 hours.

"And, third: Cooper, I wish you good luck.

"I want these folks at VALLEY to get a quick return of any data taken or you pay the price."

Outside Judge Soto's chambers, Cooper and Adams exchanged congratulations.

"Lisa, you owe me dinner for this one."

"Fine."

"How about tonight, detective?"

"OK, Jack, but the ground rules are just for old times sake. I'll meet you at our old stomping ground--Lucy's. How's that sound?"

"Eight PM."

•••

"It's Lisa. We got it, Jimmy. We got our search warrant. And it's that COBOL intercept that did the trick with Judge Soto. We'll execute the search warrant tomorrow. Charlie and Rudy are going with me; with any luck, we'll find something. Wish me luck. I'll call you tomorrow. This weekend is still on, right?"

"Take that to the bank!"

•••

Street called Joker. "You dazzled them down in Philly with that COBOL intercept. They got the search warrant. Lisa's going in tomorrow with Charlie and Rudy."

"What a waste, Jimmy. They'll go in and catch a computer virus, if they're lucky."

"I don't get it."

"Lisa, Charlie and Rudy combined have the computer literacy of yogurt. What a stupid mistake. They wouldn't know a semiconductor from the conductor of the Philadelphia Orchestra and they probably think a gigabyte is indigestion. Unbelievable! Whatever is worth finding is inside Cone's computer. Too bad, after all this work! We should be there, too."

"Yeah, you're right. Joker, can you make a flight tonight to Philly? I'll call the Chief and battle with him. Can I pick you up at MIT around six PM?"

"My bags are packed."

By eight PM, Street and Joker had checked into their hotel in Philadelphia.

Joker set up computer equipment in his hotel room while Street called Cooper at home.

SURPRISE! IT'S JIMMY. JOKER AND I ARE IN PHILLY. WE'RE GOING WITH YOU TO VALLEY FORGE SYSTEMS TOMORROW. YOU NEED A COMPUTER EXPERT. CALL ME. I JUST CHECKED INTO MY HOTEL. ROOM 115. 8:30 PM.

•••

It was 11:30 PM.

Lisa eased onto her chair and tried to balance herself on the noback white chair. She wore blue and green high heeled shoes and a green dress with blue polka dots. Her hair was braided and she wore pearl earrings, necklace and a perfume that was generous with the scent of roses

"It unbuttons on the front."

Her bra fell to the floor and she kicked it away from the chair. Polka dots covered the floor as her dress slid on top of the bra.

"Gently, slowly, you know how I like to be touched."

Cooper moved her head from side to side and was out of control.

"Oh, don't stop touching me. Move your fingers. You know the way."

"Lisa, your legs are so smooth. Do you like what I'm doing now?"

She opened her eyes and nodded.

The lights were low, wine glasses on the floor next to them and they were half on and off the chair. The darkness was pricked by the sound of her door buzzer, followed by knocking.

"Oh, fuck!"

She grabbed a shirt and wrapped it around her naked body.

"Who is it? I'll be right there."

"Lisa, it's Jimmy. I've been calling you all night. Are you OK? Let me in."

●●●

The following morning, Street clutched Cooper as she walked into the squad room and escorted her to an office.

"You sure get around, don't you?"

"Street, you're not my baby sitter and we made no promises. Who I was with and why is none of your goddamn business. I'm not your property. Don't play any guilt trips with me. I never asked for your social calendar. I'm pissed you thought you had some right to come gallivanting to my place whenever you choose."

"I thought you might be in trouble."

"Street, you've always got an answer. That's bullshit. You were nosy, or jealous, or who knows what."

"Tell you what, take a look at this." Street took out the COBOL intercept and showed the full copy to Cooper, including the threat on her life. Street had omitted that when he had paged her with the partial COBOL message.

"Why didn't you tell me about this part? You held it back."

"Yup, I did. Why worry you. I would have shown it to you today. And you didn't know this. But yesterday, I sent a copy of the full intercept to Chief Rome and she promised to pass it along to Judge Soto. You probably got your search warrant because of the threat to your life and not because of your legal eagle petting partner, Jack Adams. So, if he's your hero for a day, find a new one."

Cooper held the intercept in her hands and kept her eyes glued on it, using it as a shield so she did not have to look at Street.

"Cooper, we have a search warrant to execute. Let's do it. And your social calendar just opened up for this weekend due to a last minute cancellation from a Boston cop who took the wrong turn with you."

In the heat of the moment, a lot of thoughts went cascading through Street's head. He knew his male ego was bruised and he felt jealous. He didn't need a psychiatrist or clairvoyant to peek inside his mind and explain some of the other feelings that ratcheted through him. Street never learned how to be discreet with his feelings or conditional with anything in life. He plunged into so much in life with a mix of foolishness and naked feelings. Getting hurt was not an unknown feeling for Jimmy Street, and, beneath the anger and damaged ego, he realized how much he liked Lisa.

Chapter Thirty One: PHILADLEPHIA CHROMOSOME

OPERATION END ZONE was on a roll, literally, as the detectives and Joker drove along route 30 to VALLEY FORGE SYSTEMS. Street was in the front of the three row van and Cooper was in the rear with Smith. Rudy and Joker occupied the middle seats. A city cop drove with an unmarked police cruiser trailing. There were jurisdictional issues that Philadelphia and Valley Forge settled prior to the execution of the search warrant. The compromise was that two FBI agents would participate in the search.

Joker broke the silence in the van and launched into an unsolicited, esoteric explanation about the significance of the upcoming search. This was vintage Joker. "Hey, everyone, how about a road game? You're all from Philadelphia; so, who knows about the PHILADELPHIA CHROMOSOME and why it's a perfect metaphor for the VALLEY FORGE SYSTEMS?"

"Joker, kill the comedy scene. This isn't the time."

"Street's out of the game. How about you, Rudy?"

"Never heard of it. You made it up?"

"Wrong and wrong; but, at least Rudy's in the game. The Philly Chromo was the first chromosomal abnormality ever linked to a specific cancer and it was discovered by a doctor at the University of Pennsylvania. This chromosome 22 gives up more than it receives. And that's what we're going to do. We're going to make this place in Valley Forge tell us all sorts of things. It's going to give up a lot more than it receives. It'll receive a few extra little computer programs I brought along. That judge never said we couldn't leave things, right?"

Street glanced outside at the passing road signs like Villanova and Radnor.

"Street, recognize Radnor. That's where either TV Guide or Reader's Digest comes from. I forgot."

"Only you, Joker, would care."

Smith listened intently to Joker. "That guy is absolutely amazing or crazy or both, Street."

"Put most of your money on...crazy."

The van pulled in front of VALLEY FORGE SYSTEMS at 11:45 AM and the detectives and FBI agents moved inside. A receptionist was confronted with a sea of gold and silver badges and picture ID's and a few pages of legal documents.

"This is a search warrant signed by Judge Soto and this is your copy. We are authorized to search Rick Cone's office. Would you please escort us there."

"But, it's locked. He's on vacation."

"Under the authority of this warrant, you can either open his office with a key or we will forcibly enter. Your choice."

Ten minutes later a woman approached and identified herself as Jane Hickmont, office manager for VALLEY FORGE SYSTEMS.

"Officers, they paged me and I've got a key to Rick's office. I've also placed a ship-to-shore call to let him know what you're doing."

"That's fine. Now, open the door, please."

The detectives and Joker entered Cone's office loaded with electronic gadgets and cameras. Joker unpacked a portable computer along with a conglomeration of supplies. After a couple of minutes he connected his portable computer to the one at the rear of Cone's desk. The detectives opened and closed drawers, not knowing what documents they were looking for inside the office.

Street stood at the door with a grim look of satisfaction. "Without Joker, this search would have been a complete waste. You're all insane. This guy wouldn't leave any kind of paper trail. It's all in his computer."

"Yeah, and I'm in his computer now!"

Cooper was satisfied to sit in a chair and watch Joker scamper through a script of computer commands. He pulled a cellular phone from his pocket and talked. "Toshi, I'm using the DataStar Uplink. Are you getting copies of Cone's files? Good. We've got more coming."

At 1:30 PM, with Joker still punching commands into his computer, the two FBI agents decided to return downtown. They went in the van, leaving the Philadelphia detectives and Joker.

"Joker, come on, talk. What's the verdict?"

"Street, relax a bit. I'm still taking testimony."

"Funny."

Cooper smiled at Smith and Levin and still managed to avoid any eye contact with Street.

Finally, just before three PM, Joker announced that he had finished.

"Well, folks, I'll bet you never saw a search like this. I've got a briefcase of goodies. This computer system was very prudish and it didn't like us wandering through it's dark little secrets. Cone's computer has more traps, logons, passwords and auto destructs than I've ever seen. By the time we get back to headquarters, Toshi and DeYoe will have the extracted data ready for us."

Street and Cooper were in ugly moods and Smith and Levin remained silent as they drove back. Joker returned to the Philadelphia Chromosome and it's history, including a short discussion of the genetic basis for some kinds of cancer. The time passed quickly as all the detectives dozed off to sleep. Joker's rambling stories about genetics and computer science fiction were far more effective than bedtime stories or counting sheep.

Joker had a fax from Toshi and DeYoe awaiting him at headquarters.

FACSIMILE TRANSMISSION MIT15:33:20 PHILADELPHIA POLICE

Joker! man, you really jazzed that guy's computer. The computer in Cone's office has a selfdial to a Ridge computer, location unknown. Cone logs on with SYS. He is confirmed as a COBOL receiver. Cone's computer has two messages inside waiting for retrieval. First is notification of a COBOL message tonight. The other is warning from COBOL about a search warrant. How'd they know? CONFIRM FACSIMILE DOCUMENT RECEIVED 1 PAGE

"Yeah, I read it, too. How did they know we were executing a search? The only ones who knew were you, me, Cooper, Smith, Levin, Chief Rome, Judge Soto, and that DA smuck. Great, who do we tell about this?"

Joker had a suggestion. "Jimmy, we tell no one for now."

●●●

Street left a message for Cooper and joined Joker on a return flight to Boston.

Lisa, by the time you get this note, I'll be back in Boston. Whatever happened is history. I assumed some things about us that should not have been assumed. I want to help you solve this Ridge case. We have a message pulled from Cone's computer that shows he was warned about the police search. You've got a leak somewhere in your circle. Be careful; you've got a real mess to deal with. Street.

"Why didn't someone tell me Street was going back to Boston?"

Smith answered. "We didn't know because he never told anyone. Lisa, what's going on between you and Street? A lovers' quarrel? No big deal."

Cooper slumped into a chair and cradled her head in her hands and started to whimper. She lifted a beat up waste basket with a swift kick and swept it hand across the desk throwing a pile of papers to the floor.

"Charlie, you're so big and dumb. Typical man. Jimmy's very special to me. I messed up. I really hurt him. I couldn't hurt you guys because you've got the sensitivity level of an empty cup." She stormed out of the squad room, but not before leaving a message for Street in Boston.

Jimmy, it's Lisa. It's late afternoon. We didn't get to talk. I mean, really talk. Please call me.

●●●

Chapter Thirty Two: BELLY OF THE BEAST

00:15:05: COBOL confirms team on line. SYS is out of loop. Unplug Cooper ASAP. Crystal disconnect within next two weeks. Monitor e mail carefully during next week. COBOL clear.

•••

Rick Cone was found onboard the cruise ship Adventure of the Seas in the Caribbean, taken into custody in St. Thomas and flown to Philadelphia. His flight landed Thursday morning at 7 AM; by 9 AM, he was face to face with the detectives in a seedy looking interrogation room. Two Philadelphia lawyers from one of the city's most prestigious criminal law firms sat on either side of their client. They had never met Cone before, but had received instructions to provide him with advice and assistance.

One of the lawyers started with a little opening speech. "Detective, before you question Mr. Cone, you might consider releasing him now and reducing the chance you'll be sued for false imprisonment and a whole bunch of other offenses. So, shall we just get up and leave and chalk this up to a mistake?"

"Your client made the mistakes. Your dressed up little threat is duly noted. We met before, Mr. Cone. Do you remember?"

"Sure, you're the detective who came over and asked for my help. Remind me not to help in the future."

"You helped all right. Cone, you're part of some magical mystery club that likes to meet via e-mail in the middle of the night and plot murder."

Cone's attorneys interrupted Cooper and signaled for their client not to respond.

"Cone, do what they suggest. Clam up and keep silent. I understand these two lawyers are strangers. You keep listening to their advice. That's what COBOL expects. He expects you to take a fall for him. In the meantime, why don't you look at some of these documents."

Cooper handed over computer intercepts and a computer analysis prepared by Joker on MIT letterhead that confirmed SYS was VALLEY FORGE SYSTEMS and Cone was the contact.

Charlie Smith had been listening statue-like at the rear of the room and moved behind Cone.

"Say, detective, could you get that big guy behind me to move away. I don't like him there."

"Hear that, Charlie? Mr. Cone doesn't like you around."

Smith took over the interrogation of Cone, and it became confrontational. The detectives had prepared a surprise for Cone.

"Cone, you know we got into the computer cesspool that you and COBOL and those other night riders use. It's a two way street, so we popped off a little message to your good friend COBOL. Take a peek, Cone."

SYS to COBOL. They caught me. Police gave me immunity. You never protected me. Go to hell in cyberspace.

"That's the death certificate you sent. You've killed me."

Cone's lawyers jumped in. "Mr. Cone, say no more. That's a bluff. They have nothing. We'll have you home for dinner tonight."

Cooper stood up and swung around next to Cone, whispering in his ear. "Mr. Cone, you're free to go. Be very careful. Maybe these lawyers work for COBOL. Anyway, every one will know you're free. So, fly away, little birdie. If we never see each other again, I do have one question: how was the Adventure of the Seas? I heard it's really nice."

In his standard thundervoice, Smith made an announcement: "Get out of here, Cone; you're free. Have a nice life, or any portion thereof."

Cone looked like he was hearing the words of God journeying through the interrogation room. He slumped in his seat and dropped his head to the table with a thumping sound. Cone looked up at Cooper; his eyes were awash in terror. He was a terrorized man who looked pale despite his Caribbean tan. The detectives knew they had captured his fear, multiplied and reinjected it. This was a man going into terrorshock. "OK, OK, I want to talk. I want protection. I don't know much, but I'll tell you everything I do know. Just promise me protection from COBOL. And get these lawyers out of here."

"Mr. Cone, again, you have the right to remain silent, the..."

"I don't want to be silent."

●●●

Cone talked for several hours. When a typist came inside the room, Cone dictated a statement.

<u>STATEMENT OF RICHARD CONE</u>

I make the following statement of my own free will and was advised of my rights by Detectives Cooper and Smith.

My name is Richard 'Rick' Cone, age 43, and I am a resident of Valley Forge, PA. I am single. VALLEY FORGE SYSTEMS is a computer consulting firm I established in the early 1980's.

On or about 1984 I received an email from a person who identified himself as COBOL and said I would never know his real name. He asked if I was willing to

provide computer consulting services for him. I agreed and over the years I have downloaded data into a jump telephone service that interconnects with his computer. I never directly dialed COBOL. Each month I received a cashiers check, always from different banks, in the amount of $5,000. He originated the payment plan. I never submitted a bill based on hours of work. He wanted one monthly flat fee regardless of the hours.

During the past few years COBOL used my software to build a club of some kind and then schedules computercampfire nights. I figured that he was some rich eccentric nut that liked to play computer games.

He told us that he's affiliated or associated with the Ridge Hospital. If he's in that hospital, you wouldn't want to be a patient there.

Recently he used words like 'termination' or 'disconnect'. He used the names Cooper, Street, and Crystal, whatever that is. Again, I assumed he was kidding.

When Detective Cooper came to our offices and said some guy named 'Joker' needed to get inside the Ridge computers, well, I sent an email to COBOL using the 'jump' phone system. This guy paid thousands of dollars to me, he's my biggest client, and I owed him. I never thought there was anything wrong.

Then COBOL leaves an email that the police are going to search my offices. I retrieved it using a sea-land phone. But I never believed the email. Then it happened.

I don't know who he is, and I don't even know if he is a he.

The above statement is made under oath. Signed Richard 'Rick' Cone.

Cone was released after his statement and told to remain in the Philadelphia area.

•••

The nurse at the emergency room desk asked the young woman to fill out a form before a doctor examined her. Twin cameras swung left and right as Lisa Marie Cooper wrote her name, age, occupation, address and next of kin. Ten minutes later, a very young doctor emerged and guided Cooper into an examining room.

"Ms. Cooper, tell me exactly what's bothering you."

"Doctor, I've got severe pain in my belly. I have nausea. I've been vomiting. I feel weak. And my heart seems like it's racing. It's not the flu. I'm scared."

The doctor checked her pulse and examined her abdomen.

"Your heart rate is way up there. How old are you?"

"I'm 35. I'm athletic. This just can't be."

"Well, it certainly isn't Munchhausen Syndrome."

"What's that?"

"People who imagine they're sick and want to be in hospitals. You really are sick. It's your heart rate that concerns me; otherwise, I'd send you home. I'll admit you tonight; we'll monitor you and do an NPO regimen."

"That's what?"

"NPO means nothing by mouth. We'll give you some nutrients via an IV and then, in the morning, we'll see how you're doing. We can control the nausea and vomiting. Maybe it's food poisoning. I don't know. We'll get you all set up. We'll put you in our computer system so people can call or visit. It's like checking into a hotel, only a lot more expensive. "

Cooper was wheeled into a waiting area of the emergency room where she received a Ridge Hospital plastic arm ID. A few minutes later she was taken by two staff members up to the 5th floor and moved into a private room, 515.

"Nurse, what do I need to do to get a private room?"

"The computer printout says you're a police detective. Any officer in the uniformed services like police and fire automatically get private rooms if they're available. We'll treat you as if you were Mayor Gentry."

Cooper looked around her room and tried to use the telephone. Neither the telephone nor TV were connected. A nurse spotted her fiddling with the phone and TV.

"We'll have those up and running in about an hour. First, we're going to connect an IV and get you some liquids." The nurse wore a tag with the Ridge logo and her name, Mary Cinners, RN.

Cinners was very short--no more than five feet, with an athletic build. She was in her mid 40's and had a strong and confident look. Cooper felt safer as she watched Cinners move around the room with clarity and ease.

After the IV, Cooper was left alone for a few minutes. "So, this is the Ridge Hospital from the inside. I'm like Jonah inside the belly of the beast. Hope it turns out like it did for Jonah. Lisa, now laugh a little inside...after all, this is your performance. With the help of a doctor friend who gave me-..."

The drug was atropine and the medical examiner said it would increase her heart rate and make her breathe faster. She remembered that Dracula was angry and reluctant when she told him what she was doing. Dracula said no over and over until she threatened to find another doctor. Finally he agreed, provided she called him every couple of hours to report her heart rate.

"He said the drug would get me admitted and he was right. Shoot, if I don't call Dracula soon, he'll go bananas."

Cooper felt a darkness invading her body as she lay in bed immobilized by a sweeping sense of serenity. Was there some one else in the room with her? The moment was odorless and motionless, beautiful and non threatening. Darkness was something she experienced every day as the sun set or clouds rolled by or the lights went out. But, the darkness at the Ridge was enveloping her from the inside. For one instant, she tried to scream and there were no words as her lips moved. Then, it was black, inside and outside.

When there was no call from Cooper within one hour, Cula paged Charlie Smith.

"Dracula, that is dumb. I can't believe you did that. I can't believe she did that."

Smith dialed Levin. "Rudy, Cooper took some drug from our lame ME so she could get admitted to the Ridge. And that's where she is. Whatever happened between her and Street had something to do with this. Meet you at the Ridge in 30 minutes."

This is Street. At the tone signal, leave your message.

"Street, this is Charlie. Cooper's done it again! She got herself checked into the Ridge. That's all I know. I'm going over now. It's 6:30 PM.

●●●

18:45:00 COBOL ALERT: AUTO DIAL TO TEAM. SYS OUT OF GAME. RIDGE COMPUTER SAYS COOPER ADMITTED TONIGHT. TERMINATE HER. REPEAT. ORDER IS TO TERMINATE COOPER. RAZOR WILL COMPLY. CONFIRM DISCONNECT

●●●

"Joker, it's Toshi. Where are you?"

"I'm at a pay phone in Harvard Square. You should see the new magazines that just came in at the *Out of Town...*"

"Listen, you better find Street. It's an emergency. COBOL's back on the line. COBOL says that detective in Philadelphia was admitted to the Ridge Hospital. It gets worse. COBOL issued an order to TERMINATE her."

"Toshi, you and DeYoe keep monitoring the computers and beep me if anything else comes in. I'll get Street."

"ZEBRA COMMAND, this is Joker. I have a priority ALPHA message for Street. My verification code is JJIFI."

"Joker, we'll find Street."

ZEBRA COMMAND members like to think they're better at finding people than the White House telephone operators and that might be true. Simultaneously, Street's beeper was sounded along with calls to his home and car telephones. Every person authorized to use ZEBRA had a hot phone list that included about 20 phone numbers. Street's list included his laundry, his sister's house, the gym he used and a couple of friends. An ALPHA priority alerted every cruiser in the city of Boston to stop Street on sight.

Six minutes later, a cruiser spotted Street walking out of a wine shop at the foot of Beacon Hill.

"Street, get in. ZEBRA's looking for you... ZEBRA, Stree-t's in the car."

"Street, this is ZEBRA COMMAND. Stand by for a patch with Joker."

There's both a thrill and sick-to-the-stomach feeling when ZEBRA wanted someone with an ALPHA priority call.

The cops in the cruiser, although curious, followed ZE-BRA instructions and left Street alone in the front seat to wait for the call.

"Go ahead, Joker; Street's on the line."

"Did your atomic bomb go off? What the hell is..."

"Jimmy, we intercepted a COBOL transmission. Cooper was admitted to the Ridge and COBOL ordered her terminated."

"Street, this is ZEBRA. We have Joker on hold. Another call standing by from a Detective in Philadelphia. He says it's..."

"Put him on."

"Street, it's Charlie. You won't believe this, but..."

"I know already."

"How?"

"We intercepted a message from COBOL. That lunatic ordered Cooper terminated."

"Rudy and I are almost at the Hospital."

"Stay with her. I'll be there before nine. Do we know where Dr. Hagen is?"

"No."

"We should know."

●●●

Smith and Levin arrived at the Ridge and put down 30 feet of rubber as they skidded along the circular entrance: Welcome to the Ridge Hospital.

"Cooper, what room is she in?"

When the security guard asked if they were relatives, Smith reached over the desk and, grabbing the guard by the shirt, he pulled him out of his chair and off the ground. Levin pulled out his police ID, but it didn't matter to the guard who was looking into the face of a hurricane named Charlie.

"Man, put me down, I'll get it for you."

The guard hit a few keys on his computer. "Got it; she's in room 515. It says she is not to be disturbed."

Smith tilted his head to the right and tightened his grip on the guard and lifted him off the floor again.

"Take the elevator to the fifth floor and turn left."

Smith dropped the security guard to the floor.

The TV monitor behind the guard had stopped it's rhythmic swing from side to side and was fixed on Smith. In his 20th floor office, Dr. Hagen was taping everything.

●●●

"We're here to see Detective Cooper. Where is hse?"

"I'm Mary Cinners. I'm her nurse," she replied, her confident and assured face suddenly carrying the look of a hundred bad dreams.

"She was admitted and seemed OK. She wanted to make a phone call. We were talking. We gave her an IV. Just some fluids. I came back about ten minutes later and she was...-gone."

"Gone?"

"Oh, she's in the room, all right; but she's in a near coma. We've got a neurologist on the way and there are two other doctors inside with her. This makes no sense. They're doing some tests."

Cinners had a dazed look and seemed totally distracted.

"Detectives, what's going on?"

Cinners interrupted. "Dr. Hagen, it must be my fault. We gave her an IV and something happened. She's in real trouble now. My God, I don't make mistakes!"

Hagen had walked onto the fifth floor wearing his white jacket, emblazoned with the words, *Dr. Hagen, President*. Smith put his arm around Hagen and pressed down so hard Hagen could barely stand.

"Rudy, Dr. Hagen and I want to talk in this room. Make sure no one bothers us." Smith pushed Hagen towards a men's room.

"Dr. Hagen, are you OK?" asked Cinners as she saw Smith tugging.

"Fine nurse, no problem."

Cinners yelled. "It's not his fault. Blame me. Not him." Smith never turned back.

Smith grumbled a few words that Hagen could not understand. The men's room filled with a salty odor as beads of sweat poured down Smith's face. His eyes pillared into Hagen and he moved to within an inch of the doctor's nose. Smith's brow was wrinkled and his face screamed with contorted rage and yet there was total silence. Hagen was stone cold still, as if he were transfixed. Smith edged so close to Hagen that the tips of their noses touched. Smith's body was on fire and his biceps throbbed under his shirt. Hagen followed Smith's head as it rolled in circles. Smith grunted like he was ready to eat Hagen, ripping his limbs apart and devouring him from the head on down.

"Hagen, there's a woman in Room 515, who is a police detective, my partner, and my friend. She is very important to me, to my partner, and to a lot of other cops on the police force."

Hagen nodded.

"If that woman is not OK, this night will be your personal Armageddon. That is not a threat; it a promise from me to you. If she dies in your hospital, I will put my right hand inside your foul mouth and yank your tongue out and hold it in front of your eyes. And then I will kill you with my bare hands."

Hagen's body trembled from believing every word Smith said.

"So, now, Hagen, let's go out and see how Detective Cooper is doing, with the hope you are saying your prayers."

Smith had not finished: "You know, Hagen, we've gotten a real good education on you. I think you just suck the nipples of a lot of those Crystal Club fat cows and, when they're dry, you turn them into hamburger. Now, you've got a friend of mine in here. She's a cop, and not one of your millionaires. You better hope she comes out with a smile."

Smith kept his hand on Hagen's shoulder in a death grip just light enough so the doctor did not scream in pain. They walked into Cooper's room. One of the doctors spoke.

"Dr. Hagen, she'll be OK. I don't know what happened. Someone loaded her with morphine. Guess she could have been real sensitive to the stuff. Maybe she had some drinks before she got here. She's got an order for 5 mg. Guess that and a any bottle of wine could have done the trick. We've given her the standard treatment for a narcotic overdose. Narcan's in and she's coming around."

Smith leaned next to Hagen and whispered in a sarcastic voice. "This is where you ask the questions. OK Hagen, do it."

"Nurse, I want a list of every person who saw, touched, looked or had any access to this patient from the moment she walked through our doors. Get me that list now." Hagen looked over to Smith. But, no smile from the detective, just a menancing look.

Cooper mumbled very softly and moved slightly. Smith and Levin sat on her bed and put their ears up to her mouth.

"Hey, guys, is this heaven? I don't know what happened. The room was dark and someone came in and was doing something with the IV. The next thing I knew, my lights went out. Blank. Dark. Dead dreams. Wow. It was like someone pulled a black sheet over my face and that was it."

Cinners was in the room; she reached over to Cooper. "My dear, it's my fault. It can't be; but it must be. I'm so glad you're OK." Cooper squeezed her hand.

Hagen turned to one of the other nurses. "Call the police. This cop, the big black one, threatened me. Call the police."

Rudy's eyes lit up; he grabbed Hagen and moved him into the same room with Smith. "Hagen, you want the police? Well, I'm here."

"Get away. You cops can't come in my hospital and push me around and threaten me. I'll report all of you."

Levin flashed back to that day--so long ago--when a rogue cop had called his best friend Smith *nigger*. He punched the cop and, those long ago days, now seemed like glorious times. Rudy was usually relegated to the handsoff side of police work, with Smith handling the tough guys. Now, Rudy had a chance to show he could manage his way around.

"Hagen, you sure are determined to get yourself killed. Charlie is one of the most popular guys on the force and he's retiring soon. Now, you want to mess all that up. We've got over 1,000 cops roaming this city and Charlie knows most of them by their first name. So, do we call downtown? Want to look into 2,000 angry eyes? Or, maybe, I'll just start following you home at night. I'll make it my mission to wreck your life."

Hagen stormed out of the little room and left through an elevator.

Rudy marched out looking like he had just won the Masters. "Charlie, Dr. Hagen reconsidered and decided that he was having a bad dream. And I'll bet that lowlife snake probably wet his pants."

"What'd you tell him, Rudy? You couldn't scare a flea!"

"Watch it, big guy, or I'll give you the same treatment." Smith notched his head about 1/10th of an inch down a secret thank-you-look that both men fashioned over the years as partners.

Within 10 minutes, a uniformed police woman arrived and she was told to remain outside Cooper's door until morning and log all persons going into room 515. Smith and Levin looked into Cooper's half opened eyes. "See you tomorrow, Lisa."

"Thanks. Charlie, I've got a question."

"Yeah."

"Did someone try to kill me tonight?"

"That's my guess."

●●●

Smith and Levin lingered on the fifth floor for a while, asking if anyone unusual was seen entering Cooper's hospital room. They stopped at a coffee machine, loaded up, and headed home. The police woman stationed outside Cooper's room called Smith each hour to update her condition. Anger spread quickly through the department with news that someone had tried to kill Detective Cooper. Jimmy Street arrived at the Ridge at 9:30 PM, accompanied by the medical examiner, Drake Cula.

"I want her out of that hospital. Tell me if she's OK to move. You're responsible for getting her in; now, you get her out."

"Look, Street, this wasn't my idea. The medication I gave her had nothing to do with her deep sleep. That happened after she was admitted to the Ridge."

Street and Cula flashed their police ID for the police woman guarding Cooper's door and walked inside her dim and quiet room. Street saw Cooper lying on her side, tears on her cheeks, and facing the door with open eyes. He had brought Cooper some rumpled yellow roses a street vendor had been selling in the airport terminal. Street put the wilted and sagging roses on her bed as she reached for his hand.

"Jimmy, this can't be heaven because you're here."

"More like hell. I'm getting you out of here. I've got Dracula, and he's gonna check a few things. If he says OK, we're history."

"I wasn't thinking right. I was emotional. I didn't like myself after what happened between us. Next thing, I was here..."

"Relax, Lisa; we'll talk another time."

"Dracula, you're not used to live ones, the kind that can talk back if you prick them the wrong way. Just make sure she's OK to travel." Street moved away from the bed and watched him examine Cooper."

"Street, she's OK to travel, but I wouldn't recommend a night on the town."

Cooper was bundled in a bunch of burgundy colored Ridge Hospital blankets and the medical examiner unhooked the IV. Street popped the door open and Cooper stood there with one arm around each man.

"Officer, call police headquarters and have them inform Detectives Smith and Levin that we've taken Cooper home."

"Are you sure?"

"Do it."

Nurse Cinners called out: "You can't take her out of here like that. I'm calling security."

"Call the fuckin' White House, too!"

Street and Dracula helped Cooper slowly down the corridor towards the elevators. Street yelled out to the officer posted at Cooper's door. "Come to think of it, you'd better come with us." Now, the foursome moved into an elevator, with Cooper woozy and wobbly and barely able to move her legs. The door slammed shut and they edged down towards the lobby.

Suddenly, the elevator became a vertical coffin, bouncing to a stop between floors.

"Officer, give me your radio." Street knew what was happening and why. This was Western Union *à la* Ridge Hospital. They were on the receiving end of a not-so-subtle message from somebody in the hospital. "Bet that son of abitch Hagen did this."

"Officer needs assistance, location Ridge Hospital. Three police trapped in an elevator..."

Dracula waved his hand.

"You won't believe this, but make that three police and one medical examiner trapped. Need immediate help. Notify Detectives Charlie Smith and Rudy Levin. Do you copy?"

"We copy. The signal's not great. Assistance en route. Arrival inside five minutes. Stay on the channel."

Ninety seconds later, the elevator started to move again and slide to the lobby. As the elevator doors opened, Dr. Hagen was standing in the way, joined by several hospital security guards.

"Detective Cooper, you can't leave. You're not well enough to travel. You haven't signed any discharge papers. I insist you stay."

Cooper was barely able to lift her head. When she did, Street saw how terrorized she looked on seeing Hagen.

"Enough!" Street pulled his gun and kept it pointed to the floor. The police woman instinctively drew her gun. The hospital security guards stood frozen. The sound of sirens started to build to a roar as it seemed like all the police cars in the city were converging on the Ridge.

"Hagen, I'm Detective Jimmy Street. Let's count back from five. When I get to zero, either we're out of here or you're under arrest. FIVE, FOUR, THREE, TWO."

Hagen motioned for everyone to clear a path. At that instant, three police cars dressed in flashing lights and sirens arrived at the hospital. Street and Dracula walked through the revolving doors and into the chill of the night and into a crowd of Philadelphia cops.

Street turned and read a sign inside the reception area: WELCOME TO THE RIDGE and a bunch of flowers nearby.

"Oh, shit, forgot something!" Street exclaimed. Cooper was inside a police cruiser with Dracula and the police woman next to her. "Lisa, I left something inside. Be right back."

Street ran back into the Ridge and past Hagen and his security guards.

"Hagen, I'm taking the elevator. If you or your hacks play elevator games again, I'll sound the fire alarm."

The fifth floor was quiet. Down at the end was the police woman's chair outside a now empty room 515.

"Where are the yellow roses?" he asked. The room had been emptied of everything. Those rumpled and crumpled roses were special. But one nurse pointed to the nurses' station and to a vase loaded with the roses.

On seeing Street coming, Mary Cinners stood between him and the roses, now angry with a catch-me-if-you-can smirk on her face.

"She's gone. She left the roses. She's done with them."

"Tell you what: I'm not done with you." He grabbed the roses.

As he did, Cinners clutched Street's hand. "She left them."

"Let go...FIVE, FOUR, THREE, TWO."

After being released, Street took the roses, making sure that he also knocked the vase to the floor.

In the elevator on the way back to the lobby, Street thought: "The countdown FIVE, FOUR works every time. Maybe I should work for NASA."

He reappeared with Cooper's roses in hand and water dripping down his pants, looking like a little kid bringing roses for his senior prom's sweetheart.

"Lisa, you didn't think I was gonna leave those roses in the Ridge, did you?. By morning they'd be dead. Get the message?"

●●●

COBOL Alert. Termination of Cooper aborted. Crystal Club disconnect on schedule. Target selected. Revisit Cooper situation. Street back. COBOL off.

•••

Cooper's return home looked like the arrival of a foreign dignitary. Three police cruisers moved quickly past the Art Museum and around Logan Circle as they went southeast towards Penn's Landing to the waterfront. On Market Street the motorcade was joined by a fourth car with Smith and Levin inside.

Dracula called an internist, Dr. Sam Lee, from the Good Sam, and asked him to wait outside Cooper's apartment. With the passage of time during the trip from the Ridge to her condo, Cooper got stronger and more alert. After the examination, Dr. Lee pronounced Cooper healthy and lucky. He took some urine for a toxicology screening, but guessed she had been given an Opioid, probably Morphine. Cooper remembered a feeling of euphoria, then drowsiness and finally nothing all--symptoms consistent with Opioid intoxication.

Cooper's telephone was overbooked with phone messages and she asked Street to play them back while Charlie lifted her into bed.

"Go ahead, Jimmy, make some coffee for everyone. Can you do it without breaking any more glasses?"

"She's back alright with that snooty attitude we've all grown to tolerate. Right, Rudy?"

Message #1: Lisa, it's about 10 PM. This is Jack. Want to get together again? Call me.

Message #2: Chief Rome. Detective, I've monitored the situation all night. Thank God you're OK. You've got a blank check on staffing for OPERATION END ZONE. I'm a believer now.

Message #3: Lisa, it's Mom and Dad. The police called and said you went to the Hospital. They said you'd be home tonight. What happened. We're worried. Please call us.

Message #4: STAY AWAY FROM THE RIDGE.

Street pulled the cartridge tape from Cooper's answering machine and handed it to Smith. "Charlie, see if we can find some way to decipher this voice. Male, female, accent, age, anything is better than what we've got."

By midnight everyone cleared out of Cooper's apartment, except Street. Dr. Lee left his beeper number with Cooper and insisted that someone stay with her through the night.

"Jimmy, you were a lifesaver tonight. And you didn't break any glasses. I want to tell you about that call from Jack Adams, and about the other night. I owe you that."

"You don't owe me anything. I don't leave things undone. You opened this whole dance with the Ridge and Hagen and all the others. No one believed you, but that's changed. We'll get it done together. I've got a marathon to run in Boston in April."

Cooper kept rambling on about the Ridge and Hagen and Ginny Choate and Nurse Cinners. Then, without warning, she stopped in mid-sentence and fell asleep. Street cuddled next to her on the bed, she inside the covers and he outside. At nine AM the telephone rang.

"Hello."

"Who's this?"

"Detective Jimmy Street. And who's this?"

"I'm Dr. John Andersen, president of the Good Samaritan Hospital. My morning updates showed one of our physicians, Dr. Lee, treated Detective Cooper last night on an emergency basis. I've met Cooper and I'd like to talk with her."

"She's still a little bit out of it. Someone loaded her up with morphine or something like that and..."

"I read Lee's report this morning. Detective, I suggest you wake her up. There can be a psychological fallout from Cooper's incident. It's healthier to get her out of bed and move around. Don't let her slide into a funk."

"Dr. Andersen, I appreciate that. You hold on. I'll wake her."

"Hi, Dr. Andersen, it's me. This is real nice of you to call. I'm fine now but still a little tired. How are you doing?"

"That's the other reason I called. I'll talk to you later today."

"No, please talk now; I'm OK."

"We were just served with legal papers from Hagen and the Ridge. They've made a formal proposal to buy our hospital. The offer went to the Board of Directors. Detective, they've offered a huge sum of money. Where do they get that money?"

"We're working on that, Dr. Andersen."

Chapter Thirty Three: PARADISE LOST

For Wyatt Earl Jones, every day was paradise found, having lived everfy day to its fullest. For, each day of his 67 years on earth, Jones lived his life enjoying the attention and care reserved for royalty. His grandfather, Edward Wrightson Jones, was a 19th century Philadelphia merchant banker who saw the future, and the future was coal. By early 1905, the Jones Mining and Manufacturing Corporation owned the rights to all the major coal reserves in West Virginia. The Jones family burst forth with over achievers and the coal empire expanded into shipping and South American gold mining.

When Edward Wrightson Jones died, his trust allocated interest income to his wife and children and disposition of the principal to his grandchildren. Wyatt Jones was the sole grandchild and *FORTUNE* estimated his net worth in excess of two billion dollars. Unlike so many in such lofted positions of wealth, Jones' English schooling had prepared him well to assume control of a great fortune. He was married to his college sweetheart, a history teacher, and served in the US Army. Courted by both political parties to seek elective office, he refused but never rejected a chance to contribute to Philadelphia area causes. Several famous music schools in the city had Jones Foundation Endowments. His great passions, besides family, was classical music and wine. He could purchase any piece of property anywhere in the United States but chose to live in a modest sized condominium in Rittenhouse Square. He and his wife, Emily, were adventure travelers and had just returned from a five week journey by sea and land that circled South America, including the remote Falkland Islands.

Jones and his wife Emily had three children, who lived the American dream.

In an instant, their family dream was turned upside down inside a speeding ambulance enroute to the Ridge Hospital.

Jones had complained all day of severe stomach upset that resembled hunger pain. For days he had lived a cycle of pain, food, relief, and pain again. Finally he began to vomit blood and that's when the rush to the Hospital began.

Emily Jones reached her three children by telephone and all booked flights to Philadelphia by early evening. She called her internist and he planned to meet Jones around six PM. Then she called Dr. Walter Hagen.

"Walter, Wyatt is really sick. We're coming by ambulance. He's vomiting blood. I'm scared."

"Emily, calm down. Wyatt's in the Crystal Club; never forget that fact. We'll give him very special care. Let me get off the phone and start calling specialists in the Hospital. I'll have my medical colleague, Dr. Susan Constance, downstairs waiting for you. She'll coordinate everything, Emily. We'll get Wyatt a very special private room. See you soon and remember, he's Crystal Club.

Hagen reviewed a format sheet that outlined very specific procedures used when Crystal Club members were admitted.

Crystal Club Admittance Check List

1. **Private room with south facing view.**
   Check w/family for special meal requests.
2. **Private nurse.**
3. **PR visits by President and Chief of Medicine.**
4. **All medical reports copied and forwarded to Chief of Medicine and Dr. Hagen.**
5. **Log of all visitors to room and copy to Dr. Hagen.**
6. **Dr. Constance supervises any medical issues.**
7. **CRYSTAL CLUB support team on 24 hour standby.**
8. **Computer monitors compliance.**

9. Check financial records of Club members. Current on membership fees. Verify.
10. Notify security if needed for patient privacy.
11. Hospital phone operators never divulge information on Crystal Club patients. Advise them. Any info released only from President's office.
12. Approved visitor list. Verify with patient, family and Dr. Hagen.

When Jones' ambulance arrived at the ER, Dr. Susan Constance was waiting with several other physicians. There was no paperwork and no doubt that Wyatt Jones was the recipient of very special treatment.

"Mr. Jones, I'm Dr. Constance. We met at the Crystal Ball. Dr. Hagen will visit you after the doctors have made an initial examination. We assigned one of our Crystal Club team members to stay with your wife and handle all her needs. They're going to take you upstairs and I'll join you in a little while. Right now, our computers are printing an update of your medical history. Your private room is already set up with TV, VCR, Cable connections, a telephone and fax machine. So, let's get to work and see what the problem is."

"Wow!" Jones exclaimed. Despite his enormous wealth, Jones had always been a *Wow* person whether it was a visit with the President of the United States or a home run at Veterans Field.

•••

COBOL to RAZOR. We have a Crystal Club in the ballpark. OK to strike him out. Front Row Seats? Clear.

•••

"Walter, we've got Jones downstairs. Looks to me like his peptic ulcer. The computer says this isn't new for him. Everything's been tried. My guess is they're going to come back and recommend a vagotomy and pyloroplasty. I'm sure he didn't come here expecting major surgery. I haven't told his wife yet."

"Keep me informed, Susan. When do you think we'll know?"

"In the next two hours. They're taking him to endoscopy now. We'll see how that goes. Maybe we can coagulate a vessel. Angiography is a possibility but none of this will probably do it. My guess is we end up in surgery."

"Good work, Susan; surgery sounds right."

"Oh, you won't believe this. Guess who checked himself into the hospital about 15 minutes after Jones?"

"No time for guessing games. Who?"

"None other than Mr. Broadcast himself, Eric C. Goodman and his dog Misty. So, you've now got two Crystal Club members in the Ridge at the same time. Good luck!"

"What's his problem?"

"Same old story. He's not feeling great and reports some chest pains. Hey, with that wife, I'm surprised he's still alive."

"Keep me informed. We'll handle it all. I'll get down and do my part with Goodman."

"Dr. Hagen, now I know why they pay us. This isn't a hospital; it's a resort for the rich and we are their valets with medical degrees."

"But the money, Susan, how sweet it is. Pamper their asses."

●●●

OPERATION END ZONE was now a fully sanctioned police department investigation. Chief Ellen Rome called Boston and received a firm verbal commitment that Street could stay in Philadelphia through June 30th or to the end of END ZONE, whichever came first. END ZONE prepared a list for the FBI of every person or name they had encountered in the Ridge investigation and asked that they be processed through the NCIC (National Crime Information Center). The list was substantial and growing.

TO: FBI, PHILA OFFICE
FR: PHILA POLICE/'OPERATION END ZONE'
RE: BLANKET ID CHECK
CC: ELLEN ROME, CHIEF OF POLICE

NAME/CONTACT
Ginny Choate, widow of Steven, Crystal Club member died 6/95
Dr. Walter Hagen, President of Ridge Hospital
Dr. Susan Constance, Chief of Medicine/RIDGE
Dr. Stoltz (cardiologist)/RIDGE
Dr. Billy James/RIDGE
Dr. Markus Harmon/RIDGE
'Macky' (name on VIDEO during Roberts surgery/RIDGE empl.
'Jones' (same as above)/RIDGE empl.
M. Joy (same as above)/RIDGE empl.
O'dahl (nurse and same as above)/RIDGE empl.
Mary Cinners/nurse 5th Floor and PreOp/RIDGE empl.
Emily Rosoff, sec to Hagen at RIDGE
Celia Roberts, deceased, RIDGE empl./police source
Eric C. Goodman, Crystal Club member
'Misty', dog of Goodman (rumored to be on Prozac?)
Rick Cone a/k/a 'SYS' Valley Forge Systems (computers)
Jack Adams, asst. DA Sam Gentry, Mayor of Philadelphia
COBOL/TERMINAL/RAZOR/CHASE/SYS/SATAN/ACID/computer
Darlene Evers, rep for DATAX medical equipment
Dr. Jack Andersen, President of the Good Samaritan Hospital

Street put Jack Adams' name on the list as a goof, hoping that perhaps some drug or sex charge would show up. Cooper saw the list.

"Jimmy, I know why you put Adams on the list. You like trouble. And, if it's not in your face, well, you go out and find it. Take his name off the list, Jimmy.".

At the same time, Chief of Police Rome added some names of her own in a separate list forwarded to the FBI.

<u>CONFIDENTIAL/YOUR EYES ONLY</u>

TO: Alan Reeves, FBI Washington, DC
FR: Ellen Rome, Chief of Police, Phila
RE: Background Check/Operation End Zone

Alan, need a big favor. We've got a case going here that involves our most prestigious hospital, The Ridge. The team from Operation End Zone has sent under separate cover a request for IDs on several persons.

I want FBI to check out the team members themselves. I have suspicions. The names are: Detectives Charles Smith, Rudy Levin, and Lisa Marie Cooper, all homicide. Also Detective Jimmy Street and Edward Wilson III ("Joker")both on loan from Boston Police. This "Joker" has two pals at MIT (Toshi and DeYoe)check them, too.

Please check out Judge Malcolm Soto and Asst DA Jack Adams and Drake Cula, medical examiner. So we keep everything on an even playing field, run my name through your computer and if you find any Swiss bank accounts, well, come get me.

Thanks Alan, I owe you big time!

Ellen

•••

"Wyatt, so you've decided to come and get some royal Crystal Club treatment?"

"Walter, thanks for stopping by. What a mess this is. They're doing all sorts of tests. Your people have been terrific. What's the verdict? What do you think?"

"This tube in my nose, can't you take it out?"

"Wyatt, see that brown stuff coming out. It's a sign of slow bleeding. We call it coffee grounds. If it goes bright red, then we have to think about surgery. So far, we've been able to keep up by giving you blood transfusions. We're watching your hematocrit."

"Damn, Walter, can't any of you doctors speak English? Hema what?"

"That's your blood count. We want it to stay above 30

"Walter, 30 what? Give me a break."

"OK, Wyatt. Since when did you become a medical student. We want at least 30 per cent of your blood to be the red cells that carry oxygen."

"Why 30 per cent?"

Emily leaned over to her husband. "Wyatt, stop asking so many questions."

"No, 30 per cent. Explain it to me, Walter. What's the big deal."

"Because, Wyatt, if the number is below 30 and you bleed more, you're not going to make it to the next Crystal Club Ball."

"Wyatt and Emily, that's one of the reasons I'm visiting. I figured tomorrow morning you'd get the grand tour, looking at the Ridge from the inside. But, Wyatt, I think that will have to wait. I'll let Susan fill you and Emily in on the details."

"Mr. Jones, here's what we found."

Dr. Constance held up a colored chart showing the esophogus, stomach, duodenum and where ulcers might arise. "You've had a peptic ulcer for a long time. We don't know for sure what causes them, but we know they result, in part, from acids digesting the mucous membrane. It's a disruption in the lining of the lower esophagus, stomach, or duodenum."

Constance pointed to the point where a duodenal ulcer would occur."

Jones cracked a reassuring smile for his wife's sake. "Walter, it sounds like I don't get to try some selections from that Crystal Club menu you're always bragging about."

"No, Wyatt, but we'll give you a raincheck to come back for dinner a la Ridge. Go on Susan, tell Wyatt how we plan to take care of this problem."

"Mr. Jones, you've been on a merrygoround with this problem for years. In the past, you've had an endoscopy and upper gastrointestinal barium X ray and stomach acidity tests. You eliminated alcohol and you don't smoke. You've tried the regimen of five or six small meals a day. You've tried drugs to reduce the amount of acid being formed in the stomach."

"Well, so now what?"

Hagen interrupted Constance. "You're bleeding, now; and, if we can't handle it, the best course of action is surgery. Drugs usually can handle this. Not this time. We can reduce the acidproducing capacity of the stomach using a procedure in which we cut the nerves responsible for regulating acid production. We call that a vagotomy and it's usually combined with a pyloroplasty which widens the stomach outlet. We need to oversee the bleeder now and do the V & P to stop it from happening again. You'll be uncomfortable for a while after the operation, but that's out best chance to get you a major upgrade in quality of life."

"So, you're saying surgery, Walter?"

"Yup. That's what I'd do."

"When?"

"Hopefully, tomorrow. Although, if the bleeding increases, we'll go sooner."

Emily held her husband's hand as Constance and Hagen discussed some of the details such as which doctors would be available.

"Wyatt, Dr. Constance and I are talking about scheduling and so forth. We've got some specialists in mind. You'll meet with the Chief of Anesthesiology and he'll either handle it personally or bring in his assistant. Have you met Dr. Harmon or Dr. Stoltz at any of our Crystal Balls?"

"If I have, I don't remember them."

"I may ask them to drop by, also. They're both doctors of world class quality. I don't know if they're available. Both of them travel and teach a lot. Get some rest tonight and I'll see you and Emily tomorrow. Emily, I understand your kids are flying in town." Hagen took some burgundy colored plastic badges from his pocket. "Give them these Crystal Club passes. They'll get special privileges when they're visiting...things like valet parking, use of the private dining rooms. Our preop room for Crystal Club members is burgundy, too."

Jones lifted his hands up. "Time out, Walter. I appreciate the thought; but, that's not how Emily and I brought our kids up. No special privileges of any kind. If they can't park their own cars and eat in the cafeteria, then I'm really in trouble."

Next stop for Hagen and Constance was Eric Goodman's room.

"Eric Goodman, what a pleasant surprise."

There was Goodman, sitting in bed with his dog Misty on the corner with her head on the sheets.

"Eric, as usual, you've outdone yourself. They've got everything for me. Computer. Special telephone lines. And Misty's customized dog house. This Crystal Club deal looks better each time I'm here."

"Maybe this time we can find out what's wrong so there won't be more visits. We love having you Eric, but, hospitals aren't fun. We've ordered a complete examination tomorrow, toetohead. This time, we'll find what we're all looking for. You know Wyatt Jones, don't you?"

"Wyatt, sure. Now, that's money. He makes the rest of us in the Crystal Club look like peasant farmers. I'd trust a check from the Jones Foundation more than one from the US Government. What's his problem?"

"Eric, talk to him yourself. You know, doctor-patient privacy. He's a few doors over. We'll see you tomorrow."

Hagen and Constance returned to the 20th floor.

•••

Joker relayed the COBOL Strike Out message to OPERATION END ZONE and that night they punched out calls to everyone on the list gathered from the Crystal Ball.

Charlie spoke first. "Got him. It's that TV guy, Goodman. His housekeeper said he checked in with his dog Misty. She thought maybe we could help her locate Goodman's wife. She's supposed to be at the Plaza in New York on a shopping trip. She's registered but doesn't answer in her room."

"I've got one, too." Cooper had spoken with a housekeeper at the Jones residence. "Wyatt Earl Jones was admitted tonight. It sounds serious."

"Is that *the* Wyatt Earl Jones as in Jones Foundation and Jones Library and Jones Zoo?" Rudy already knew the answer.

Chief Rome arrived in the squad room just before nine PM.

"Well folks, now, what do you suggest? Cooper radioed me and said there are two of these Crystal Club members inside the Ridge. Based on that computer intercept, assuming it's reliable, we better do something fast."

This was the moment of real choices and real lives. Mistakes now could cost someone their life. OPERATION END ZONE acquired a deadly serious mood as they sat around and talked.

Street stood up and spoke. "If I were calling the shots, which I'm not, I'd take a copy of Joker's COBOL intercept and show it to Goodman and Jones and tell them to get the hell out of that hospital."

"Detective Street, I don't know how things work in Boston." Chief Rome looked irritated at his remark, "In this city, we have slander and libel laws. In this city you don't go parading through hospitals telling patients to evacuate because some computer whizkid at MIT says so. You're a visitor and we appreciate your contributions; but, it's our city and it's our case. You're here sort of in exile. Street, you seem to be some kind of rogue cop, a buckaroo on the loose. And we're babysitting you. I don't mind telling you; I resent it. Am I clear?"

Street and the other detectives were stunned at the anger riveting through Chief Rome's words.

"Chief Rome," Cooper rose to Street's defense. "Street helped save my life at the Ridge. This Joker is for real. Those patients at the Ridge are in danger."

"Cooper, don't get into Street's garbage. We don't need a Boston cop to fix a Philadelphia problem. He's only in town because of politics. He's a real promoter...of himself. And the sooner he's out of here, the better."

Street absorbed the last remark with dwindling composure.

"Chief Rome, I don't know where all this anger comes from. If you weren't such a kiss ass, you would have told Mayor Gentry NO when City Hall asked you to babysit a so called Boston rogue cop."

"How dare you speak to me that way?"

"Easy. I just did."

"Street, out! I'll call the Mayor's office and expedite your departure to Boston."

"Sure. Get me out of town just when the Ridge case is getting hot. Rome, that's pretty sharp. You don't want a Boston cop around. Do what you have to do. But, you better do something about those guys in the Ridge. They were admitted in a somewhat vertical position; but, if you don't move fast, they're coming out horizontal."

Street packed his briefcase, looked over at Cooper, and left.

"Chief, you came down real hard on Street. Why? And why now?"

"The Ridge is our case--plain and simple. I answer to a mayor who would freak out if his newspaper read BOSTON COPS HELP CRACK RIDGE HOSPITAL CASE. Understand?"

"Chief, without Street and his friend, we may not solve this case. Think about that."

"I already did. Now, back to the Ridge. Aside from Street's stupid idea, what other suggestions do we have?"

Rome acted like she was on sick leave. Her behavior was staccato. She shuffled around the room, unable to remain still. "OK, I'm excited. This could be a career making case."

Smith suggested they get some undercover cops, with doctors from another hospital, and go undercover. They could visit Goodman and Jones and perhaps persuade them to leave the Ridge. The other option was to get a court order to lace the hospital with listening devices and hope to catch the killers, if any, in the act.

When the meeting ended, Chief Rome had made her decision. They would wake up Judge Soto and cover the hospital with bugs and telephone taps. Undercover agents would get the work done during the next 24 hours.

●●●

Street arrived at Cooper's condo just after midnight.

"What happened to Rome? She's out of it!"

"Strange, I've never seen her that way. Rome called Judge Soto and they'll get a court order to put bugs in the hospital. They'll be working by tomorrow afternoon."

"Lisa, Rome has sentenced those men to death. She can put all the bugs she wants in that hospital. Makes no difference. The killers are computer nuts. They don't get on telephones or talk in the open. This is a big mistake. We should reach their families and warn them."

"No can do. Rome is off the wall. If I do that, I'm off the case and off the force."

"I'll do it. She doesn't sign my paycheck."

"Lisa, I'm going outside. I'll call from my car. I don't want any phone calls coming from your place. Wait inside."

●●●

There's a gossamer here. A web. Street pondered. How were they killing these people? Joker and Cooper had described the inside of the Ridge. They took pictures.

Street transported himself into the hospital with his eyes closed. He used the pictures taken inside the Ridge to guide him.

"OK, Street, you're so smart. Take the walk; talk the talk. You figure it out. No one else will. Limited access. They've got to do that. These guys check in at the Ridge. They get royal treatment. They're moved to Crystal Club suites. Then what?" Street was into it now. "They die. They're in these plush rooms, dining better than Le Bec Fin, with Hagen all over them. Now, where? The operating room. Last stop. No. This isn't quite non stop service. They go to that purple room with the painted ceiling. That's where they take Crystal Club members before surgery. Very private. Very special. Very ugly. And it's prime real estate. Right between the OR and procedure rooms. Not non stop, but it's their own private travel lane. Just like those HOV lanes on highways. Crystal Club members only. Regular folks need not apply. And lock-tight access. That purple room is where they say their good-byes before going under the knife."

●●●

Street sat in his car and pulled out the list of Crystal Club members with the names Goodman and Jones circled. It was late, but Street called anyway. The Jones family was staying overnight in a special hotel-like suite for Crystal Club family members. Goodman's wife was in New York.

"Lisa, two phone calls and two big, fat zeros. Well, I tried."

"Yeah, you did, Jimmy. Let's give it a rest and see if the wiretaps work."

Cooper's phone rang. "Great, who's that at 12:30 AM?"

"Yes, Chief, I understand. Sorry about that. We better do something."

"Lisa, was that my close friend, Chief Rome?"

"Yeah, it sure was. Judge Soto rejected the request for wiretaps. He ruled it a gross violation of the rights of privacy of everyone in that hospital. That's it, Jimmy. Goodman and Jones are in that hospital naked, without any protection."

"Lisa, they're already dead."

Chapter Thirty Four: KNIFE OF THE NIGHT

The office was filled with Hylocereus and Nyctocereus, both nightblooming cacti. This was night school in night gowns. Assembled in the darkened office were stalkers of the night whose nigrescence and blackened eyes mirrored the green reflection from computer screens. This was the unholiest of black holes. The office was the embodiment of neglect of the human spirit. The mission of those gathered was to kill inside a hospital.

"Jones will die. Use the same protocol we used with Choate and Roberts. Confirm that the team is ready."

A woman rose from the table and walked towards the door without a word.

"And this will be it. No more after Jones. I can't live with myself. The blackmail is part of the nighthell you created. I don't care any longer. Tell everyone what you know. My life is over. You've raped my head. My body never meant anything. Your drugs imprisoned me. No more. I just don't care."

The men at the table stood as she left.

Chapter Thirty Five: FAREWELLS

COBOL confirms termination of Crystal set. TERMINAL is ready. PRIMUM NON NOCERE ? Clear.

•••

Street, I faxed you the latest COBOL intercept. They're sick. That Latin phrase is part of the Hippocratic oath that doctors take. It translates: First, Do No Harm'. You better move fast."

"I'm working on it, Joker. Now, Chief Rome wants me out of town. She popped her cork last night. I'll give the intercept to Cooper and see what she wants to do with it."

"Charlie, we've got to send someone in to talk with Goodman and Jones. We owe them that much. If we're wrong, and Hagen's a new Mother Theresa, what harm have we done. If things go wrong, and we did nothing, that's a lot worse."

"I say we go. I'd rather take my chances with the Chief than with my conscience."

•••

Hagen and Constance waited in Jones' room with his wife and kids for the anesthesiology team to arrive. A young looking man, no more than 35, walked in and introduced himself. "Mr. Jones, I'm Dr. Stieglitz. I'll handle your anesthesia. I've got a couple of questions for you." Stieglitz fired off a series of standard questions given to preoperative patients. "Mr. Jones, have you ever had anesthesia before?"

"No."

"Are you allergic to anything?"

"Nothing."

"What medicines do you take routinely?"

"Other than Tylenol sometimes, I don't take anything."

"Do you smoke or have you had kidney problems?"

"Nope."

"What about your teeth, are they false?"

"No, they're the real thing."

Dr. Stieglitz explained that Jones' entire medical record, as supplied by his private physician, would be reviewed.

The following morning, Dr. Stieglitz said he'd return and give him a tranquilizer, probably about four milligrams of Versed, delivered IM--intramuscular. The next day's surgery was expected to take approximately two and half hours.

Jones was alone in his room when the door was pushed slightly open. A man stuck his head through the side.

"Wyatt Jones, are you awake?"

"I'm up; who's that?"

"We've met before; but, never like this."

Eric Goodman walked into the room, clothed in his white and burgundy Crystal Club bathrobe.

Goodman smiled and asked if he could sit and talk for a few minutes.

"Sure, come in. My wife and kids are due here soon. I'm trying to stay awake."

"So, Wyatt, we're both Crystal Club members. They've got two of us at the same time."

"Guess so."

"Say, listen. Is there anything I can do for you? With all the doctors in and out of your room, I'd guess you're going under the knife."

"You guessed right."

"Hey, I don't mean to intrude. I just want to be, well, neighborly if that's possible in a hospital."

"So, what's your problem Goodman?"

"No big deal. They're running tests. No surgery or anything. At least as far as I know. Say, I think this probably isn't a great time Wyatt; so, good luck tomorrow." Goodman reached over, shook Jones hand, and walked out.

When Goodman returned to his room, he saw the silhouette of a huge man standing at his window. He was so large his frame blocked most of incoming sunlight, and the room was in a partial eclipse.

"Who are you?"

"Mr. Eric C. Goodman, President of KEYSTONE Broadcasting? It's a pleasure to meet you. My name is Detective Charlie Smith, Philadelphia homicide."

"You said homicide; you must be kidding."

"No, I need just a couple minutes of your time. It's very important we talk now."

"Is everyone OK?"

"It's you we're worried about, Mr. Goodman. Say, I didn't know they allowed dogs in hospitals."

"They do if you're in the Crystal Club."

"Your dog is so quiet. She's very well behaved."

"She should be."

"I know, thousands of dollars in obedience training."

"No, thousands of dollars in PROZAC."

"No way!"

"You bet. It's the newest thing. Who needs obedience schools."

Smith started to explain the specific reason for his visit. "What I'm going to tell you is strictly confidential. We don't want you to share it with anyone. Do you understand?"

"Sure."

Then Smith outlined the history of Crystal Club deaths at the Ridge and the coincidence of deaths in June.

"That's preposterous! Hell, it isn't even June, anyway."

"Whatever month it is, if you're in the Crystal Club, we think you're in danger in this hospital."

"Detective, maybe you think it's April Fools Day. I've been in and out of the Ridge lots of times. Do I look dead?"

"Not yet."

"That's not funny."

"Mr. Goodman, all we ask is that you consider transferring to another hospital."

Goodman's dog started to bark.

"I thought you said she's on PROZAC."

"Not enough, I guess. Detective, you're looking for trouble spreading rumors about this hospital. I appreciate your concern, but you should go."

Wyatt Jones' room was a few doors from Goodman, and detective Smith knew the number. He walked in and found Jones surrounded by his wife and three children.

"Hi, who are you?"

"I'm Detective Smith from Philadelphia homicide."

"OOPS, Emily I told you they'd catch me."

Everyone in the room, including Smith, laughed. A sense of humor within 24 hours of major surgery is one definition of grace under fire. Smith instantly liked Jones.

"Mr. Jones..."

"Wyatt, as in Earp."

"Wyatt, I'm here because we're concerned about you and Mr. Goodman. I'm not here to alarm you. But, we're investigation the deaths of Crystal Club members in the Ridge. It's an investigation only, and no one has been charged with anything. Let me be blunt: would you consider leaving the hospital and seeking medical care somewhere else until we're finished?"

"Wow, detective, you sure know how to get a man's attention." Jones wife Emily added: "Tell me more detective. Who died? When?"

"Well, Mrs. Jones, in June of last year two Crystal Club members died. Did you know Steven Choate or Jonathan Roberts?"

"No, how about you, honey?"

"Detective, the name Choate sounds familiar."

"We reviewed a list of Crystal Club members who died in the Ridge and almost 40% died in June. That's made us suspicious."

"Well, it's not June."

"Mr. Jones, that's not the point. We think this demands a complete investigation. And while that's in progress we think you might consider getting medical assistance in another..."

Dr. Susan Constance pushed the door open and stopped the conversation.

"Mr. Jones, we apologize for this man's behavior. We've called the Chief of Police to stop this harassment. It's outrageous."

"He wasn't bothering me. His story is far fetched but meant no harm."

Constance touched Smith's hand. "Detective, if you'll go outside, I think you'll find your Chief is waiting on the phone."

Smith picked the phone up and, to his surprise, it was Chief Rome.

"Detective, I just got a call from the Mayor, who got a call from Dr. Hagen. He said the Ridge is considering legal action against the department for this damn fool stunt of yours. Now, I couldn't do anything to that jerk Street, but I can deal to you. Smith, effective immediately, you are suspended. Return to headquarters and turn your gun in. And if Cooper and Levin are involved, they're out, too."

"Chief, you're sentencing these two men to death. What's wrong with you?"

"That's all, detective."

Emily Jones heard the commotion in the hallway and came outside. Smith was at the telephone with his eyes covered.

"Detective, we appreciate your coming to the Hospital. I'm sure Wyatt is in good hands."

"Mrs. Jones, he's in someone's hands. Good or bad, I don't know."

As Smith walked away and Mrs. Jones returned to her husband's room, Dr. Constance stepped in front of the detective. "Had a bad day?" Her half-faced, sugar-smile looked so repugnant that Smith thought it smelled.

•••

The Thursday morning sunrise at 6:02 AM was 45 minutes away and darkness enveloped the Ridge. A few lights, like lighthouse beacons in a cold morning drizzle, punctuated the night as the very first morning buses moved through Chestnut Hill. Jones and Goodman slept.

And it was peaceful.

One hour after sunrise, at 7:03 AM, OR #5 was humming with activity as a patient was wheeled in for his emergency surgery. Dr. Hagen watched his TV monitors scan OR #5 as the procedure started. The bottom right corner of his video recorded the elapsed time of the surgery. There was no sound. At 14 minutes and 24 seconds into the surgery, the patient's blood pressure began to drift down to dangerous levels. Blood and fluids were administered, then ephedrine and next a dopamine infusion. His heart was failing; his circulation collapsing. The BP monitors clearly displayed the unfolding drama. For the next one hour, the battle raged. Hagen watched until the patient was pronounced dead and removed from the operating room

•••

05:35:00 AM: RAZOR to COBOL. Crystal disconnect is successful. Time to rise and shine. COBOL confirms message. Well done. COBOL is clear

•••

"Street, it's Joker."

"What time is it?"

"5:45 AM."

"What's up?"

"Toshi just got another intercept from COBOL at 5:35 AM. It says CRYSTAL DISCONNECT IS SUCCESSFUL. Street, they did it. They killed those Crystal Club guys at the Ridge."

"Holy shit!"

Street reached Cooper at her apartment. "Lisa, Joker just called and said he got a COBOL intercept in Boston and our Crystal Club members are dead. They've been disconnected."

"Jimmy, I'll call the Hospital. What's Jones wife name?"

"Emily."

At 5:50 AM, Cooper called the Hospital. "Hi, this is Emily Jones and my husband is a patient. How's he doing?"

"He's in the Crystal Club, isn't he?"

"Yes."

"One moment, please."

"Mrs. Jones, good morning. Your husband is resting and doing well. His surgery is scheduled for 7:00 AM."

"Thank goodness. Bye."

Cooper called Street. "Jimmy, they bought it. They never asked for ID. They thought I was Emily Jones. He's fine. No problem. False alarm."

"That means it's Goodman. He's dead."

"I'll call again. Do you know his wife's name?"

"No. No. Just call and tell them you want to know if he's awake. Tell them you're the dog's...who cares. Tell them you're supposed to pick up Misty and bring her home."

At 5:55 AM, Cooper called Street for the second time. "Jimmy, are you sitting down?"

"Lisa, I'm lying down. Go ahead. I'll bet Goodman's dead. That damn Chief of yours is a fool. We could have done more."

"Jimmy, Goodman is gone."

"I knew it."

"No, I mean gone as in checked out of the Hospital, PROZAC Misty and all. They said Goodman was discharged at 5:45 AM and then picked up by his driver. He's alive!"

"That's impossible."

"Not if this whole COBOL stuff is one giant hoax. Both Goodman and Jones are alive."

"I'll call Joker."

"Toshi, get me Joker; it's Street in Philadelphia."

"Jimmy, so who's dead?"

"You are Joker. Everyone is fine. This whole computer thing is a big hoax. Cooper called the Hospital before 6. Jones is fine and Goodman has already checked out."

"Impossible."

"That's fact. Not computer muck. This whole COBOL thing was too wild to begin with. It's a figment of someone's sick-after-midnight computer fantasies. Man, we look really dumb on this one."

"Street, how much sleep have you had?"

"I forget."

"Translated, not much, right?"

"So what?"

"Because, listening to you, Street, well, damn, you weren't Street."

Street spoke with Lisa on the phone. "Tell you what, this is called a major league; we're sorry, sir. I'll meet you at the Ridge. We're gonna apologize to Hagen."

"No way."

"Lisa, trust me; saying I'm sorry is free and it might get your friend Smith off the hook. Let Hagen enjoy his vindication. But let's do it early, before Chief Rome arrives at headquarters. And call Smith and Levin on the way and tell them to get over to the Ridge. Maybe, that'll help."

"OK, I'll meet you there, 8 AM. Street, are you going soft on me?"

"Not a chance. You know better."

•••

Street and Cooper arrived at the Ridge just before 8 AM.

"I called Smith and Levin. They're not too happy about this idea; but, they're on the way over. We're eating a lot of crow today."

"This is Detective Cooper and Street. We're here to see Dr. Hagen. I assume he's in the Hospital."

The security guard called upstairs. "He's in the Hospital. He said you can go upstairs. Take that elevator to the 20th floor."

Cooper and Street talked about their little speech of repentance; and, as they did, Dr. Hagen appeared with Dr. Susan Constance, Emily Wyatt and her three children. Detectives Smith and Levin arrived at the same moment.

"This is a bad time. Emily's husband, Wyatt, died at 7:30 AM on the operating table."

Chapter Thirty Six: JABBERWOCKY

Apology canceled!" With that, Street and the other detectives returned to headquarters, overflowing with questions.

"Lisa, Joker's intercept of COBOL's message reads 5:35 AM. So, almost two hours before the Ridge says Jones died, COBOL is spreading the word in that sick computer world he lives in. And COBOL says a Crystal Club member has been disconnected 30 minutes before you call the Ridge and ask about Jones and Goodman. And the Ridge says everything is OK. We've got a timeline problem here."

"It could be the Hospital operator didn't know about Jones' death."

"For two hours--they didn't know? And Hagen said Wyatt Jones died on the operating table at 7:30 AM. But COBOL knows he died two hours earlier. What am I missing?"

"Hagen must have a video tape of the surgery. Let's get a look."

"OK, back to the Ridge. We'll call from the car. And why don't we call Chief Rome, that super sleuth of American homicide. I wonder if she can spell the word: apologize?"

•••

The two detectives were lead to Hagen's office by a security guard. Hagen was quiet, contrite, and seemingly very upset.

"Detectives, this is horrible. I've got the video tape and you're welcome to watch it and take it with you. And, detective Cooper, you're feeling better I assume?"

"Sure! I'm out of your Hospital."

"Look, I know how this looks. But, understand, it's all crazy. I'm going to call the Mayor and apologize for what I said about you and about the other detectives. That's all history."

Cooper leaned over and whispered to Street. "Major attitude change today."

Hagen had coffee brought into his office and started to play the video tape. Now, it was Street's turn to whisper. "Think the coffee is safe? Lisa, take a sip and I'll watch."

Cooper leaned under the table and pinched Street's leg. "Cute."

The tape's IBOX in the lower right hand corner displayed the patient name, time, date, and those present in the operating room. According to the video, surgery started just after 7:00 AM and the electronic monitoring equipment went wild a few minutes later. The IBOX listed the names of the doctors and nurses in attendance.

For a split second, Cooper had the thought of Conspiracy; then she remembered that the names of the doctors were different from those of Choate' and Roberts' failed procedures. Cooper's beeper sounded and she left the room to call headquarters. After a few minutes she returned and remained standing.

"Dr. Hagen, you may remember Detective Charlie Smith."

"I do. We had an unfortunate argument. No hard feelings. Is he still suspended?"

"As a matter of fact, no, he's not. And I'm sure if Charlie could be here, he would *never* say, no hard feelings. But, Dr. Hagen, Charlie isn't here. And Charlie isn't at police headquarters. He just called me from Judge Malcolm Soto's chambers and read me what the Judge dictated. Charlie will hand deliver them within a few minutes.

Application of Philadelphia Police to Autopsy the Remains of Mr. Wyatt Jones.

GRANTED: Judge Malcolm Soto

I hereby ORDER the Ridge Hospital, Philadelphia to make proper arrangements so that the Medical Examiner's office of the Philadelphia Police shall claim the body of Mr. Wyatt Jones for the purpose of performing an autopsy, which shall occur no later than 6 PM this date. The body of Mr. Jones shall remain in the custody of the Ridge Hospital until said autopsy is completed.

"So, Dr. Hagen, no hard feelings?"

"This is outrageous. The Jones family has already informed me that they are taking custody of the body and plan to cremate it."

Cooper clarified the issue for Hagen. "Perhaps you don't understand how all this works; so, I'll explain. We are investigating a suspicious death. Any interference by you, the Jones family, or anyone in this hospital may be considered obstruction of justice. Hagen, people go to jail for things like that."

"I'll call Mayor Gentry. This is criminal."

"You might be right on that point."

●●●

Smith arrived a few minutes later in the lobby with both the court order and the medical examiner. "Lisa, how did Hagen like the news about the autopsy?"

"Charlie, why don't you personally deliver the judge's order to him? That would be a nice, personal touch."

Cooper saw 'Dracula' talking with some doctors and nurses. "So, what's the deal."

"It'll happen now in the morgue, downstairs. Want to watch?"

"I'll wait. Just let me know."

"Lisa, how about a walk? We're in Chestnut Hill; so, let's see the sights other than this place."

Street and Cooper walked through Chestnut Hill, passing the old mansions, shops and restaurants, art galleries, train stations, and famed arboretum. Time moved quickly as they strolled along the cobblestone streets.

"You know, my favorite Boston detective, you have really turned my life upside down. Jimmy, I remember the first time I saw you jogging through the snow. You looked so silly. So, well, Street, you're unlike anyone I've ever met?"

"Thanks, but that's not so easy to believe. You meet lots of people. That Jack Adams or whatever his name. And who knows how many more."

"Like you meet lots of women. But, there's only one Street. You're sensitive, childlike with that Mickey Mouse watch you refuse to lose. And how many homicide detectives collect teddy bears? You're tough, honest, damn stubborn at times, and so loyal. This isn't the right time for all these words. They just came out."

"Keep it going, Lisa; it's fun, especially if you change your mind later."

"Which reminds me. Before I change my mind, I saw a great teddy bear for you in the police gift catalogue--the next addition to your collection."

"You'll get me investigated with too many of them."

"Don't understand."

"I just heard about some marauding marbleheaded doctors claim adults who collect teddy bears have repressed desires as child predators and molestors. Next they'll close Disney world. Every day, a new theory and a bunch of selfrighteous doctors hiding behind their white coats. Lisa, they're the ones to worry about. You know what's the wild part of all this. These doctors march into some government office, plunk down their perverted theories, and, next thing you know, the government is on the case. The great teddy bear caper. Thanks in advance for the teddy bear. I'll keep it and take my chances."

"Yeah. And in a couple of weeks, I'll be in the Boston Marathon. If this case breaks open, I'd like to have you come up and see the new teddy bear on display."

Cooper's beeper went off as they stood outside a book shop near the Hospital.

"That's Dracula! Now, we get the answer."

Dracula was in the lobby waiting for them. "Sorry, guys, this Wyatt Jones died from heart failure. There are no signs of drugs or anything suspicious."

"Jimmy, I think I've got a stomachache and headache all combined. Let's get out of here and think about this."

•••

Rick Cone from VALLEY FORGE SYSTEMS waited for Street and Cooper at headquarters. Cone was on a very short rope and still subject to possible criminal charges. Cooper had called him from her car.

"Mr. Cone, here's an intercept from COBOL, your middle-of-the-night computer friend. He's graduated to big times now. See the timing sheet: 5:30AM.

His computer buddy, RAZOR, confirms that a Crystal Club member has been disconnected. According to a video tape we've just seen, that Crystal Club member whose name is Wyatt Jones died almost two hours later. Go ahead, educate us."

"Detectives, I told you before all this stuff is way beyond me. I just thought this was a rich eccentric who got his computer advice anonymously and used the middle of the night to play out his fantasies."

"You said, he."

"I assume so. No reason. Wait. There is a reason. COBOL uses computer language with a military edge to it. There's something about the type of words he uses. Like code words from the military--you know, commandos, that sort of thing. So, I think it's a man."

After Cone left, Cooper called Eric Goodman's home.

"Mr. Goodman, please."

"He's not here; may I take your name."

"This is Detective Cooper, Philadelphia police. Where is he?"

"Oh, he's at Channel 31, working."

"I'll call him there."

Twenty four hours earlier, Goodman was in a hospital only a few feet away from Wyatt Jones. Goodman checks out and goes to work and Jones is checked into the Hospital morgue for an autopsy by the Philadelphia medical examiner. Why Jones and not Goodman? Why not both?

"Channel 31 TV, your ten o'clock news station."

"Mr. Eric Goodman's office, please."

"Betty Brinkerson, may I help you?"

"This is Detective Cooper, Philadelphia police. Is Mr. Goodman there?"

"He is, but can't be disturbed right now."

"Disturb him. Tell him it's Detective Cooper, as in Philadelphia homicide!"

"Detective, I can't talk right now. My bankers are in town and we're in a very important meeting. Maybe you read about it in the papers. KEYSTONE Broadcasting is buying some radio and TV stations in the south. I can talk later, OK?"

"Mr. Goodman, did you know that Wyatt Jones died today at the Ridge?"

"No. What happened? I just talked to him yesterday. Nice guy. Very quiet. Very rich."

"He died this morning during surgery. Another Crystal Club member is now dead. Don't you think it's time we talked. You're a very lucky man. Why you're alive and Jones is dead...well, who knows? But, I wouldn't be cavalier about it."

"This is one hell of a wake up call. I just checked out of the Ridge this morning. Tell me when we can meet."

"You name it."

"Four PM here at Channel 31."

"See you then."

Almost invisibly, Chief Rome settled into a chair in the squad room. Her hells-bells way had vanished sometime between her lacing of Street and news that another Crystal Club member at the Ridge was dead. Chiefs, Presidents, and Generals don't wear regrets in high fashion, and Rome was not practiced in penitence. Smith's suspension as a renegade cop was a marker of Rome at her worst. Her treatment of Street showed the same inclination to discount people first, then conditionally reprice their value later. Rome's reputation as a lance throwing lampoon of a Chief was well established in the department. Most figured that Mayor Gentry named her chief because it was politically correct. Rome was never as good as the Mayor had hoped or as inept and disloyal as her cops imagined. She wallowed in a murky middle ground.

"Confession time, folks. I want everyone out of this room except Cooper, Street, Smith, and Levin."

Rome waited as the room was cleared.

"I'm not going to waltz around. I screwed up. Street, I hope you'll stay on board until we figure out what's happening. We wouldn't be this far without you and Joker. Charlie, you know I lifted that suspension. You showed initiative and that you cared. You showed some real guts inside the Ridge. I apologize."

"Accepted, Chief. Thanks." Street nodded in agreement.

"Well, don't smile yet, folks. You're doing an FBI background check on the names of people associated with the Ridge. But, I asked a friend at the FBI to check all of you. I apologize for that, too."

Street measured the reaction of everyone in the room. Cooper seemed most upset unless there was something she was not telling.

"Tell you what, Chief, about the background checks, you did the right thing. I would have done the same."

Rome finished. "We have a job to do. We've got resources available but we must get something more than computer print outs about a death that could have been a coincidence. We need more; so, let's go out and get it."

Street asked, "So, what do you think, Lisa?"

"JABBERWOCKY."

Street looked at Cooper, Smith and Levin before answering. "You know what, Lisa, I agree one hundred percent. You expressed my feelings exactly. Say, does anyone have a dictionary handy?"

Chapter Thirty Seven: THE GEODESIC DOME

Street and Joker were collaborators of different stripes, united in common respect and in an insatiable need to match wits with evildoers whose exotic diversions confounded others. Street was like an older brother and Joker was the son that Street never had and always wanted. Every time Joker concocted some incredible new invention in his MIT laboratory, he showed it first to Street as if seeking a father's nod of approval.

For both, the word, stymie, was their clarion call and the Ridge renewed memories of the labyrinth of dead ends they negotiated in the Charles River Medical Center murders. Sometimes, the sheer fun of the chase tempted Joker to consult at no charge. That was an erasable thought.

So, it was natural and comfortable when Street reached Joker at MIT. "I'm stumped, my friend. The answer is in our face and I can't see it." When Street issued his, I need you, it was like Street inviting Joker to Disneyworld.

"OK, get me the airline ticket and I'm there."

Street made a couple of phone calls, wrestled with a few *kvetching* superiors, and got approval for Joker's return to Philadelphia.

"You know, Street, this is getting expensive with you and Joker. We're taking money from our undercover fund and the guys in vice aren't too pleased."

"Tell vice when they need a hidden mike that won't fall out of their pants and get them killed, they should look for audio shops in the Yellow Pages. Joker's electronic gizmos have saved so many asses in vice they ought to fly him first class with a limo waiting and a massage at the hotel."

"Don't you know how to take a yes for an answer? You got it. He's OK to fly. He's OK for hotels and all the other stuff. Have him stop by vice and they'll get him the cash. You don't mind if we use cash on this deal, do you? As it is, our necks are way out."

"Joker, it's STAY ALIVE in '95--that's our theme. We're gonna dig in and do this right. Get down here and bring all your toys."

"Jimmy, we're gonna build a GEODESIC mousetrap in Philadelphia."

"Shit, can't you ever use English without all those words. What the hell is a GEO-something?"

"GEODESIC, Jimmy! It's the shortest line between two points. We're going to build a simple trap and connect points one and two. Point #1 is where we are in the I-don't-know-and-can't-prove-it zone. Point #2 is where the killers are. See you tomorrow."

"Lisa, case solved!"

"Are you crazy?"

"Joker's coming back to Philly with a GEODESIC DOME. COBOL and the others in this killing spree are finished."

"Tell you what? Call Chief Rome and tell her the case is solved because computerhead in Boston is coming down here with his, whatever..."

"GEODESIC DOME. Get with it, Lisa!"

"Jimmy, have you been drinking?"

Chapter Thirty Eight: THE SMILING COBRA

It was an extraordinary meeting at police headquarters as eleven persons crowded into Chief Rome's office for the late night meeting. OPERATION END ZONE members Cooper, Street, Smith and Levin were joined by Joker, two FBI agents, a police psychologist, Dr. Drake Cula, and assistant DA Jack Adams.

Rome deferred to Cooper. "Lisa, you started this whole Ridge thing; so, you've got the floor. Tell me what you plan."

The plan was exquisitely simple, patterned after Joker's idea of finding the shortest line between two points. Cooper proposed a refinement on her ill fated admission to the Ridge with a faked illness. END ZONE and the FBI would fabricate a blue blooded dossier for a police detective, get him into the Crystal Club with a $250,000 donation and send him into a Ridge Hospital that would be rigged from top to bottom with Joker engineered electronic monitors. Hagen was a prime suspect and an attempt to kill the detective infiltrator was at least possible, if not probable.

Judge Malcolm Soto had signed an application for electronic monitoring and the FBI promised to get the devices into the Hospital and assist in round-the-clock maintenance. The necessary money and personnel were ready and the estimated cost was in excess of $100,000.

Selecting the detective, turned Philadelphia blueblood, was more problematic. It was too dangerous to use any one from the Philadelphia area. The FBI offered an agent from Washington and Street suggested some one he knew outside Philadelphia.

"This person knows his way around hospitals; he's polished, meticulous and smart. He's also my friend and I want him protected like the President of the United States. Change that, I want him better protected. I'll call him." Then Street outlined some conditions, assuming his friend took the assignment. No insult to anyone here, but, this person will be known only to myself and Joker. Everything done to create this Philadelphia blue blood will go through me or Joker. If that's agreed, I'll call him. Or, maybe my friend is a she. So?"

Chief Rome asked. "We can't OK a civilian going into the Ridge."

"He or she is not a so called civilian. I just said this person is smart and polished and you assumed they're not a cop."

A wave of low level laughter rippled through Rome's office.

Cooper and the other END ZONE members preferred Street's choice versus an FBI agent.

"OK, I'll let you know in the morning."

●●●

"Mickey, do you miss your old partner?"

"Not really, Street. OK, a little."

In his entire career as a detective, Street had been teamed with only three people. His first partner divorced and retired to live alone on Cape Cod. His second partner was forever alive inside Street's soul. Street and his partner stumbled on a drug deal in a seedy part of Boston's South End and found themselves kneeling on a sidewalk with guns to their heads and druggies joking about who to kill first. Then they killed Street's partner with a fusillade of bullets to the head. Like Jackie Kennedy in the hours after the assassination of her husband, Street refused to take off his blood spattered shirt. The blood stains from that night soaked into his body and Street often endured a surreal sense that he was bleeding from the inside out. He reconciled that the pain and what ifs of that night would remain inside his soul forever. Street was offered a psychological discharge from the Boston Police based on stress, but that would have been surrender.

Mike *Mickey* McCoy was his third partner and a man whose white-picket-fence life gave Street hope that not all detectives ended their lives divorced, alcoholic, alone, stressed out, or unhappy. Mickey married his college sweet heart, didn't cheat, and lived every day for her and their two children. His desk was littered with Little League photos, including one with Street and Mickey in Red Sox uniform shirts. Street was not much of a baseball coach, but the day he wore his holstered gun to practice was part of little league lore. When league officials saw a newspaper picture of a guntotting little league coach, they suggested Mickey find a new assistant coach.

Mickey's wife, Judy, always made Street feel like a member of the McCoy family. She never asked anything from Street except, "Jimmy, please take care of Mickey."

"Mickey, just say no and it's between you and me."

"Hell, I can't say no to nothing."

"We need an out of town cop to take the identity of a Philly blueblood who returns home and joins Hagen's Crystal Club. The FBI handles everything on this from drivers license to social security number to condo address and bank accounts. Then you check into a Ridge Hospital which the FBI and Joker have converted to one huge recording studio. If you even sneeze wrong, half the Philly police force will be in your room before you get the Kleenex."

"Jimmy, sounds exciting and..."

"Wait a minute, the more I talk about it, the less I like the idea of pulling you away from Judy and the kids."

"Hey, I'll talk with Judy. I like the challenge. What about Boston? Have you cleared any of this upstairs?"

"Yup. They're still afraid of all the dirt lying around from the Charles River case. Now, I didn't blackmail anyone; but, it's amazing how sensitive they are these days. Bottom line is the Chief and the Mayor have a nice, unwritten understanding about your partner. When this Ridge case is done, Joker, you and I will return to Boston and the Mayor and Chief have a ton of IOU's from the people down here. Every one lives happily ever after."

"Street, like I said, count me in. I'll talk to Judy tonight. I know her; she'll worry. So, expect a phone call."

"OK, talk with the Chief and he'll work out the logistics. I think the FBI will do your ID switch up in Boston. Forgot to tell you: only Joker, me, and a couple of FBI agents know you're the new millionaire in town. Mickey, we have a new name for you."

"Tell me."

"Ernest Boron Samuels."

"What the hell kind of name is that? Never mind, I forgot. Joker's down there with you."

"You got it. Boron is a chemical agent, and the initials EBS is Joker's enigma. If you figure it out, let me know. That kid can't do anything simple."

"Hey, don't knock it. He saved your tail."

"See you in a few days, Mr. Ernest Boron Samuels."

•••

McCoy met with his superiors and then went to FBI headquarters in the Kennedy Federal Building in Boston. During the three hour meeting, several agents outlined the protocols of the Witness Relocation Program and how those procedures would be similar to the new identity program created for McCoy. His fingerprint file in the NCIC would be switched so that if stopped for a traffic violation, the name Ernest Boron Samuels would come back. Agents, with the approval of Philadelphia police, moved one million dollars into a New York bank the FBI used to transfer funds. A check for $250,000 was prepared for delivery to Hagen at the Ridge. McCoy had a new temporary address assigned and it was the Ritz Carlton Hotel while he ostensibly was house hunting. To simply matters, McCoy would meet Hagen as a trust fund baby returning to Philadelphia and his roots. The FBI used a long standing, and secret cooperative agreement with the Mormon Church in Salt Lake City to create a family history for the new Samuels. He was given an array of charge cards, a golf handicap card at an out of town course (12 handicap) and pictures of family members. Arrangements were made for him to call his family in Boston using an 800 number that would prevent anyone from tracing the calls.

Ernest Boron Samuels arrived in Philadelphia and settled into the Ritz Carlton. Street and Joker arranged to meet McCoy for the first time at a local gym.

"Mickey, we've come a long way from Boston. Here we are, three guys in white towels sweating oceans in this Philadelphia sauna."

"Mickey, who? You and Joker are in the honored company of Ernest Boron Samuels."

Joker gave Mickey a gentle push. "So, Mr. Philadelphia BlueBlood, did you figure out what your name stands for?"

"Boron, I know--it's a chemical agent; so, I guess, way back in the Samuels family, we made our billions in chemicals."

Street added: "Sure, Mickey, as in fertilizers!"

"Mickey the EBS initials represent the Emergency Broadcast System...that's what you'll be inside the Ridge--our private broadcast station roaming the corridors and transmitting data to a van in the parking lot."

END ZONE planned for Mickey to make several high visibility visits in the next couple of days, including the Good Samaritan Hospital, Eric C. Goodman at Channel 31, Mayor Gentry and a few high powered law firms. END ZONE expected Hagen would pick up the scent very quickly and initiate a contact with the newly arrived Ernest Boron Samuels.

Goodman and Gentry both called Hagen and asked if Samuels had visited the Ridge. "As a matter of fact, no. Wonder why. I'll find out." Goodman mentioned that Samuels had visited with Dr. John Andersen at the Good Sam.

"RITZ CARLTON, may I please direct your call."

"I'm Dr. Walter Hagen. Could you please ring Mr. Samuels' room."

"Sorry, there's no answer. Could we take a message?"

Hagen gave the telephone operator his office and home phone numbers.

"Joker, it's Mickey. We've got a nibble. Hagen called and asked if I'd be his guest for lunch at the Ridge tomorrow. This guy wastes no time. This new FBI identity had better hold up."

"Hagen's office will be your rumpus room. It'll be a party."

•••

McCoy was met downstairs in the Ridge lobby by Dr. Susan Constance and escorted upstairs to Hagen's 20th floor office.

"So, you're Mr. Samuels. This is a great honor. I asked our research department to get me a history of your family. It's great that you've returned to city where your great grandfather got his start."

"Dr. Hagen, I'm the only direct descendant left and Houston did nothing for me. I'm bored looking at chemical plants and ships. I want to leave my mark here in Philadelphia."

"We'd like to show you our complex. We have a new facility, the Eisenhower Clinic of Health Sciences; it's our first venture into a structure that we think will sweep the country. You check in at 8 AM, no food the night before, and when you check out by 5 PM, you receive a preliminary report on your health profile. Two days later, you get a more extensive report including specific recommendations on ways to extend and improve the quality of your life. The cost is $2,500 and it's a complimentary service for our Crystal Club members. Why don't you try the Eisenhower clinic as our guest?"

"That's very thoughtful. I was over at the Good Samaritan and met with Dr. John Andersen. They sure don't have anything like this Eisenhower Clinic."

"Mr. Samuels, you'll find the Ridge is the hub of medicine in this area and we offer many services that are unavailable elsewhere. By the way, did Dr. Andersen mention that the Ridge is seeking to acquire the Good Sam?

"As a matter of fact, no."

"Dr. Constance is going to give you a tour, and then, let's meet for lunch in our private dinning room. Susan, are you all set?"

"Yes, Dr. Hagen, we'll meet you in one hour. Is that OK Mr. Samuels?"

"Let's do it."

Outside the Ridge, two FBI agents, Street, Cooper and Joker listened to the conversation in stereo. McCoy wore a hidden microphone and another had been placed in Hagen's office by an FBI counter intelligence agent working as replacement for a sick employee of the Hospital's cleaning service. The FBI arranged for several Hospital employees to call in sick during the past week, and replaced each one with an electronics agent. None of the employees was sick. All had received a phone call telling them they won roundtrip transportation to New York, $500 in spending money, dinner and tickets to a Broadway show. They were called instant winners and failure to use their prize meant forfeiture.

By the time McCoy was visiting, so many electronic devices were planted that some of the frequencies started to cause interference and were disabled. The Ridge had been converted into one giant radio station.

"Emily, this is Walter. Please come in."

"Has Data Universe completed the background check on Mr. Samuels?"

"Yes. The preliminary report was faxed to us while he was in your office. Here it is."

DATA WORLD: MR. ERNEST SAMUELS
PRELIMINARY REPORT/RIDGE HOSPITAL

Mr. Ernest Boron Samuels: Residences in New York City/Palm Beach. Credit report summary states Samuels assets in various trusts. Sources say annual income from his trusts exceed $125 million. Assuming a conservative return of 5%, trust value aggregate is more

than $1 billion. Single. No children. Lived in Houston, Texas. Current address is Ritz Carlton. Real estate contacts say he is looking at area estates. No criminal record. No cars owned. Full report within next 5 business days. 4/2/95. Report filed by RMK.

"Our Mr. Samuels belongs in the Crystal Club."

Dr. Hagen entertained McCoy for lunch with half a dozen department heads in attendance.

"So, Mr. Samuels, what did you think of our Hospital?"

"Dr. Hagen, it was very impressive and I'd like to take you up on that offer to spend a day at the Eisenhower Clinic."

"That's excellent, and I'll have Dr. Constance make the arrangements for later this week, if that's convenient."

"I'll check on dates and someone will call back."

Hagen and Constance escorted McCoy downstairs and watched as he entered a dark blue Lincoln Town car drive away. Within a minute, McCoy's cellular phone rang.

"Mickey, that's an Oscar nomination!"

"Hey, Jimmy, first let's do the movie. One thing about Hagen, he sure smiles a lot."

"A smiling Cobra. Keep your hands in your pockets."

Chapter Thirty Nine: PROTOHUMANS

Extinction is forever.

As the END ZONE team reviewed the tapes of McCoy and Hagen, a queasy feeling overcame Street. One of the voices on the tape was his partner and friend, not some anonymous under cover agent. And McCoy was in Philadelphia because Street called him.

"Mickey, that was a great job. You know, I was feeling a little..."

"You were worried. Right? Hey, Jimmy, you're not the only detective that sticks his neck out. I'm a detective by choice. I know the risks."

"But I promised Judy to look after you. I'm wondering is this whole thing a bit too dicey? Did you tell Judy? Did you tell her everything about this deal in Philly?"

"I did. And she said it's OK because I'm here with you."

"Great! Now, I feel worse. This is no ordinary doctor. The Ridge makes the Chamber of Horrors look like a Sunday at poolside. Be careful."

"Fine. You know tomorrow is Eisenhower Day at the Ridge. I get the once over from head to toe and everything in between."

"We'll be listening. You'll go without a portable mike tomorrow. But we'll hear everything. There are more mikes in that hospital than patients. Mickey, you sure won't be alone."

•••

The following day, McCoy checked into the Eisenhower Clinic; and, for the next eight hours, he felt more hands on his body, needles in his arms, and faces in his face than ever before. At 5 PM, the examination was completed and Dr. Hagen came downstairs to discuss the preliminary results.

"So, how was it, Mr. Samuels?"

"Dr. Hagen, please call me Ernest. Shoot, if I let your folks fiddle with my body all day, we sure can go by first names."

"Ernest, tell me, what'd you think of our people?"

"They're amazing, Walter. I've never met so many doctors and nurses in my entire life. With all that care and attention, maybe I just won the Presidency of the United States. OK, what's the verdict? Will I make it to tomorrow."

"With flying colors. They gave me a checklist and there were a few things, none of them serious. During the colonoscopy, they removed a couple of polyps, all of which are pre cancerous. That sounds scary but it's no big deal. There was one remaining polyp not removed because it was difficult to reach and the report recommends it's surgical removal at your earliest convenience. All your vital signs are great. We'll have the whole report in a couple of days."

McCoy reached into his pocket and took out a check and handed it to Hagen.

"No. No! This day at the Eisenhower is on the house. It was our way of introducing you to the Ridge."

"Walter, look at the check. It's not for $2,500."

Hagen took the check back and unfolded it. "Wow! $250,-000."

"Eric Goodman told me about your Crystal Club and he thought there might be a chance to get in. So how about it?"

"Ernest, we're honored that you'd want to join. I'm sure there's a place for you in the Crystal Club; so, let me be the first to welcome you. Come on upstairs; you've got doctor's permission for a little celebratory drink."

"Walter, let's go. Wait one minute while I tell my driver to come back in an hour."

Outside, in a dark van, Cooper flashed a big thumbs up to Street.

"He's in. That was great."

"Lisa, he's in all right but that never was my concern. Getting him out is."

"What you need, my Boston friend, is a home-cooked meal, some quiet music mixed with a bottle of red wine. You need to relax. Eight PM my place, OK?"

"Sold."

•••

"Jimmy, our lives: are they just mirrors of other cops now gone, forgotten, or rotting away on pensions and social security? We're probably just the latitude and longitude on a map that never changes. We dance our dance and then the music stops."

"That's a pretty heavy way to start the night."

"Better think about it. I do and it scares me. Who really gives a damn about what we do? I want more, Jimmy. I want to be a painter, a painter of lives and hopes and dreams and maybe even kids some day. Do you ever think like that?"

"I think plenty and that's usually when I get in trouble. I have nightmares about my dead partner. Hell, he goes where I go. I think about my exwife and a lot of what ifs."

"What about you, not others, just you, Jimmy?"

"I'm a cop. I love it. I love Nantucket, my place in Boston, and the Marathon."

"You're still not answering my question."

"What is this, 20 questions? I'm not on a witness stand."

"But you're also not a witness to your own life. You find it tough to look inside. Or maybe you never did that."

"Are you now Dr. Cooper, psychiatrist?"

"You can joke all you want, but it's just another way to be evasive. I care for you and you're not getting off the hook. So tell me about you."

"Lisa, maybe tonight isn't a great time for either one of us; so, I'll just head on back to my hotel."

"Go ahead and run. But your partner is still dead and your wife is still divorced and you're still a prisoner inside yourself."

Street slumped into a fluffy chair and looked up at the ceiling.

"No answers up there, Jimmy."

"OK, I'm scared too. Some days I love being detective and other days I want out. The busy days and the days with risk are easy, but the slow quiet ones are hell. Now I'm sweating plenty about Mickey. I put him in harm's way. I'm responsible. Maybe I shouldn't have told you he was my partner. I promised myself no one would know, but I had to tell someone. I'm so afraid for Mickey."

"Give him the credit he deserves because he's a detective and a damn good one. Stop carrying the whole world on your back. Relax and let go; take some chances. Not chances at work, but in life."

"You know, Lisa, I'm a virgin!"

Cooper looked and laughed.

"I mean, I'm a virgin in things like talking. A lot of this is new to me. I can talk the talk with the guys; but, you're different."

"Jimmy, you do the talking and I'll do the listening. Let yourself go."

At 11 PM, they realized there was no dinner, just a bottle of wine and some crackers. Street talked and couldn't stop. Cooper rubbed his neck while he moved across the whole playing field of his life.

When Street had no more to say, Cooper lowered the lights and they eased onto the floor in a cuddling position.

"Tears in your eyes?"

"Yup. You did it, Lisa. I don't know how you could listen the way you did."

"Easy. I care a lot about you. My life can never be the same again. There's so much about you that's special and different."

"Jimmy, let's make love tonight? I want you closer to me than any person in the whole world."

Street moved his hands across Cooper's breasts and down her stomach and across her legs as he unbuttoned her shirt. She released his belt and moved his zipper down--his pants off. Their lips locked in a long passionate kiss after which Street moved his tongue into her left, then right ear as she moaned. His fingers came in and out of her mouth as she sucked on them like sugar coated lollipops.

The next thing Street recognized was a big teddy bear nestled next to him in Cooper's bed.

"How did I get here?"

"We started on the floor. Maybe you sleepwalk."

"What time is it?"

"Eight AM."

"I've got to meet Mickey at nine."

●●●

6:13 AM. COBOL on line. RAZOR OK. TERMINAL good. CHASE is on. SATAN here. SYS and ACID absent. Crystal disconnect # 2 authorized. Good target now in house. RAZOR to COBOL. Why not go slower? SATAN to RAZOR. I'll answer that one. Cash. We need it. These hospital suck up money. We have to pay for the drugs stolen by the doctors. COBOL to SATAN. Silence. Talk and you'll give your identity away. You're the key. We'll need a third disconnect by 6/30 then relax time till next year. COBOL is off.

●●●

Street drove towards a second rendezvous with Mickey in his gym's sauna. En route, he received a call from Smith at headquarters. "Joker said there's another COBOL intercept and another Crystal Club disconnect authorized."

"Charlie, remember that night when we got all the license plates at the Crystal Ball. Take the list, split it with Lisa and Rudy and start calling, fast!"

Ten minutes later, Smith called back, his voice trailing off. "This is gonna take all day, and that's if we're lucky. We can always go back to the Ridge..."

Street interrupted. "...and run up and down the halls crying, All Crystal Club members, duck! These people killed outside the Hospital (your police friend Celia was killed at home). Maybe they're franchising to new locations. And find Goodman first. If he's anywhere near that Hospital, he's a sure target."

•••

8:05 AM. RAZOR to COBOL. STAND BY. COBOL AT REMOTE LOCATION. Disconnect #2 completed without incident. Clear. COBOL to RAZOR. Excellent.

•••

OPERATION END ZONE continued a frantic search for any Crystal Club members in the Ridge while Street plunked down in a sauna with McCoy. Before they started to talk, Street's beeper sounded and he called Smith at headquarters.

"Street, this is brutal. We've only reached about 30 Crystal members so far. I called Mayor Gentry's office because I figured he's got a list of members but he's in Chicago at a mayor's conference. I tried the Chief but Rome's up in your hometown giving a speech to some women's group. At least you don't have to worry about Goodman 'cause he's nowhere near the Ridge. His secretary thinks she may have a list of members that she can fax over. If not, she'll call Goodman when he wakes up."

"When he wakes up? Charlie, if he's not up by now, he's probably extinct!"

"No! Goodman is in LA at a TV convention."

"Just curious, Charlie; but, where's Hagen? Is he out of town, too?"

"Funny you ask. I thought of that. Surveillance at the Hospital reports he arrived at 5:30 AM this morning. Hagen is definitely in town."

"Well, at least Goodman's safe. Maybe we can keep him and his Prozac-eating dog Muffy or Misty alive. Keep me informed. Thanks Charlie."

"Street, the dog's name is Misty."

"Great! Earthquakes. Floods. Fires. Maybe Hagen and the Ridge will get a freebie with Goodman in LA." Street rejoined McCoy in the sauna.

"Joker got another intercept that reads like an invitation to afternoon tea; only the message is DISCONNECT. We're trying to find any Crystal Club members inside the Ridge and so far it's a big fat zero. COBOL must be a little tight for cash. Guess it's those quarterly Federal returns."

Street cracked a smile and expected a laugh from McCoy.

"Wow, Street, go back and check that list of Crystal Club members who have died and see if any fell in two week periods before March 15th, June 15th, October 15th and January 15th. Damn, you might be surprised."

"Are your serious?"

"Just a hunch. No, wait. Even if they did that, they wouldn't get the cash right away. The gifts would take time to go through the legal system, unless they found some way to discount the future cash in a will and convert it to instant cash, say 80 cents on the dollar. They might pull that off with some foreign bank if they had binding legal documents and if they had proof the deceased had the money to fund the gift. Hey, anything is possible. Even miracles, Jimmy."

"Look, Mickey, I've done some more thinking about this tangle I've got you in and..."

"...and, Street, for the first time in my career, I feel alive and at the front of a big case, not riding shotgun for you. You've got to respect that, OK?"

The two detectives set a tentative date when Mr. Ernest Boron Samuels would enter the Ridge as a patient and try to lure the Crystal Club killers.

"Mickey, I'll check the date out at headquarters. So, how's it feel to be a billionaire, riding around in a limo?"

"You get used to it."

"Mickey, you're a $50,000 a year cop; so, don't get used to it."

●●●

OPERATION END ZONE met the next morning to talked strategy for the upcoming sting at the Ridge.

Charlie held up the morning paper. "Here it is folks. Read all about it."

The obituary page had a very small story on a Howard Hughes type recluse named Lawrence James:

> **Philadelphia inventor Lawrence James died yesterday at the Ridge Hospital after a long illness. James was 89 years old. He and his wife, the late Ellen James, had no children. James is best known for his invention of a device that lead to parallel processing for computers. He served in counter intelligence during World War II. James lived alone and in later years was never seen in public.**

"This one was easy," Smith said.

Street read the obituary, then turned his head up from the paper. "Yeah, but the next one at the Ridge isn't going to be easy. In fact, the next one is a bomb that's gonna blow up in their faces!"

"Listen, the man going into the Ridge as our human guinea pig is a friend of mine. I know his wife and I've coached his kid's little league team. So, this sting is a lot more to me than a chance to nail who ever is killing these Crystal Club members. Hell, I don't give a damn if we ever catch the bad guys. All I worry about is making sure that my friend goes in vertical and comes out the same way. Get it?"

One of the FBI agents had a few reassuring words. "Detective, I've had many friends from the Bureau who've gone under cover, dealing with spies, traitors, killers, druggies, and kidnappers. Your friend will be fine. In fact, I'll tell you a story, which I promise to deny, about an incident a few years ago during a sting. It might explain how we handle these situations."

The FBI told the detectives about a drug deal in a Chicago warehouse. The drugs were payment to a man who worked in the Chicago Mercantile Exchange--a swap of drugs for information of crop prices. The drug dealers worked for a major commodities trader; the man with the crop prices was an employee of the US Government.

"We had an undercover agent inside who was wired and posing as another government employee who had the advance crop production figures. Those numbers are worth hundreds of millions of dollars. If you get them in time to take a major commodities position, well, one of the drug dealers recognized our agent and the last thing we heard was swearing, some punches, and then the wire went dead. We were inside the warehouse in less than sixty seconds."

Street stood up in anger. "Great story. You lost your agent, right?"

"Wrong. We found our agent backed against a wall with a gun to his head. We had ten agents inside that warehouse, each one packing a Rambo assortment of weapons. Three drug dealers and the dirty US Government official were inside and they wanted to take our agent as hostage. They threatened to kill him."

Street was getting impatient. "So, you negotiated and everything turned out OK, right?"

"Detective, you'd never make it on a game show. Shut up and listen to the rest of the story." The FBI agent put himself in the shoes of the agent in charge and reenacted what happened.

"You've got our guy. You can kill him and we can't stop you. Here's how it's coming down. We're gonna kneecap one of you right now unless you release our guy within 15 seconds. If you kill our agent, we'll kill everyone in the warehouse. If you release him, you'll live. And if you tell any of this story, we'll deny it. We protect our own.

"The drug dealers stood motionless with their weapons drawn and refused to take the gun away from the agent's head.

"Do him! BOOM. BOOM.

"Two blazing shots rang out from behind the agent in charge and one of the drug dealers fell to the floor with his left leg almost severed at the knee. The right leg, from the knee down, was lying on the floor.

"I'll wait 15 seconds more and we have an instant replay.

"The FBI undercover agent was released and the drug dealer bleed to death.

"Street, that is a true story. You'll never read about it and you'll never hear it on a radio talk show. But it happened for real and it wasn't the first time and it won't be the last. So, yeah, your friend is taking a chance going inside the Ridge Hospital. But, tell him this story and he might feel better."

Joker leaned over to Street when the FBI agent sat down. "Do you really believe that story?"

"I hope it's true because it makes me feel a lot better when I think about Mickey going inside the Ridge."

"We have to talk, Jimmy. I've got some crazy theories."

"You and the word crazy are lookalikes. Let's talk."

"Jimmy, I said crazy. It's safer if we don't talk here."

"First, hospitals aren't safe, and now, you're telling me police headquarters isn't. What is safe?"

"My computers. They don't lie."

●●●

The Boston duo left headquarters and found a greasy spoon a few blocks away. Lost in their own thoughts, they began to talk as never before, although Street had a sinking feeling that Joker's word crazy translated into his word, danger.

"This last COBOL message is an e-mail enigma."

"What's that mean?"

Joker pulled out a copy of the last COBOL intercept with the words, **COBOL at remote location**, yellow lined.

"We've never seen those words used before. I always thought COBOL was at a fixed location. Frankly, I figured COBOL was Dr. Hagen."

"Me, too."

"When this intercept came over, Hagen was at the Ridge and that could not be his remote location. At the same moment, Chief Rome is in Boston speaking at some women's group and the Mayor is in Chicago and Mr. Goodman is in LA."

"Crazy was the right word. That's absurd. Are you saying one of these three is COBOL? Lots of other people were also out of town. Maybe that DA that Cooper knows, Adams, was out of town."

"He's different. You've got a grudge with him because he was engaged to Cooper. Think about Chief Rome. What do you know about her?"

"It's not my business to know anything about her. She's wired into the politics of this city. That's it."

"What about the mayor?"

"Other than the fact he and our mayor are buddies, he could come from Mars, for all I know."

"And Goodman?"

"He's got a dog on PROZAC, a wife who loves to shop in New York, a broadcast company and one other thing."

"What's that, Jimmy?"

"He's got a lucky charm somewhere. He's dodged a few bullets inside the Ridge and I guess he won't be so lucky the next time around unless we stop these Crystal Club killings."

Street and Joker fiddled with their coffee and kept bouncing ideas back and forth.

"Joker, we've been reading these intercepts from COBOL. Can we send COBOL a message even though we don't know where he or she is?"

"Maybe. We could go to VALLEY FORGE SYSTEMS, get Cone's computer and use it. I'm sure we could. So, how come I didn't think of that?"

"Because it was a simple idea."

The message Street and Joker wanted to send was peek-a-boo-I-see-you. A preemptive strike might worry COBOL enough to close down the killings, at least for a while. Street knew that could take McCoy out of harms way.

COBOL. This is the Philadelphia police. We're going to take a megabyte out of your game. We know who you are. When we can prove it, we'll put you away. One more Crystal disconnect and we'll have our proof. We already short circuited SYS. Razor, Chase, and Terminal are going, going. COBOL. The games are over.

"OK, Jimmy, let's do it."

They hustled back to headquarters, grabbed Cooper and left for VALLEY FORGE SYSTEMS. The reception area of VFS featured a landscape of computer screens manicured with cyberland paraphernalia. The reception area was a combination cybermall, cyberspace of gadgets, amber colored lights and a large computer printed signature slogan from Rick Cone: WE ARE THE PROTOTYPES.

"Translate, Joker."

"He says this is the archive of archetypes as arcane as that may appear!"

"Holy, shit! Joker, just once in my life, could you please speak in English for us lonely mortals."

Cooper translated. "The sign says this place is a so called original. Cone thinks whatever they do here is special, like first of a kind. How's that?"

"Thank you."

Cooper asked the receptionist to ring Cone's office. "Tell him it's Detective Cooper."

"I can ring, but no one will answer. Mr. Cone put a message on our computers two days ago that he was home sick and not to disturb him. He signed the message, RICK NEPTUNE'. Strange huh, but Mr. Cone always does things his way. He's a real prankster."

"We'd like to go to his office, please."

"I don't know about that. Mr. Cone didn't give permission."

Cooper tossed the copy of a signed statement on Philadelphia Police letterhead towards the receptionist. "Read this. After, you let us into his office."

She scanned the document and saw Cone's signature. "OK, I'll let you in. But, what's all this about?"

"It's confidential."

Cone's office was unlocked; it was dark, with the only light coming from a computer screen behind his desk. The message scrolling across the screen was purple against a green background.

COBOL welcomes the Philadelphia police to SYS. Come in and look around. Enjoy the sights. Say Goodbye Neptune.

Joker summarized the chilling thoughts of everyone. "This is not good."

Cooper and the others rushed outside into the reception area. "Give me Cone's home address and start calling him. If you reach Cone, tell him to lock his doors and stay put until we arrive."

Cone lived near Pottstown about 20 miles northwest of Valley Forge. Cooper called for State Police assistance as they raced along Route 422, with everyone wondering what they had found. When they arrived, the front door was unlocked and after knocking the detectives entered Cone's farm. The inside was as ultra modern as the outside was rustic.

There were computers everywhere, each scrolling a message simultaneously in the same hideous purple on green color they saw in Cone's office.

Say Good-bye Neptune. COBOL.

The house filled with state troopers. One asked: "Is this somebody's idea of a sick joke?"

One of the troopers outside yelled. "You better come outside."

Near the back door, set in a stoned patio, was a huge built in the ground Jacuzzi bubbling hot water and steam into the air. Through the mist was a man dressed in a dark business suit with a very proper tie and blue shirt, floating face up in the Jacuzzi, with his eyes open. The man was Rick Cone and he was dead.

Joker told Street. "Neptune is the god of the sea. In this case, it's a Jacuzzi. We've got a killer, computer wizard, medical nut and comedian all rolled into one package. Boston's looking better every minute."

Dracula arrived in his ME van within two hours of the phone call from Cooper and began his medicolegal autopsy.

During the two hour wait for the ME, it was an eerie site in the farmlands of Pottstown. The outside temperature was less than 40 degrees and Cone's body continued to drift in circles inside the Jacuzzi as a steam fog rose while a gurgling sound drifted near the still running Jacuzzi. According to police procedures, in suspicious deaths, absolutely nothing can be moved or touched until the crime scene unit arrives. The police photographer, a young woman new to the department, started shooting ID pictures with time and date imprinted on each shot. Cone floated counter clockwise around the Jacuzzi every couple of minutes but remained in a face up position.

"Jimmy, before the ME arrives, I'll guarantee this was murder."

"Looks like it; but, we'll have to wait."

"No need. Come on, I'll prove it." Cooper followed Street and Joker to the edge of the Jacuzzi.

"This is the Jacuzzi auto timer still positioned at ten minutes. Someone disabled the timer so this guy could broil indefinitely. The ME is gonna have a tough one guessing time of death because the temperature in the Jacuzzi eliminates the value of a body temperature test. Smart killer. Unless this guy was in the habit of taking Jacuzzi baths in Armani suits, it's simple to guess he was deposited here. I doubt they'll find enough water in his lungs to show drowning. On the other hand, they might just find some residue of a sedative and trauma to the trachea. Strangulation."

"Joker, did you have a front row seat to this?" Street looked around and noticed Cooper had vanished.

"Where's Lisa?"

"Beats me."

Street went inside the house, now packed with both State and local police.

"Anyone see Detective Cooper?"

One of the local cops answered. "You mean the broad with the cute body?"

Street cut a nasty look at the cop. "No, I mean the female detective as opposed to a beerbelly, out-of-shape, half shaven, bad breath Saturday morning cartoon cop like yourself!"

"Hey, asshole, what kind of fuckin' thing is that to say to a fellow officer of the law?"

Joker looked on with pride as Street finished the conversation. "And I forgot, to add: low-life-language to half-shaven."

"Want to talk outside, buddy."

Another local cop moved the two men apart, pointing to a bathroom on the first floor. "I think she's inside there. She didn't look too good."

KNOCK. KNOCK. KNOCK. "Lisa, are you in there? Are you OK?"

There was no answer and Street pounded on the door. "Lisa, answer me or I'm coming in."

"I'm sick, Jimmy. Don't come in." Her voice trailed off and Street forced the door open.

Cooper was lying on the floor, her head perched on the edge of the toilet. From the smell, it was apparent she had vomited. Street closed the bathroom door.

"This is sure romantic, isn't it, Jimmy?"

"You, OK? These aren't pretty sites. For the first year on the force, I vomited like clockwork. Show me a crime scene and show me a bathroom. My first partner did the same thing I'm doing. He found me hiding in a bathroom so I could come out with my tough guy cop image. When these stop making you feel sick, it's time to get out of the business."

Street sat down on the floor of the bathroom, holding Cooper's hand, and rubbing her neck. He held her warmly in his arms while her head rested on his shoulder. For almost a half hour, they sat on the floor.

"Jimmy, I was thinking of my dad's pharmacy back in Long Island. I could have called for a prescription; but it's gone."

"It's gone; but I'm not. I'm here with you. And I'll stay with you until you feel better and I'll walk out into that room of other cops with you. Feeling better?"

"Yeah. There's some toothpaste already open on the sink. Can you squeeze me out a dab?"

"This guy Cone must have been a health nut. The toothpaste has all these pictures of cows and birds. The label must say All Natural ten times. I'll push out a stream. Nice color, sort of like a green and white woven together."

He stuck his finger out with the toothpaste on it and Cooper leaned down to lick it off his finger. Street pulled his hand back in a jerking motion.

"Bitter almonds. Smell it?"

"Cyanide?"

Street picked the tube up, careful to try and not disturb any latent finger prints remaining on it. The top was off and there was a visible, but hard to see, puncture mark right in the middle of a brown cow decorating the tube of paste.

There was knocking on the door. Street recognized the voice of the over sized cop. "Say, Detective Street, are you trying to clean up the broad? Maybe she's getting potty training. Want me to help?" he asked derisively.

Joker heard, too, and motioned for the State Police to come over. "That big cop, the one with the vacant mind and a sewage mouth: he's looking for trouble."

Street emerged from the bathroom with Cooper standing behind him.

"You know, we could smell your foul breath through the door. So, get out of our way."

The State Police stepped between Street and the local cop.

Cooper held the tooth paste in her hand and turned it over to the State Police. "Give this to our ME when he arrives. He answers to the name, Dracula, Drake Cula."

Street added: "And tell fatso with the big mouth that Dracula offers free medical service for cops like him. Why doesn't he come in about 2 AM and we can do a complete brain work up and have him back to the zoo by 2:05 AM."

When the local cop heard Street, he lunged for him, but was restrained by two State Police officers. One of them turned to the local police commander. "Your guy is contributing nothing at this crime scene. Get him out of here."

"You can't order us around in our own town."

"He's out of this house or under arrest. We're counting. 5432..."

Street and Cooper watched, straight faced.

"Hey, that's my line", Street said.

"What line?"

"The countdown: 5432. It works everytime."

The State Trooper winked and flashed thumbs up.

Dracula arrived as they spoke; the State Trooper handed him the toothpaste, which was now in a plastic evidence bag.

"Dracula, we're out of here."

•••

In a darkened and sound proofed studio-like room in downtown Philadelphia, a small gathering of people began. The center of evil can be a silent, almost tranquil place and that was true today. Those assembled spoke in low voices with no anger or emotion. Like an opportunistic infection, these persons were pathogenic only because society's immune system was unable to expel them. However, the meeting was itself a reminder that their killing ways were no longer untraceable like optical illusions.

"We have enjoyed a great opulence of opportunity during these past years, but that environment has been comprised by a convergence of bad luck. SYS was compromised and probably much of our computer systems. That's why we meet here."

Present in the room were three men and one woman.

"We will complete one final Crystal Club disconnect and close down for the remainder of the year."

The woman stood and spoke while the men remained seated.

"You've already done enough. You've raised the cash necessary for the Hospital in 1995 and the money markets can provide a cushion for years to come. Why take more chances?"

Now, a man stood, and, as if orchestrated in musical chairs, the woman took her seat. The man cut an imposing look as he answered the woman.

"You cannot bathe yourself in the luxury of conveniences when your body and soul are dirty. Nothing was ever written in hieroglyphics or anything spoken in some foreign tongue. You feasted at my table, taking the money. And, what did it buy? You are a high priestess and you coveted that role and accepted all our help. Your moral virginity was sold to us a long time ago and your eyes were always open. The lowest common denominator of this enterprise is money and power and each of you has calculated the risks. There is no EXIT door."

Again the woman rose and spoke.

"There is no way you can keep me in this, against my will."

For a couple of minutes, the room was locked in silence. The man waited till she sat and this time he stood with a ghostly aura that enveloped him. His eyeballs were big and they moved in a chilling circle within his sockets. Whether intentional or uncontrollable, the effect was the same: terror! He walked from his chair at the head of the table and put his hands on the woman's shoulders, pinning her. She looked straight up towards the ceiling with her furrowed forehead and saw his gaping nostrils and eyes looking down at her.

In a singsong way, he continued, his voice climbing and descending as his lips curled and closed while his eyes widened and narrowed.

ARE YOU THE LUCIFER, THE MORNING STAR? ARE YOU PENITENT MY SWEET THING? SO LATE, TOO LATE. PERHAPS YOU'RE OUR LITTLE POLTERGEIST. ARE YOU REALLY IN PUZZLEMENT AT THE DEEDS WE HAVE DONE?

As he rambled, with words that seemed connected and then disconnected, the men seated exchanged looks of bewilderment. "He's on the cliff. Is this a meltdown?"

"AND SO, MY ROSE, REMEMBER, ROME WAS NOT BUILT IN SEVEN DAYS AND THIS JOURNEY FOR YOU IS A WORK IN PROGRESS. SINNERS WE ALL ARE AND ALWAYS SHALL BE. WE MADE OUR CHOICES. IF YOU CHOOSE TO LEAVE, THEN YOU SHALL LEAVE. EXTINCT!

Suddenly, the singsong ramblings ended and he sat at the table. With everyone now seated, he issued some final words.

"We will complete our mission. We will continue to communicate using our computer link and CHASE will insure the security of the link now that Cone is gone. So, I'm sure this final Crystal Club disconnect will be executed. What I want now is a status report on the police investigation from RAZOR."

Police Chief Ellen Rome provided a summary of the undercover operation in progress, including details of everything she knew.

●●●

"They know another Crystal Club disconnect is planned and Street has a volunteer ready to go into the Ridge. You must be very careful."

Rome did not have a map with the location of listening devices inside the Ridge, but warned COBOL that the hospital was wired from top to bottom.

"So, we have adummy pill, our own little placebo ready to visit us at the Ridge. We must welcome him. It's larceny of a Ridge hospital bed. Such a shabby little enterprise, probably engineered by our friends, Street and Cooper.

Chapter Forty: THE UNRAVELING

Deception is like the Pantheon in Rome--circular.

The act features a person who earns trust through deeds and then pirates that trust. There are few people immune to the temptations of deceit and the holy grail of it's rewards. Detectives know that the decay rate of deception can be infinitely slow, with many evildoers content to take their sins into eternity. Solving a crime, more exquisitely known as decapitation of the deceitful, demands a mixture of courage, instinct, luck, and timing.

Do doctors practice a genteel form of deception as they seek to comfort a patient with reassuring words, knowing that disaster is the likely outcome?

Do cereal makers promote deception with adorable drawings of animals which enclose boxes of overpriced, sugarcoated nothingness?

Do airline captains counterfeit the truth when they fail to tell passengers that the ice storm at their destination slightly reduces the chance for a safe flight?

It is accepted as gospel that government and the politicians that practice the art of governance expel deceit more frequently than their own bodily fluids.

Cops are immersed in deception each day of their lives until it becomes either a numbing feeling or an addictive acquiescence.

•••

"So, how was your weekend back in Boston? Did you miss the limo and all the billions of dollars you don't have?"

"It felt great to get out of this pressure cooker, Jimmy."

"Now, it really starts. Everything is ready and we figure you'll check in this weekend with chest pains. Any second thoughts about all this?"

"None."

"Joker gave me this think piece and you ought to see it. You know him: he doesn't think the way we do."

"Which is probably why he saved your life in Boston. Let me see it."

TO: Jimmy
FR: Joker
RE: Mickey & The What Ifs

Everyone in END ZONE better start thinking about the what ifs in this sting. If there's a conspiracy, we can't be sure when they'll strike at Mickey, or even if they will.

Who do we have inside the Hospital to keep an eye on Mickey? Those listening devices are limited. I'd like a few sets of eyes in the Hospital.

We've got COBOL, RAZOR, CHASE and TERMINAL running around loose somewhere. They seem to have an inside ear with police.

Despite what the FBI says, I don't think this sting is a sure thing.

"So, what do you think?"

"Joker sure knows how to make someone feel uneasy."

All week, the END ZONE team reviewed the weekend admission of McCoy into the Hospital. The only ones who knew his identity remained Street, Joker and Cooper.

The weekend approached and, as planned, McCoy flew back to Boston to meet with Boston Police doctors who had prepared a medical cocktail designed to get McCoy admitted to the Ridge.

At police headquarters, the END ZONE was called *en masse* upstairs to Chief Rome's office.

Rome spoke like a coach at halftime. "Just a few words of good luck to all of you. I know we've kept this compartmentalized as they say in the FBI, so none of us know all the details. But I called you together because, based on equipment and manpower demands, it appears you're almost ready to go forward. Is there anything I can do?"

Cooper flashed a smile at Rome. "Chief, we wouldn't be this far without your help. Remember that first time we spoke and you gave me the OK? That meant a lot."

"Lisa, tell me something. If I had said No, would you have given up this whole Ridge thing? I doubt it."

"You're probably right, Chief."

"I'd like to talk privately with Street after this meeting ends."

As everyone filed out of the Chief's office, they looked back at Street sitting alone, seemingly lost in his thoughts.

"Detective, we've had our problems; and, before you send in...forgot his name...I want to clear the air."

"Chief, you didn't forget because I never told you who's going in. Nothing personal, but it's a friend of mine and I feel better this way."

"Regardless, when you came to town, you were a baby sitting chore. You've come a long way and we'll be sorry to see you leave. Maybe we can have dinner when it's over. Next week, how's that sound?"

"That's fine with me; but, it may not be over next week." Street left Rome's office and called Joker from a pay phone.

"I've just spent 15 minutes with Ellen Rome and all of a sudden she's full of questions. With Mickey going into the Ridge, I don't trust anyone. See if she's got any deep, dark secrets we should know. Call Martin in the Boston FBI office and ask him to keep the inquiry very quiet."

Upstairs, Chief Rome placed a call to the Chief of Detectives in Boston.

"Street and Joker are fabulous. You should be very proud of them, Louis. They've made the difference on this case.

You'll get them both back in a few weeks, or at least that's my best guess."

"That's what I hear, too. Street and his partner up here, Mickey McCoy have really been running up a big telephone and travel bill. Ellen, I hope your budget can handle it."

"Sure it can, Louis; this is a giant case and it's probably going to put your boys back on the morning talk show circuit."

Rome heard a loud sigh. "Just what Street doesn't need. This time the glory should be spread around."

"Louis, can you fax me biographies of Street, Joker, and the other fellow..."

"Mike Mickey McCoy, Street's partner and a great detective. Ellen, you got three for the price of one. I'll send the info down ASAP."

"Louis, I'll have my secretary give you my private fax. We need to keep this sting at the Ridge quiet."

"Done. Take care, Ellen, and stop by when you're in town."

•••

RAZOR to COBOL. We have ID on next Crystal Club disconnect. May be police undercover agent. Identity confirmed. Please advise. COBOL to team. Proceed as planned and disconnect. COBOL out.

•••

"Joker, it's Toshi and we've got another intercept. They know about the sting. They know you're sending in a cop. Better get to Street."

Joker reached Street and relayed the contents of the intercept.

"That's it. Call the damn thing off! Let's meet with McCoy."

A few hours later, the three met and discussed the intercept. This time, Street brought along one of the FBI agents.

The FBI agent started. "Street, you're over reacting. This COBOL probably knows we're reading his computer messages. This is to scare you off."

"It worked."

"OK, who knows the identity of your friend?"

"Just Joker and I...and Cooper. Sorry Mickey; I told her. But, I trust her. I needed someone to talk with."

The agent interrupted. "Now, don't go convicting the innocent. Detective Cooper is clean. She's been checked out and we'll double check again. I think you've got a case of butterflies. We've got the Ridge so wired I'm surprised the electricity is still on."

Street turned to Mickey. "So, how do you feel?"

"I say it's still a go. I've got confidence in the work we've done and the protection I'll have inside the Hospital. I'm ready."

The decision was made to continue. Within 48 hours, Ernest Boron Samuels, billionaire and newest Crystal Club member, would be admitted to the Ridge, suffering from chest pain.

•••

Saturday, 3:30 PM, a gray unmarked police car moved towards Penn's Landing on the Philadelphia waterfront. Inside the car were Street, Joker and an FBI agent. Through the rear view mirror, Street spotted a car he thought was following them.

"Hold on, we're gonna make a few turns."

Street accelerated and sped down a one way street in the wrong direction as the other car followed.

"That does it!" Street slammed on the brakes and rocked to a stop on the curb. He and the FBI agent flew outside the car with weapons drawn, charging the other car and pointing their guns at the driver who made no move to escape.

"Cooper, what the fuck are you doing?" Street yelled as he told the FBI agent to holster his gun.

Cooper jumped out of her car and put her face into Street's. "So, you think maybe it was a mistake to tell me about Mickey? So, you're not sure about me? You've got a lot of nerve. And now, you're keeping secrets."

"Calm down. Wait a minute."

"I will not calm down."

A small crowd formed along the sidewalks. The FBI agent held his badge high, instructing everyone to keep moving.

"Lisa, I've always trusted you. Someone gave you the wrong impression. One of the FBI agents asked how many people knew about Mickey and I told them about you. No big deal."

"If it's no big deal, then tell me--go ahead and don't lie; tell me where you're going right now. Go ahead. I'll wait till hell freezes over."

"We're going down to Penn's Landing."

"You're full of shit. Ready for a swim or maybe some pictures of the Delaware?"

"No, we're actually going down..."

"You're going to meet Mickey and you never called me. You didn't call because you didn't trust me. Or maybe yourself. Am I right?"

"Yeah, we're gonna meet Mickey. I didn't call because, well, uh, I just didn't."

"OK, am I going or not! And if the answer is no, don't you ever call me, talk to me, look at me, or even think of me."

"I'm sorry, Lisa. I should never have gotten my partner involved. Of course, I trust you. Come with us."

Cooper parked her car and joined Joker and the FBI agent for the ride. Standing outside a coffee shop was McCoy, who climbed quickly in the car. They drove over the Ben Franklin Bridge, east onto the New Jersey Turnpike, and north to the first rest area.

The sun was setting and the rest area was packed with tourists and truckers. Highway rest areas, like the busy ones on the New Jersey Turnpike, have an ambiance similar to airport terminals. Thousands of people coming and going in an anonymous American ritual celebrated with burgers, fast food, fast drinks, and rest rooms whose walls are decorated with condom, ladies hygiene and fragrance dispensers. The rest rooms are uniformly gray or green tile. Truckers with week long growths of hair and dirty jeans sip coffee next to men and women wearing Fifth Avenue designer clothes.

Street wanted a few minutes alone with McCoy. "Joker, take the car and fill it up. We'll meet you inside in a few minutes."

"So, Mickey, here we are, two Boston cops on the New Jersey Turnpike."

McCoy laughed. "Yeah, where else?"

"Listen, Mickey; I gotta do this now. You have to listen and I have to talk. OK?"

"All ears."

The two men walked to the outer perimeter of the parking lot and bundled against the raw cold winds.

"Mickey, we've been friends a long time. And no one could ask for a better partner. Yeah, I get carried away and steal the spotlight a lot and I guess that's just me. Now, I've got you in the spotlight; except that's inside a hospital. And, Ernest Boron Samuels, it's a hospital that has a real bad track record with Crystal Club members."

"But you made me rich, Jimmy."

"Funny. I can't bring myself to find much that's funny about my friend and partner going in harm's way while I'm sitting on my ass in some van listening for voices in the night. And I promised to look after you. Hell of a job I'm doing."

"Hey, Jimmy, if you didn't call your partner; then, who could you call?"

"What I'm thinking is that we could call this sting off; get someone else like an FBI agent, and you could stay on the case. You just wouldn't go into the Ridge. How's that sound?"

"Sounds like my partner is all twisted with guilt, nerves, stress, and maybe a little love? So, this is the Cooper you've talked about. She seems real special, and, take it from a married man, I see the look, and she's got it for you."

"Mickey, Cooper's not the subject. You are."

"No, actually you are. These things you say are demons inside you. You have to deal with them. Maybe Cooper can help. I took this job to make a difference and I know the risks. I've talked about it with my family and they know I love this job. I even love my good buddy, my partner. So, thanks for caring. You've said your peace and I've said mine. Let's get this job done and get back to Boston before Joker blows up something in Philly by mistake."

Street had tears in his eyes and McCoy watched as they dripped to the concrete parking lot.

"If anything ever happened to you, Mickey..."

"Nothing will. That's a promise and you know I'm good with those."

They walked inside the restaurant and saw Joker, Cooper and the FBI agent huddled in a corner eating a pizza.

"Jimmy's told me everything about you, Cooper. Is it all true?"

With a smile towards Street, she answered. "No way is it true. He didn't tell you everything?"

McCoy motioned to Cooper. "Can we talk outside for a couple of minutes or do I need to ask Street's permission?"

"My pleasure. How often do I get invitations like that from billionaires like the famous Ernest Boron Samuels."

McCoy and Cooper walked outside, leaving Street to finish the pizza with Joker and the agent.

"Jimmy, what's that all about? What does Mickey want with Cooper?"

"Who knows, Joker? Don't you have her wired?"

"That's not funny."

"Joker, I thought one out of three Americans were wired by you and plugged into one of your MIT computers."

McCoy and Cooper walked the same perimeter path around the parked cars.

"Cooper..."

"It's Lisa."

"OK, and it's Mickey."

"For a while it's Ernest..."

"I got it. Lisa, I want to talk with you about Jimmy. I want you to know how special he is to me, my family and a lot of other people. He's different. I know he treats you well, but you've got to get past that protective wall to really see the sparkle."

"Oh, I've been working on that and he doesn't make it easy."

"He doesn't make much easy. But you have to know where he's coming from. He worshipped his dad, who was a cop and never got to say goodbye when he was gunned down on a stake out. His exwife turned ice cold and really changed when Street said he wanted a family. I didn't really know her, but other guys did. She used to work in a travel agency and was cute as a button. Then, she just changed. She was obsessive-compulsive. There's some fancy name for it. Sex became dirty for her. They say she washed her hands hourly and kept calling Jimmy at headquarters. He tried to help her get better and even went to a psychiatrist with her. She wanted no part of it."

"Jimmy never talked much about her."

"That's because he hurts so much inside. He thinks it was his fault. That guy carries around a lot of guilt. And did he tell you much about his partner--the one who was killed?"

"Not a lot. He just said it was a drug deal that went bad and they were in the wrong place at the wrong time."

"Well, that's true. What he didn't tell you was he kept tracking down the killers on his own time. He pursued them and that wasn't good enough. He went after their suppliers and up the line. Street became a one man vice squad, working on his own time. When it was over, Street was the hunter and almost 20 guys went to jail. Most of them had no idea what happened that night when Street's partner was killed. The guy is ferocious. He's blood-loyal."

"Mickey, there's also a little kid inside that man. I've seen and felt it. And I like it."

"Do you know his eyes are different colors? We sometimes call his dog eyes.

"I've seen the real thing, Mickey."

"Lisa, I want a promise from you."

"I'm listening."

"Street's all wound up about this sting. If anything ever went wrong, he'd blame himself."

"Nothing will go wrong."

"Show me where that's in black and white. Lisa, promise me you'll always be honest and gentle with him. If anything went wrong, you tell Street that it wasn't his fault and that I'd do it over again. And tell him thank you for the chance to get into the spotlight. But I've got a warning, too."

"A warning?"

"Loyalty is the blood that runs through his veins. If someone hurt his friend, his partner, his family: well, Street is a storm all bottled up. Take the worst hurricane, mix it with a blizzard, add thunder, lightning an angry wave of tornadoes and you just begin to get Street on your radar scope. I used a word before, blood-loyal, and I meant it. For Street, it would be *BLOOD GAMES*. It's his ugly side; but trust me, it's there."

"Mickey, thanks for caring. I don't ever want to see that side of him. I promise he'll be OK and, Mickey, you'll be OK, too. You guys from Boston get pretty intense. Except Joker."

"Joker. That's a whole other story. For those answers, just look up to the stars."

Cooper put her arms around McCoy and gave him a big hug and a kiss.

"Lisa, that's what Jimmy needs most: hugs."

"He must be very special to have a friend like you."

"He is."

●●●

"Chief, this is Sanders. I followed Street as you asked. Detective Cooper met him in town along with that guy Joker and an FBI agent. They stopped down at the waterfront and picked someone up and went to Jersey. I parked near them in a rest area. They were there about one hour. Then they climbed back in Street's car, and this guy--I've never seen him before--he gets out. That's it. Do you want me to write up a report for the department?"

"The only report is in your head and I want you to forget it."

"No problem; it's forgotten."

"Detective Sanders, was that fellow they picked up about five feet ten inches, dark hair with blue eyes?"

"Chief Rome, it sounds like you were in the car with me."

"Sanders, good job. Keep it quiet."

Rome fiddled through papers on her desk and looked at the faxes sent from Boston. She recognized Street and Joker and then there was the third man. She looked at his file:

Mike Mickey McCoy. Detective. Homicide. Married. Children. Three awards for valor. Partner is Jimmy Street.

"Gotcha!"

Encrypt. RAZOR to COBOL. ID on the undercover agent is Detective Mike Mickey McCoy. the real McCoy. Transmitting picture and complete description. Does he match any Crystal Club member ID's? What if he checks into Ridge? COBOL to RAZOR. He doesn't check out. They can't catch us. COBOL to RAZOR. Well done.

•••

Mr. Ernest Boron Samuels and his driver pulled into the Emergency Entrance of the Ridge Hospital at 2:30 AM. The driver, an FBI agent, helped Samuels into the waiting room.

"My man is really sick. Chest pains. He wanted to come here. He's in your Crystal Club." He spoke the magic words.

Within seconds, a swarm of doctors and nurses surrounded Samuels. The receptionist in the Emergency Room typed in his name, Ernest Boron Samuels, and up popped CRYSTAL CLUB. While Samuels was cared for, a call went to the home of Dr. Walter Hagen. Hagen insisted that he was advised, day or night, when a Crystal Club member checked into the Ridge.

"What's the first read? BP sounds OK. Heart rate, too. Look in the files. We just did a complete work up on Samuels. Keep me advised. And get Dr. Constance out of bed and tell her to get to the Hospital."

Huddled in a van parked outside the Hospital were detectives Street and Cooper. Smith and Levin would take the next 12 hour shift. Two FBI electronics specialists were crowded in the van along with Joker.

"We've got excellent telemetry. NASA would be proud. McCoy's watch is sending out a voice signal and also monitoring his heart rate. His data looks fine, except for the medical cocktail we gave him."

Street felt a bit more relaxed as he listened to his partner's voice.

Two hours passed during which time a series of tests were conducted on McCoy.

"Dr. Constance, it's almost 5 AM Sunday morning. Afraid you won't get a copy of the *Times*?" The residents assured her that Samuels was fine and probably the victim of some bad food and long hours away from his pillow.

"We've admitted him. He's Crystal Club. Hagen will want to visit him tomorrow and turn this non event into a PR bonanza. You know Hagen! Keep the cash coming."

"Where is Samuels?"

"We've sent him up to a Crystal Club room...or suite. It's better than the Ritz. And he'll have company."

"What?"

"They didn't tell you?"

"No."

"Misty, the Prozac Dog, is back with Goodman. The guy's been in here so many times, maybe he just needs a place to sleep. Actually, we're going to prep him for surgery."

In the van there was a bolt of excitement. "Shit, they're gonna finally kill Goodman in the OR. That guy finally hit some bad timing."

Encrypt. COBOL to team. Crystal Club disconnect is ready. Team members confirm. RAZOR. CHASE. TERMINAL. COBOL off. SATAN. CODINE.

Joker received a phone call from Toshi and DeYoe in Boston informing him that they had another intercept, except this time they could only provide part of COBOL's message.

"COBOL is trying to encrypt. Trying to hide the contents of his computer messages. We retrieved the words *Crystal Club* and *the real McCoy* and *disconnect.*"

Street pondered the words and turned to one of the agents inside the van. "How do we know they're going after Goodman?"

"It's logical. He's got a real medical problem. He's the one they're going to wheel into surgery. As they say, he's the *real McCoy*. We've got so many rooms wired that we can monitor Goodman along with our man."

Street walked outside the van and tried to guess which lighted window was McCoy's room. He wandered around the parking lot waiting for the first bits of light. Then Joker's voice rang out. "Street, get in here fast... Jimmy, listen to what we just picked up."

We'll bring Samuels in for an angiogram. We'll do it at 7 AM. Better safe than sorry. Agreed. Let's get his consent.

It was 5:45 AM. "There's more. They took McCoy's watch off. We're getting no reading on heart rate. But, we've got other wires in the room. He's fine. That room is like a radio station."

"Prove it."

"Relax, Jimmy. There's a nurse in there, telling him about the procedure. They gave him a light sedative."

Street grabbed one of the FBI agents and pulled him outside the van. "What's your next move? Tell me now or I'll march in there and get my partner out."

"They're gonna take two people into procedure rooms this morning. We let them go that far and then seal everything off. We've got our own people inside that hospital."

"Why didn't I know that?"

"Everyone's got his secrets. We've got agents inside the hospital working on the phone lines. We disrupted their main switching yesterday and that gave us the chance to bring our people in. In fact, we've got two agents on the floor with Goodman and McCoy and a couple more just above the OR. We've also got a video monitor snaked through an air conditioning duct so we can see when they take your guy out for his procedure."

Street raced from one emotion to another. Fear! Excitement! Cooper put her hands on his shoulders and rubbed them.

At 6:30 AM, the van's audio equipment started to sound like a chatter line.

Let's move Goodman. And do something with that damn dog. This hospital is turning into a petting zoo.

Then the talk turned to Samuels.

He goes into Cath Lab #3.

●●●

McCoy looked up and down.

"Who picked out that purple color?"

"Mr. Samuels, you don't like our colors? Well, not to worry."

McCoy's thoughts flashed back to Boston and wife and kids. If only they could see him now. Multibillionaire, treated like royalty, and in this purple room.

McCoy looked up. Their faces were covered with masks. Dead eyes.

"Say, how come the masks?"

"Relax, Mr. Samuels, just a precaution. We're in the surgical area. Now, I'm going to give you something that will really relax you. Sort of like a scotch before the sun rises. Cocktails before 5 AM? Enjoy the moment."

McCoy wasn't enjoying the moment.

"We're going to give you some morphine to smooth things out."

McCoy felt a slight burn and then a pleasurable rush.

"Samuels, can you hear me? McCoy can you hear me?"

McCoy felt someone lift one of his eyebrows. "Welcome to the Ridge, Detective Mickey McCoy."

McCoy powered his eyes open, like lifting two garage doors. He was terrified. "My name isn't McCoy. It's Samuels."

"Detective, I'm Dr. Tara Tuls. Just here to make sure you're relaxed. Call this a free consultation. Any fears of death?"

McCoy heard laughter in the room.

"Oh, we're really careful about our guests at the Ridge. We don't want to treat the wrong patient, do we Detective McCoy?"

"They're listening outside. The hospital is surrounded. Street, help me."

"Detective, Street can't hear. We thought you'd like a room with peace and quiet. So, we disconnected the listening devices. And that camera is carrying our show. Nice touch. We're running a little video show for your friends outside. We taped it yesterday and it's playing now. What they're watching looks just like what they expect--a blockbuster!"

McCoy tried to scream. Nothing happened. He heard words around him.

"Ready every one? Give me a three-way stopcock and a sixty cc syringe. Let's pump this one up with air. Flat tires, anyone?"

McCoy lifted eyes again, ever so slightly. The room was purple with stars on the ceiling and it was floating. He felt a bubbling in his arm. He thought of his family. He felt no fear even though he knew the morphine was killing him with pleasure. "My God, they're killing me!" he exclaimed without panic. It was the morphine.

"More air. Keep pumping that air into his blood. His heart can't take much more. How's our Michelin man doing?"

McCoy started to gasp, trying to breathe. His body stiffened. McCoy's eyes popped open.

"Is he dead?"

"Yup, he's dead. And he's ready for his angioplasty."

"Anyone got the time?"

"5:30 AM."

"Great, time for coffee before we wheel him into the Cath Lab."

●●●

Joker's eyes were glued to the TV monitor as he saw them wheel McCoy out. Joker tugged at Street with a reassuring smile as they watched.

"Mickey looks fine to me. His eyes are open. See Jimmy; he's smiling. It's hard to tell with those TV monitors. Not great quality."

"That picture makes me feel a little better. But, where's the FBI?"

One of the agents in the van answered. "As soon as your partner goes through the OR doors, the sting begins. Our agents will seal the room and we'll do an inventory of everything and everyone in that room. Our proof breathes inside that room."

"And what if it's Goodman?" Street asked.

"He's covered, too. This is the bigs--we're ready to go. Chief Rome is on the line for Cooper."

"Detective, I know this is the time. Are you set? We've pulled out all the strings. Sometimes I think half the FBI is with you. Good luck. I'll be watching."

"Thanks, Chief. You know, there are two Crystal Club members in the Ridge. We can handle it. I really appreciate everything you've done."

"Detective, you don't know the half of it."

•••

The doors to Cath Lab #3 swung open. From the upper right hand edge of the TV monitor, the detectives could see McCoy wheeled inside. Except McCoy, everyone was covered with surgical hats and masks. Two nurses and one doctor were waiting for McCoy inside the Cath Lab as he was wheeled in.

Audio from listening devices in Cath Lab #3 reached the police van loud and clear.

"Mr. Samuels, you look bright and chipper this morning. They've explained the procedure and it won't be much of anything. You'll be conscious the entire time but too drowsy for anything other than a chance to yell if we cause any pain. And you know: no pain for Crystal Club members!"

Cooper watched transfixed as Street remained still.

"Jimmy, they're kidding with McCoy. He'll be fine."

"Hey, Joker, I didn't hear Mickey speak."

"Of course not; he's on morphine. He's spacey."

The commander of the FBI sting listened and prepared to issue the command for the sting to start. He turned to Street. "Well, why don't you do the 100 yard dash now; by the time you make it to the OR, we'll have it flooded with agents and electronics folks and your partner will be waiting, safe and sound. A little groggy."

Street jumped outside the van and ran towards the front entrance of the Ridge. The run was closer to 200 yards. "Go, Jimmy go, run, run; this is a sprint, not the marathon," he said as he coached himself to within about 50 yards of the entrance, all the while listening over his headphones the command issued from the van.

"This is FOX. The hunt is on. Get the dogs. FOX standing by."

Street threw his hands up in the air and jumped with joy. "Nail those bastards. Mickey, I'm on the way. Hang in their buddy."

Street exploded through the front doors of the Ridge with a police ID dangling from his neck and a blue and gold POLICE emblazoned on his wind breaker. From his left and right FBI agents popped out of cars and rushed through the hospital doors and up the stairs. The Ridge security guards were pushed to the floor, and there was action three floors up with the small team of agents already in the Hospital.

"FOX TWO to command. Get us some doctors fast. FOX TWO to command. Copy."

All the detectives were monitoring the channel and the call from upstairs was weird. "Doctors?"

"Command to FOX TWO. Are you nuts? You're in a hospital. Why Doctors?"

Street interrupted the chatter between the van and FBI agents. "Who needs a doctor? What's wrong up there? Come back, someone? Who copies me?" No hearing anything come back in his earphones, he and Cooper reached the third floor and its procedure suites.

His eyes glued to an agent in front of him, Street grabbed the agent's shoulders. "What happened up here?"

"One of those Crystal Club guys is dead. Fuckin unbelievable! Not posssible."

Street collapsed onto his knees and then dropped his hands to the floor as Cooper kneeled beside him.

"Jimmy, hold on, hold it together. We don't know who it is." She motioned for the FBI agent to stay with Street, who was now rolled in a ball with his hands over his head and his feet tucked into his stomach.

She ran into the Cath Lab which had an incredibly surreal look. The room was hot with overhead lights brighter than any sunny day she had ever seen. In one corner of the Cath Lab were four persons with their hands held high in the air. These were doctors and nurses pushed up against a wall like cheap Saturday night hustlers. Ten or more men and women wearing FBI blue and yellow jackets moved quickly around the Cath Lab. Cooper looked and listened.

"Kill those damn lights; they're cooking us."

Orders were coming from all directions in a state of organized panic. Cooper asked herself: "Was this what Parkland Hospital in Dallas was like when they brought Kennedy in?"

"Take these four and put them in separate rooms. Lock down all the equipment--no one touches anything."

One of the female agents screamed: "My God, the BP shows he's got a pulse. He's not dead."

Another FBI agent answered. "I don't give a fuck what that piece of equipment says. This guy is gone."

"But it shows a pulse, and blood pressure. He's got to be alive."

The FBI agent took her over to the table and slammed her hand around the man's hand. "OK? he's not breathing. Tell me about his pulse."

"None. He's dead."

Cooper moved towards the Cath Lab table, all the time feeling like she was going to vomit. She looked down at the man whose eyes were open with a slight smile, and saw Mickey McCoy.

Cooper spoke to herself: "Lisa M, got to be strong. Strong for Jimmy. Strong. Don't get sick. Don't throw up." Cooper looked around and couldn't see a familiar face until she looked up and saw a small viewing area partially suspended over the OR. Street and Joker pressed their faces against the glass window looking at Cooper.

Street's face moved from side to side and she read his lips: "No, No, No."

Joker had his hand around Street as tears rolled down his eyes. Then Cooper moved her head up and down and mouthed, "Yes, Yes, Yes."

•••

"This is Detective Cooper. Find Smith and Levin and get them over to the Ridge now. Tell them it's an emergency. And find Chief Rome. Wake her up, too."

Cooper's thoughts spun like a merry-go-round and her first worry was Street. "Got to find Jimmy." By the time she looked up from the OR a second time, Street had vanished from the viewing area. Cooper, however, had a hunch where he was headed. Grabbing an FBI agent, she raced up to the 20th floor. "If Hagen's in his office, Jimmy will kill him stone cold dead."

Cooper popped open the door to Hagen's office, half expecting to find the doctor sprawled on a table, dissected alive by Street. Instead, the office was dark, except for the luminescence from the TV monitors along the wall.

"Where's Jimmy? Can anybody hear me on the radio? Where's Detective Street?"

"Lisa, this is Joker. He's outside in the parking lot behind one of the dumpsters. An agent is with him and he's sick."

Cooper rushed outside and saw Street sitting on a curb with vomit on his shirt and tears pouring out his eyes.

"Oh, God, Mickey! Please not you. Let's switch places. Make it me. Not you, Mickey!"

Cooper cradled Street in her arms for half an hour as he cried himself dry of tears. Joker stood and watched from a distance.

One of the agents in the van walked over and quietly guided Joker into the van.

"Are you OK, kid?"

Joker offered no words in response.

"If you're not, then get OK fast."

Joker scanned the agent's face.

"Kid, look at the video. Your guy gets wheeled out of his room and into the OR--and he's still wearing the monitor watch we gave him--the one that reads out his heart rate? Remember we said it showed nothing, but no one worried since we all figured he wasn't wearing it. He was!"

The electronics team stopped the video, isolated, then enhanced the section of video when McCoy was wheeled out. His watch was on.

Joker's eyes popped wide open. "Then, why was the BP monitor in the OR showing that he was fine. One of your agents thought he was alive. I remember her screaming. That's not possible. You can't be dead and alive at the same time. Dead is before and after alive. Or after. Anyway, it's all wrong."

Joker thought about getting Street. Instead, he remained motionless on the curb. When Cooper looked up, her eyes said: "Stay far away!"

Smith and Levin radioed they were en route to the Hospital and asked to talk with Street.

"Charlie, this is Joker. He's really sick. He's on the curb with Cooper. He needs time to get himself together."

An agent in the van reminded Joker that procedures required that he immediately contact superiors in Boston and advise them about McCoy's death.

"I'll do it. Street can't."

"ZEBRA TEAM, this is Joker. Urgent. Contact the Chief. Use secure lines. No press. No nothing. We're at the Ridge Hospital in Philadelphia. Me. Jimmy. Mickey. Mickey's dead. Murdered." Joker threw the phone to the floor.

Within five minutes, the Mayor of Boston, the Chief of Police and Detectives were all conference on a phone call.

"Jimmy Street! We want him on the line."

Joker motioned to Cooper with his hand up to his ear. Cooper shrugged her head from side to side. "No, not right now!"

Then Joker walked over and nudged Street up from the sidewalk.

"Jimmy, the Chief is on the phone. Talk to him. Do it for Mickey. We've got to think about his wife and kids. Please, take the phone."

Street went inside the van and put the phone to his ear.

"Jimmy, we're all on the line. We know what's happened. We're sorry. Are you OK?"

Street uttered not a single word and Joker spoke into the phone. "Chief, he heard you. He'll be OK."

"Listen, Street, pull yourself together. You've got no choice. Get back to us with more information. No word will leak to the press and make sure that's the same in Philly. We've dispatched a crew to Mickey's house for notification."

Street listened silently.

"This is a great loss. Chief Rome down there is gonna be very upset. We just sent her some photos of you and Joker and Mickey. She was getting set to make all three of you..."

"What do you mean, photos? You sent her photos of Mickey?"

"Jimmy, this is Louis. Chief Rome called me and started talking about what a great job you and Joker were doing. The way she talked, I assumed you told her about Mickey. I told her Mickey was the other cop helping you. So what if she found out?"

"When?"

"Within the last 48 hours. Jimmy, Jimmy, are you there?"

Joker picked up the phone. "Guys, he's gone. He's out of here."

•••

Street raced to his car at the far end of the Hospital parking lot as Cooper and Joker charged after him.

Cooper yelled through the car window."You can't go. Your dead partner is upstairs in the Hospital."

"And your dead Chief of Police is home sleeping. You better stay away from this, Lisa."

"No way. I'm not gonna let you make a mistake. I'm going."

With those words, Street rolled up the window and sped off.

"This is Detective Cooper. We need an APB. Subject is Detective Jimmy Street and he's driving a gray unmarked. He's probably looking for Chief Rome."

Rome was in her car driving to headquarters and heard Cooper's warning to police dispatch.

"Cooper, this is Chief Rome. What's wrong?"

"Our under cover at the Ridge is dead. You don't want me to say anymore on the radio. We've got an APB on him."

"Cooper, you've got my cellular number. Use it now!"

"Yes, Chief, stand by... Chief Rome, this is Cooper. Street's out of it. He thinks you might have had something to do with McCoy's death."

"Is he threatening the Chief of Police of Philadelphia?"

"I guess you could put it that way."

In seconds, Cooper heard Rome with an All Channels on the police radio. Every beat cop, rolling cop, detective or anyone with a police radio heard her call to arms.

"This is Chief Rome. We've got a renegade cop loose somewhere in the city and his name is Jimmy Street. I guess I'm his target. Detain and arrest Street. Consider him armed and dangerous. He may be a threat to himself as well. Shoot to kill if necessary. Street is a weapons expert. I want a detail to meet me downstairs when I roll into headquarters. Rome is clear."

When she arrived at headquarters, a battery of detectives and cops met her downstairs, surrounding her in a human wave as she went to her office upstairs. At the same time, Cooper, Smith, and Levin were convinced that Street had walked off into a twilight zone between reality and fantasy.

Joker remained in the FBI van outside the Hospital and listened as detectives and federal agents interrogated every one in OR #3. He also listened to his instincts which convinced him that Street was wild with rage, but not crazy. Joker knew it to his core, that Street was a hunter, that, although wounded through the stomach by McCoy's death, he was neither delirious nor dilusional.

Street parked his car a few blocks from Rome's condo and went to the doorman downstairs.

Flashing a badge so quickly the doorman could never tell Boston from Philadelphia, Street said. "Don't worry the other people in the building. The Chief had a death threat this morning and they sent me here to guard her door. Just tell me the floor and I'll plant myself outside."

"She's already left for headquarters."

"I know that. We don't want anyone getting in! OK, now the floor?"

"Third floor, number 3 F."

Street went upstairs. Withiin two minutes, he had jimmied the lock and was inside.

Everything was an opiate for Street and he felt sedated by the sense that he was finally inside the womb of the monster they were chasing. When the phone rang, Street was mesmerized by the sound of Rome's sweet and seductive voice. Suddenly, he was slapped across the face with an unexpected bolt.

"This is Joker. Jimmy, I know you're there. Pick up the phone."

"Joker, how'd you know?"

"After all this time together? I'm on my way over. Don't fiddle with her computer." In less than 30 seconds Joker was gone.

Street went through the apartment, looking at photographs, notes on the refrigerator, and everything else. There was nothing. Joker knocked on Rome's door. "Jimmy, open it up. Let me in."

Street cracked the door open just wide enough to let Joker slide through, and the two embraced.

"Joker, he's gone. Mickey. My partner's gone. Again! Why me?"

"You stay cool, man. You'll make your mess when it's time. It's not the time now! Where's the computer?"

Street pointed to a computer in the bedroom on a small table with a printer. Joker was at the keyboard before Street said a word.

"Jimmy, I'm going into her memory. She's got a retrieval system, which means I can do a memory trace. It's like an engram--we're going into the computer's memory banks. Call it brain surgery with a keyboard."

Street sat on Rome's bed with his head between his legs, sobbing on and off as Joker worked on the computer.

"Street, get me one of those computr gadgets over there."

"So, what did you find?"

"The Holy Grail of this COBOL search."

"Explain."

"Better you see for yourself."

As Street peered over Joker's shoulder, he scrolled the last several COBOL messages. Surely Rome must have thought the messages erased, but they went into hibernation within the labyrinth of cyberspace.

"Rome didn't know it, but her default program requires that all erased data is saved for 48 hours. So, she'd erase. If no one retrieves the document in within 48 hours, it is gone forever. You've got enough here to nail her ass. And by the way! Chief Rome is **RAZOR**."

Street never said thanks. But the look was the look.

"Joker, take your gadget and get the information to Cooper, Smith, Levin and to Louis up in Boston. You can tell him that his fat mouth killed Mickey. Never mind. Don't do that. Take this stuff downtown and make copies."

"What about you?"

"I've got a few phone calls to make. Can you stop Rome's computer from erasing anymore?"

"Already done."

"You know none of this stuff proves anything. We're in here illegally."

"That's your department."

"Joker, find out what they're doing in Boston. I'll call Mickey's house in a little while. When I'm done here, I'm going back to the Hospital."

Joker left the condo and returned to police headquarters. His artful computer handiwork arrived before he did.

Street dialed headquarters. "Get me Chief Rome. This is the condo office in her building. It's an emergency."

"Chief Rome, what's wrong."

"This is your **holocaust** calling--Street! I'm inside your condo. Go ahead, send all the police you want. I'm inside your computer which is the same as being inside your rotten polluted head. Call off the APB. You've got fifteen minutes to get your ass here and we'll talk. Your computer has a good memory. I've read your wet dreams chitchat with COBOL and TERMINAL and CHASE. I want names. Fifteen minutes! Understood! RAZOR?"

Street blackened Rome's condo, shut off the computer, unplugged every appliance and unscrewed all the light bulbs. It was dead dark and dead quiet. Having emptied his holster gun, he kept his leg gun loaded as he listened on the police radio's APB on him being called off. Having turned the radio off, Rome waited 13 minutes.

Joker arrived at headquarters a few minutes before Rome returned home. He took the floppy disk from Rome's computer and played it for Cooper and the END ZONE team. He also sent the files to the FBI van at the Ridge.

Rome entered her condo and reached for a light switch, flicked it, but nothing happened.

"Street, I'm alone. I did what you asked. I didn't kill your partner. I just went along. They were blackmailing me."

Suddenly, Street reached with his hand from behind the door and tossed her head first through the living room until she smashed into a chair. Her room was soaked in the kind of black that seems to eat up light. Up was not up and down not down in the room. Street had placed blankets over her drapes and the condo was darker than the inside of a coffin.

"Street, where are you? I did what you said. I'm here. Let's make a deal."

On pronouncing the word, deal, Rome felt herself lifted off the ground by two huge hands and hauled into the bathroom. In the next second, Street submerged her head inside a toilet bowl, vehemtly holding her head under water until the gurgling slowed to a trickle. He flushed the toilet and yanked her by her hair. As she started to scream, Street forcefully stuffed a bunch of toilet paper in her mouth.

With every passing second, Street fought not to surrender to the animal inside. He really wanted to devour Rome; he wanted desperately wanted to kill her.

When Street turned Rome's computer on, and the screen provided green and purple light for the room, Rome saw Street with gun in his hand, the silencer attached, and pointed at her.

"Rome, I'm gonna dig a Panama Canal from your right ear to your left ear unless I hear answers."

Rome's eyes were ablaze in fear while Street was red hot angry. For several moments, he imagined what it would feel like to kill her. He took his gun out and pressed it hard against Rome's right ear.

"Chief, you might even hear this despite the silencer. Or maybe you won't hear anything when I dig the canal through your head."

"Wait, I'll tell you everything. Please. Don't do this."

As he pulled the trigger, Rome's body contorted on hearing the sound of the trigger. Because she heard the sound, Rome also knew she was still alive. Street pulled the paper from her mouth and looked at a pathetic, wrinkled, washed out woman. Rome's body muscles twisted in wild turns when Street pulled the trigger, wetting her pants at that instant. Urine was dripping down her legs and the stench immediately infiltrated the room.

"Jimmy, are you in there?" It was Cooper with Smith and Levin. Street opened the door. "Joker showed us the files.

Thank God you didn't kill her! It smells in here. What happened?"

As Cooper said those words, she looked at Rome. Erupting forward, Lisa reached over and dug her fingernails into Rome's face, carving out five deep canals across her forehead down to her chin. With blood dribbling down, Cooper recoiled in horror. "Oh God, look what I did. That's sick," Cooper said as she turned to Smith.

Smith peered down at Rome, perfumed with the stench of toilet water and urine and carved across the face by Cooper. "Better you, Lisa, than me. If I had touched her, she'd be dead."

Street pulled the delirious Chief of Police up and tossed her onto a coach. At that instant, it hit him that Rome was the Chief of Police. "Rome, we want names."

"You can't do this to me. This is police brutality. You're all going to jail for this. You're all out of control. Nothing in my condo is admissible by law. Now that I think about it, you've got crap. You're the ones going to jail." Rome reached into her pocketbook and took her ultralight portable phone.

Smith took the phone and crushed it under his enormous feet.

"Rome, this is police brutality and you're the author. And you're right, we're all going to jail, but only to insure you've got a rotten cell. Give us answers or I'll just toss you out the window and claim temporary insanity." Street turned to the other detectives. "I don't want you here now. She talks or she flies. You better get out. Wait downstairs. If you see the Chief flying out the window you'll know she's dead, and you'll know she never gave up the names of her partners.

Rome watched the detectives leave. Cooper turned to Street. "Fuck her, just toss her out the window. We've got the files anyway. Do it for me! Do it for Mickey! Let her fly!"

Outside the door, Smith took Cooper's hand. "What kind of bullshit was that, Cooper? Talk about good-cop-bad-cop. You scared me."

"Charlie, I wasn't bluffing. I wanted to toss the bitch out myself."

The detectives waited downstairs. In 30 minutes, Street walked outside with Chief Rome handcuffed.

"I've got it all."

Cooper squeezed Rome's head as she guided it into their car for headquarters.

Radio dispatch at headquarters heard the kind of thunderclap words that reverberate in memory like Dallas in November of 1963 or NASA in 1969 with Armstrong on the moon.

"Dispatch, this is Detective Cooper. En route to headquarters with Chief Rome under arrest. Request contact Judge Soto, US attorneys office, FBI, and appropriate agencies. Get the assistant Chief. Contact Mayor Gentry. Cooper 465 off."

The city room at the *Inquirer* erupted. Someone picked up part of the conversation from a police scanner. Across town, several of the newsradio and TV stations heard the transmission as well.

A young intern rushed to the assignment desk with the police scanner in his hand. Pushing away the reporters huddled around the assignment, he turned the volume up.

"Someone, get a tape recorder. Tape this. I can't believe what..."

"This is dispatch 465. Come back with your transmission. What's wrong with Chief Rome?"

Street took the microphone. "Read our lips. There are five people in this car and one is wearing handcuffs and under arrest for murder. Detectives Street, Cooper, Smith and Levin are here. We've got Chief of Police Ellen Rome and she's under arrest. You're taping this; so, play it back a few times till it sinks in. And get a judge. We're arriving in a few minutes. Chief Rome has been read her rights. Do you copy now?"

"Dispatch to Street. We copy."

A caravan of news cars converged on police headquarters. Radio and TV stations interrupted their programming with bulletins. Even Beethoven on the classical music station got bumped off the air.

> THIS IS A NEWS BULLETIN. WE HAVE BEEN INFORMED BY WIRE SERVICES THAT THE PHILADELPHIA CHIEF OF POLICE HAS BEEN PLACED UNDER ARREST FOR MURDER. DETAILS ARE SKETCHY AT THIS TIME. STAY TUNED TO YOUR CLASSICAL MUSIC STATION AT 95.7 FM AND WE'LL HAVE FURTHER DETAILS. NOW BEETHOVEN'S SYMPHONY NO. 5, AS PERFORMED BY THE DETROIT SYMPHONY ORCHESTRA.

By the time Rome was brought into headquarters, there was a ring of reporters outside. She was hustled inside, past stunned cops and into an interrogation room.

"I have a statement to make." Rome's personal attorney had heard the news and was on his way. "I'll wait for my attorney."

With headquarters overrun by swarms of reporters, Street commandeered the 2nd level men's room and OPERATION END ZONE assembled. He had taken notes as Rome spoke but didn't want to talk until they were at headquarters.

"Rome was rambling a lot and saying *everyone* was a conspirator with her. We'll have to sort all this out. Where's Hagen?"

"Not at the Hospital. We've been looking for him."

"Rome claims Hagen is **CHASE**. That still leaves us **COBOL** and **TERMINAL** . And **SATAN**? I'm going over to the Hospital. We should have an APB on Hagen."

"Where are you going in the Hospital?"

"I'm going to see Mickey. They took his body downstairs and I need some time alone with him. Keep looking for Hagen. If I find him first, he's dead. Correction--he's dead after he tells me how all these Crystal Club members were killed so conveniently without any trace. Joker's coming with me."

Cooper knew Street was not bluffing. "Jimmy, if you find him, don't do anything you'll regret."

"Like turning him over to the courts so he can get himself a dream team of lawyers and plea bargain his way to a few years in a mental institution? That I'd regret. If I find Hagen, I'll have no regrets. This is one doctor who's not going to keep me waiting."

Street and Joker left the room, and Cooper issued a warning to Smith and Levin.

"Call the FBI in their van and see how the interrogation of those people in the OR is going. Maybe they know where Hagen is. I know Jimmy, and this is no bluff."

Chapter Forty One: 'TO MY GRAVE'

Street and Joker arrived at the Ridge and went inside the police van. FBI electronics agents were playing back video and audio tapes from the Ridge. Joker asked for the tape that showed McCoy being wheeled out of his room to the Cath Lab.

"Whether that was a mistake or not, Mickey had his watch on. And it showed no pulse. We thought he wasn't wearing it. Jimmy, I think they killed Mickey in that fancy purple room. That special preop room. They put a smile on his face and wheeled him into the Cath Lab. Once inside they prepared a show, including flashing lights from the BP monitors and other equipment to make it look like he and the other Crystal Club members died during a procedure or surgery. These folks never made it out of the purple room alive."

The FBI agent confirmed part of Joker's story, telling Street that the two doctors and nurses already confessed. They knew some Crystal Club patients were wheeled in dead and they were paid or blackmailed to pretend a surgical procedure was in progress as Hagen taped it upstairs. Electronic equipment in the OR was controlled by a panel under the surgical table and doctors manipulated it to show a patient doing well, then decompensating in some way and finally diving into cardiac arrest.

The doctors and nurses had drug habits and an assortment of other problems including alcohol. One of the doctors was HIV positive and was threatened with exposure and termination if he failed to help. One had a bad habit of soliciting children on the Internet. Each one received money and continuing threats of disclosure. It was an ugly group and they rationalized their way through this medical desert since the patients were already dead when they came in.

While the FBI interrogation continuied, medical records were being exhumed going back ten years. With Judge Soto having expanded the search warrants, the entire Hospital was open territory for the police.

Street went inside the Ridge for the first time since his partner was killed. Joker went upstairs while Street went into the basement morgue.

Cooper asked the FBI agents to keep an eye on Street to make sure he was OK. What she really wanted was some protection that Street wouldn't find Hagen.

Street was in the morgue for almost an hour talking to Mickey, crying on his shoulder, begging forgiveness and asking his dead partner what to do next? Street provided all the answers. The ME was gone and Street had the morgue cleared out so he could be alone with Mickey. When the phone rang in the morgue, Street picked it up.

"Street, this is Hagen. I thought I'd find you downstairs with your partner. I want to talk. I can give you information in trade for help. I'm not the only one in this. Can we cut a deal?"

"You and that fuckin' bitch love to cut deals, don't you? We'll talk, but it's you and me. Alone!"

"Street, I'm in the building where they'll never find me. There's a staircase upstairs to the roof. You can't get onto the roof without the code. It's 334. I'll be there in 20 minutes."

Street told no one and made it to the roof before Hagen. The roof was black tar with all the usual rooftop equipment including an array of satellite and microwave dishes. A three foot high protective brick wall ringed the roof. There was also a one foot ledge beyond the brick, plus lawn furniture and even a broken down outdoor grill atop the roof along with a spattering of graffiti. Beyond the ledge,it was straight down to the parking lot.

The view was superb with the Philadelphia skyline visible atop the backdrop of trees and homes. Street looked out and pondered the moment, his radio filled with police commands and all sorts of chatter, including the search for Street himself.

"This is Cooper, come in all positions. Has anyone seen Street or Hagen?"

Street flipped his radio off and waited for Hagen as he tried to understand. "He's a doctor; he takes an oath; the others downstairs in the OR: they also took the same oath. Doctors. Nurses. These are the high priests and priestesses of America, more exalted than the President. I understand a bad cop, a rotten politician, a weasel corporate type. But, doctors? Now, these slime killed my partner. They took a husband from a wife; they took a father from his children; they took a friend from me."

Street's rage was building inside as he kept looking at his watch. "Twenty minutes. He'll never show. This is a waste. He's baiting me."

Across the black tar top of the Ridge in the far southeast corner, Street saw the outline of a man standing close to the three foot brick wall. Street saw Hagen standing there wearing his white medical jacket.

"Don't come any closer, Street."

Street was within 20 feet of Hagen, with both men standing on the inside edge of the brick wall. Below in the parking lot, several of the detectives spotted Hagen and Street.

The police radio crackled. "Up on the roof, we've spotted Hagen and Street. They're talking. That's it."

Five minutes later, as word spread through the Hospital about police activity, two television ENG (Electronic News Gathering) trucks arrived. In ten minutes, the parking lot was packed with radio and TV news crews.

Without warning, Hagen mounted the three foot brick wall. "Stay away. I mean it! I've got nothing to lose." Hagen was sweating and Street thought he had taken some drugs, based on the way some of his words slurred.

"This is Street. You copy down there?"

"Go ahead."

"I think we've got a jumper. It's Hagen. He's flipped."

Cooper came on the line. "Jimmy, they're sending up some people to talk with him."

"Don't let them do it. He's ready to fly."

Downstairs, TV cameras zoomed in on Hagen and Street. A couple of the TV stations went live with the story. "This is Johnny Desmond at the Ridge Hospital in Chestnut Hill. We interrupt our programming to bring you this Action 7 News exclusive. On the roof, 23 stories up, is Dr. Walter Hagen, President of the Ridge and perhaps the best known hospital president in America. With him is Detective Jimmy Street. From what we know, Street is a consultant with the Philadelphia police and is a member of the Boston police. We also know that during some sort of under cover operation earlier today, a police detective was killed inside the Ridge.

"We have been assured by police that all patients in the Ridge are safe and receiving appropriate medical care. Do not come to the hospital. Access has been limited to police only. You will be turned away at the Hospital entrance.

"Stay tuned to Action 7 News. Now back to the studios."

Cooper and the other END ZONE detectives joined Joker inside the police van where one of the monitors was picking up the video feed of Hagen and Street on the roof.

Hagen jumped off the brick wall. Now only one foot of roof separated him from the parking lot below. He held onto the wall as he wavered back and forth on the edge while Street moved within a few feet from him.

"Hagen, JUMP! Your life is ruined. You're not a doctor. You're Lee Harvey Oswald in a white jacket. You've got the right idea: JUMP and show me some balls!"

Hagen wiggled his head in disbelief. "Aren't you here to talk me out of this?"

"No way, Hagen. You killed my partner. You're just a corpse on the 23rd floor roof. Now, do it: JUMP!"

Down below, TV cameras focused on Hagen and Street as they spoke.

"This is Action 7 News back at the Ridge where the drama on the roof continues. A brave police detective is trying desperately to convince Dr. Walter Hagen not to jump. That detective, Jimmy Street, must be using every ounce of courage to try and talk Hagen down--knowing that his friend and partner is dead inside the Hospital. According to our police sources, Hagen may be responsible. As we go back to our studios, the situation is that one man is inches from destruction while a detective is trying to talk him back to safety. Stay tuned to Action 7 News.

Joker leaned over to Cooper in the police van. "Lisa, can you read lips?"

"As a matter of fact, yes. I studied it in high school."

Across town at the Good Sam, another lip reader watched TV with both a sense of amazement and vindication.

Joker observed: "Well, Lisa, my man, Street, seems to be saying JUMP a lot. I guess he's trying to convince Hagen not to jump."

Cooper, howver, knew the truth. She held Joker's hand tight as she alternately looked at the TV monitors and then turned away. She spoke into her police radio. "Jimmy, if you can hear me, it's Lisa. Get off that roof. Be careful. Think of us down here."

Street was wild with rage. With each passing second, his thoughts flashed back and forth between a dead partner lying years ago on a desolate Boston sidewalk and another dead partner just floors below inside the Ridge. Inside Street's head, his anger burned so hot he thought his skin would bubble and his hair melt.

"Come on, Hagen, stop the delay. JUMP!" he commanded. "You killed with such much ease; now, what's the problem? JUMP! or spend the rest of your life in prison and be brutalized by inmates looking for every orifice God created on your slimy body. I'll make sure you get a real nasty prison assignment. The roof is fast. In prison, death is daily affair," Street emhasized--no pun intended.

"Hey Street, if I jump I'll take all my secrets with me. You'll never find the others. Maybe they'll keep killing."

"Hagen, we've got Chief Rome with all her computer files. You're useless now!"

"Don't you want to know how your partner died?"

Those words--salt on an open wound--cut across Street's body and mind. "Get it off your chest, Hagen. What happened?"

"I orchestrated it, but COBOL issued the orders when Chief Rome tipped us Ernest Boron Samuels was your partner from Boston. He was dead in his room. He had an IV in. We just gave him a BOLUS of air. A few times we used a BOLUS of potassium on Crystal Club members. It's perfect. No trace. No evidence. And I've got one more surprise for you, Street, if you wish to hear it!"

"Hagen, time to JUMP. I don't care about your surprises."

"Street, the biggest surprise is--I'm not going to jump. I'm coming in. Now, everyone knows how upset I was with all the deaths in the Hospital. But no one can prove anything; it's all circumstantial garbage. Computer transcripts aren't fingerprints. What I told you, I'll deny. I'll be out of here and in the parking lot sooner than you think. When I'm driving home, I'll think of how pathetic you are, Street. This is your dead end."

Action 7 News once more. Street has apparently succeeded. Dr. Hagen has put one foot, now two, on the brick wall and is climbing back. Street has climbed the brick wall to help Hagen.

Street watched as Hagen moved his legs slowly onto the brick wall. When he had both legs on the wall, Street jumped up and grabbed Hagen by the hand.

"What are you doing? Let go of my hand! I don't need your help to get back in. Street, when all the noise settles down, we can talk. I'll bet we can work out some kind of deal..."

"Fuck you, Hagen. You said you'd be in the parking lot soon, and you were right. What goes down, never comes up. Now, fly Hagen, fly!"

Street lunged at Hagen, while everyone watching from the parking lot thought Hagen was trying to jump and Street was fighting to stop him from jumping.

Street bumped Hagen off the roof and watched Hagen flip over and over until he slammed dead weight into the parking lot. Although Street watched Hagen's whole trip down, what he saw instead was the face of his dead partner.

BULLETIN FROM Action 7 News. We've had a horrible end to the drama at the Ridge. Just as Dr. Hagen was coming onto the roof, he apparently changed his mind and started to fight with Detective Street. The detective, risking his life to try and save Hagen, failed in keeping Hagen from jumping to his death. We'll have more updates during the day and a complete wrap up during our 6 and 11 o'clock news. This is Action 7 News.

The parking lot filled with doctors and nurses from the Ridge. Patients peering outside their windows looked away in horror. Hagen's body, tangled in ivy that his limbs caught on the way down, smashed into a blue and white zone restricted for handicapped parking. Police ringed the body as news crews jostled to get pictures.

Cooper and the END ZONE team stood at the rear of the crowd with Joker holding her hand. "Cooper, you and Hagen have come a long way. You one way, and Hagen the other. Right now there's someone who needs you."

Cooper moved past Hagen's body and into the swarm of people in the Ridge lobby.

"Street, if you're on the radio, this is Cooper. Where are you?"

Two words popped over the radio. "Hagen's office."

When Cooper entered, she found Street sitting at Hagen's desk, glaring at the TV monitors. The 20th floor had been emptied of people.

"Lisa, what makes a man at the top like Hagen slide into the gutter? It makes no sense."

"Hey, he was probably in the gutter way before he set foot at the Ridge. Jimmy, don't think because you're in his seat, in his office, that you can get into his head."

"Lisa, I need help. I need to understand. I have trouble saying goodbye and I can't do that with Mickey until I understand."

Cooper reached out and held Street's hand. They talked for what seemed a lot of time. She sat with him during the phone calls to McCoy's family, and heard Street's ramblings over his not wanting to return to Boston for McCoy's funeral alone. But. sometime after 3 PM, Joker knocked and entered into Hagen's office.

"OK, Jimmy, you're always asking; so, now I am."

Street looked at his very preoccupied young friend. "I need to know what happened on that roof. You kept using the word JUMP."

"OK, Joker, I owe you the truth. Hagen faked his little suicide routine. He bragged about going free. He knew the evidence was circumstantial and not easy to prove. Translated into big city law and order--that spells plea bargain. He taunted me with it and made fun of Mickey." Street stood up from Hagen's desk, stood next to Joker, and put his arm around him. "I used the word JUMP. I told him to go for it. When he started to back-off, I grabbed him. Hell, bare minimum I was going take both of us down. I didn't care. So yeah, I pushed him. Murder One. You and Lisa better let everyone know."

Cooper and Joker both saw the devastation inked under Street's red and darkened eyes. Together, unrehearsed, they said: "To my grave!"

"To my grave. What's that mean, Lisa?"

"Jimmy, to my grave."

"Joker, you tell me."

"Jimmy, it means, to my grave."

Street understood what they meant.

"Yeah, and I have to live with what I did. So, it's to my grave."

Street looked at Cooper and Joker and again they repeated the phrase.

"We're not done. SYS--we found dead floating in his Jacuzzi. RAZOR--we nailed with her own computer. CHASE was Hagen and he's dead."

Cooper asked. "Where did that nickname come from?"

Street answered. "That's a wild one. I'll tell you in a minute. We've still got COBOL and TERMINAL running around; we know who they are. All we have to do is catch them. And we've got two more: ACID and SATAN"

Cooper asked again: "So, where did CHASE come from?"

"Eric C. Goodman. Eric Chase Goodman. Goodman gave Hagen the code name CHASE."

"If Goodman did that, then Goodman's in on this?"

"Goodman, according to words of wisdom from Chief Rome in between dunks in her toilet, was COBOL. It's a financial term for business language. And I'll introduce you to TERMINAL after we round up Goodman and his Prozac dog."

Street recounted the squeezed out words from Chief Rome about Goodman and his hospital stays. He was almost always in the Hospital when a Crystal Club disconnect was in progress. The Ridge provided him with a computer in his bedroom and that's where all those messages came from. Not from Hagen, but from Goodman. It seems Goodman's appetite for money to build his broadcast group was exceeded only by Hagen's hunger to stuff the Ridge. Goodman and his KEYSTONE Broadcasting were major recipients of loans from the Crystal Club venture fund and those loans kept getting larger. If Hagen ever pulled the plug, KEYSTONE would have tumbled like a feather tower.

"So, who's TERMINAL?"

•••

Street escorted Cooper and Joker to McCoy's floor. He asked Smith and Levin to meet him there.

"There's a shift change coming at 4 PM. Let's watch."

By now, the Ridge was the lead story across the nation. The Vice President of the United States had lunched with Dr. Hagen at the Ridge a year earlier and proclaimed him a hero of American medicine. But now the Vice President was working on a new statement. As the story of the Ridge built, doctors and nurses continued to take care of patients and do all the routine things that never make the news. And then at 4 PM, the shift change was in progress.

Street went to a phone and got the codes from hospital wide paging. Before he did so, Street called police and told them to lock down the Hospital. Street waited until just after 4 PM, checked the computer log in sheet, and proceeded to make an announcement over the public address system:

"THIS IS DETECTIVE JIMMY STREET. TESTING 123. CAN YOU HEAR ME? SOME OF YOU ARE SICK, SOME OF YOU ARE IN OPERATING ROOMS, HELL SOME OF YOU ARE IN THE CAFETERIA. TODAY WE CLEANED OUT AN INFECTION IN THIS HOSPITAL. IT WAS THE WORST KIND...IT WAS HUMAN. WE'RE ALMOST DONE WITH THAT JOB. THERE'S JUST ONE LITTLE SPECK LEFT TO CLEAN UP. NOW YOU CAN ALL HELP BY TELLING US WHERE NURSE MARY CINNERS IS. THANK YOU."

In less than five minutes, several nurses and two patients pulling and tugging at Nurse Cinners and delivered her to Street.

"You killed my friend Mickey. You put a syringe of air into an IV and killed him. And you've done it before. I heard from the detectives that you bragged about never making a mistake."

Cinners stood silent and mean. "Fuck you--you can't prove a thing."

"You're TERMINAL. You're the one who actually kills while the others issue orders and secret commands in the middle of the night. We can prove everything." Street ripped off her name tag and nurse insignia. He then reached for both his guns and handed them to Cooper. "I did that for my protection. I don't want a gun in my hands now."

Cooper reached out for Street. "Don't ruin your life, Jimmy."

Cinners was held by Smith and Levin.

"Bitch, who's SATAN? And who's ACID?"

"Go the hell. You're the pyscho detective."

Street grabbed Cinners close to him. "Bitch, can you feel my heat. Smell my breath! You just gave me ACID."

"Fuck you!"

Street grabbed his radio. "Joker, this is pyscho Street."

"Are you nuts?"

"Pyscho. Hey, remember the red head? The psychiatrist! Bet she's ACID. Tell them to round her up and get her in custody."

Cinners yelled. "Lucky guess."

"Joker, we've got a confirm on Dr. Tara Tuls. She's ACID."

"Street, what about SATAN?"

Street took Cooper's hand. Holding it gently, he lookd into her eyes. "Lisa, Good-by."

Chapter Forty Two: GOOD-BY

When Jimmy Street reached out and took Cooper's hand and said good-by", both their lives changed forever.

He resigned from the Boston Police force before his plane landed at Logan Airport. Cooper resigned from the Philadelphia Police Force before her plane to Boston took off.

Cooper won a special appointment to the Boston Police force--no longer a desk jockey detective.

At age 50, Jimmy Street, former detective, entered a six year medical studies program that could make him a resident by the time he was 56. He headed back to school with the hope of finding peace and quiet in academia.

Cooper, on the other hand, found a nice place to live in Boston, a beautiful condo on Beacon Hill that just happened to have the same address as Jimmy's.

Detectives Charlie Smith and Rudy Levin found new addresses in Boca Raton, Florida where they try to catch every fish in the southern Atlantic.

Mayor Sam Gentry was destroyed in the next election.

Eric Chase Goodman continues in the TV business as TV repairman at a state prison in Pennsylvania.

Nurse Mary Cinners is imprisoned somewhere in the western United States. The US Marshal's service gave her a new identity because there were so many attempts on her life. It seemed an unknown detective had spread the rumor that Nurse Cinners still had access to drugs and when she could not produce, she was inmate-punished. She is serving nine life sentences, consecutively.

Dr. John Andersen, President of the Good Samaritan Hospital, performed one final, official act before retiring. He acquired the Ridge Hospital and dropped its name.

Curious thing, though, because he kept the Crystal Club, he was appointed guardian of its money and mission. Dr. Andersen had convinced the Good Samaritan Board of Directors that the famed Crystal Club was the wave of the future in medicine.

All his dreams fulfilled, Dr. Andersen sent one final email message into the nothingness of Internet space. It was addressed to all and camouflaged with a fake address.

"To all who may venture forth, be it known that the torch has passed."

Signed: **SATAN**